FEARLESS

FEARLESS

FERN MICHAELS

WHEELER PUBLISHING
A part of Gale, a Cengage Company

Copyright © 2020 by Fern Michaels.
Fern Michaels is a registered trademark of KAP 5, Inc.
Wheeler Publishing, a part of Gale, a Cengage Company.

Wheeler Publishing Large Print Hardcover.
The text of this Large Print edition is unabridged.
Other aspects of the book may vary from the original edition.
Set in 16 pt. Plantin.

LIBRARY OF CONGRESS CIP DATA ON FILE.
CATALOGUING IN PUBLICATION FOR THIS BOOK
IS AVAILABLE FROM THE LIBRARY OF CONGRESS

ISBN-13: 978-1-4328-7656-2 (hardcover alk. paper)

Published in 2020 by arrangement with Kensington Books, an imprint of Kensington Publishing Corp.

Printed in the United States of America
1 2 3 4 5 6 7 24 23 22 21 20

FEARLESS

PROLOGUE

Lubbock, Texas
Now

Anna Campbell accepted the friend request from Laura Jones, a common enough name. Possibly, she was a friend of a friend, or someone who followed her vlog on YouTube, *The Simple Life.*

Accepting the request, she then clicked on the name to see if there were photos to put a face to, possibly reminding her who Laura Jones was.

She read through the woman's Facebook bio, then once more. This was a mistake. It had to be. She drew in a deep breath, slowly letting the air of uncertainty pass through her dry lips. Chewing on her bottom lip, she pointed the cursor to the photo tab. Afraid, yet knowing she couldn't stop now, she double-clicked on the link. Heart racing, she viewed the images. One by one, still shots of the woman's smiling face grinned back at her. She clicked on one photo, realizing it had been taken just a few hours ago.

This whole thing was impossible, yet she couldn't deny what she was seeing.

She clicked through the pictures, each image tearing apart the life that she was trying to put back together. She stared at the images again.

No way this could be real. Photoshopped, most likely. Yes, it had to be. Maybe one of her viewers had decided to play a cruel joke on her after all the publicity she had received lately. With over 6 million subscribers, it's highly likely that some were haters. The vlogging community was like any other in that respect. People disagreed. Respectfully. Or not.

Clicking the white back arrow, she viewed the pictures a third time. With a few clicks of her mouse, she was able to enlarge the photos.

No. This was not some crazy subscriber trying to rattle her.

This was the face of a woman she'd seen on Daniel's phone. The photos that were discovered in Renée's luggage after the fire. Dark brown eyes, thin lips pressed together with deep grooves furrowing above her upper lip. Dull gray short hair, choppy, as if it had been cropped with blunt scissors, the ends uneven. In one of the photos, she smiled, showing protruding teeth yellowed from years of nicotine. Using her thumb and index fingers to enlarge the picture, Anna saw old acne scars and knew this was *not* Laura Jones. She closed the window, brought up the search engine, typing in her name, then hit PHOTOS. Almost 2 million hits according to the info displayed on her screen. She scrolled through several of the blue hyperlinks and clicked on the first page. Yet none of the Laura Joneses she saw matched the face in the photographs.

Anna pulled the Facebook pictures back up. In all, there were seven, each a different pose but with the same background, the same pale pink blouse. If this were a joke, someone had gone to great lengths. She recognized the Sun 'N Fun home and garden show, the charity fund-raiser she herself had been at earlier that night. It raised money for Habitat for Humanity, an organization near and dear to her heart. An auction open to the public. Laura Jones had obviously also attended it, given the background in the photos. Anna tried to recall if she'd seen her, or possibly spoken to her. Almost three thousand people had attended, and while she knew it was impossible for her to have spoken with that many people one-on-one, those whom she did speak to usually left an impression on her one way or another.

Searching her memory, she guessed she'd spoken to thirty or forty people, mostly women, but there had been a few men. She would have remembered if one in particular stood out. If they had, she would have mentioned it to Mandy during the drive on the way home, as they'd had a short chat. They'd gotten into this habit a few weeks after the accident.

Her days were long and the nights sometimes longer when Christina had one of her rough nights dealing with being cooped up in the den for so long. Though they weren't as frequent as they'd been after the accident, she still had them once in a while. Long gone were the days when Christina would spend the evenings by herself in her room, reading Harry Potter books and texting with her best friend, Tiffany. It absolutely enraged Anna when she thought about what had happened. She wanted to kill the son of a bitch who had done this to her, but she knew these were idle daydreams and nothing more. Even so, there were many nights when she would lie awake plotting ways to rid the world of the evil it contained.

The woman in the photographs had not been the topic of any late-night discussion. Only once had her name come up during the time she had a relationship with Ryan, if you wanted to call it that. Anna had expressed sympathy over the tragedy, then moved on. She knew from personal experience that life wasn't always fair or kind. When life bombarded one with bushels of lemons, Anna knew that with perseverance, often the sweetest of lemonades resulted. Her life was testimony to that.

Ten years into her first marriage, her husband, Wade, had died in a motorcycle accident on his way home from Woodworks, the furniture store in Corpus Christi where he'd built and sold custom-made furniture for yachts and boats. A lifelong dream, shattered in seconds on a wet, slick road. After months of wallowing in the dark depths of despair, Anna had had no other choice but to pull herself out of her grief-induced depression and find a way to provide for her daughter. Without Wade, there was no furniture store, no income. With a degree in marketing, and little experience, she'd started a vlog about grief, which became an immediate success. When she began vlogging full-time, it had afforded her many sponsors and provided her a decent income. After two years, she'd branched out into cooking, and more lifestyle vlogs, and again, her ideas were so well received, she'd zoomed straight to the top of the vlogging world, her recipes and decorating videos reaching viewers across the globe. She'd been a guest on all the national morning shows, the cooking networks, and a few of the late-night talk shows. And more often than not, she was recognized in public, which to this day still surprised her. Once she became financially successful, she sold the home she and Wade had purchased in Corpus Christi and built a new, modern, upscale home in Lubbock, complete with her own recording studio. She hired a film crew, an editor, and found a manager to direct *The Simple Life's* future. After years of long days and late nights, she was pleased with her success, her ability to provide for Christina and give her the best life possible.

Why now? she thought. How many more lies was she going to uncover?

Part One

CHAPTER 1

Before

"Mandy, you know I can't leave Christina. She's only thirteen," Anna said to her best friend and assistant.

"Yes, you can. I'm quite capable of caring for a thirteen-year-old, I'll have you know. This cruise is just what you need. It'll be fun. Just because it's a singles cruise doesn't mean you're going to find a significant other just like that."

Anna laughed. "I think that's exactly what it means. You can't put thousands of single people together, on a singles-only cruise ship, and not have expectations. It sounds fun, but it's not really my cup of tea."

"You've never even been on a cruise," Mandy teased. "You might surprise yourself and actually enjoy being waited on hand and foot. Meeting new friends is simply a bonus."

"Then why don't *you* go?" Anna asked.

"Because someone has to keep you organized, and besides, I'm dating Eric exclusively now."

"Hmmm, and when did this happen? I thought he was just a guy from the gym." Mandy Martin was a total babe; she attracted men like bees to honey. At thirty-five, she'd never married and loved the single life. Anna was lucky to have her on her team. *Tall, blond,* and *buxom* were three words to describe her. Add in kind, smart, and a huge heart, and this was who Mandy was.

"He was. At first. That's what happens, Anna. You date, you find out you're compatible, then boom, you sort of commit to date one another. Easy peasy."

"Does this mean what I think it means, or am I being old-fashioned?"

"Probably not. It means we're going to see what happens. When you're dating five or six guys at once, it's time-consuming. Not so easy getting to know any of them, you know?" Mandy said.

"No, I wouldn't know from personal experience, but I get the picture," said Anna. "I would feel completely out of place, not knowing anyone."

"My point exactly! You'd be in the same boat, literally, as the other guests. You mingle, you see someone who interests you, say hi, ask his name. Say something cutesy, or you could go the traditional route and just introduce yourself. Whatever works. It's the perfect solution for you."

Anna thought her life was as close to perfect as one could get, given her circumstances. Being a single parent had its moments though she'd been lucky so far. Anna adored Christina and knew her daughter felt the same way about her. At thirteen, she was tall, like Wade, who'd been six-four. Christina was five-eight already, but that's where the similarities ended. Minus her height, she was a carbon copy of Anna. With her reddish brown hair, aqua-blue eyes, full lips, and olive skin, Anna often thought of her as a mini version of herself. They laughed about this, Anna telling her at least she would know what she might look like when she was her age. At forty-one, she hadn't aged too much; but she knew that in this age of fillers, plumpers, and sunscreen, Christina's generation would age exceptionally well if they took care of themselves while they were young. Living in Texas, sunscreen was a necessity. She had used it most of her adult life and insisted that her daughter do the same.

"So, you'll go?" Mandy interrupted her

17

thoughts.

Sighing, she knew that if she didn't give her an answer, Mandy would never let up. *And why not?* she thought. They were weeks ahead with her filming schedule; school was out for the summer. Christina would be fine without her for a few days. For Christina's thirteenth birthday, Anna had given her an adorable tabby kitten whom they'd christened Mr. Waffles because of his wafflelike coloring, and now she spent most of her free time with him. So she doubted she'd be missed.

"Give me the details, and I'll start packing," Anna said, enjoying the surprised look on Mandy's face.

"Seriously?"

"Yep," she replied, grinning. "I need a break. After what I've been through the past couple of months, it will be a relief." Anna had been stalked for weeks, probably by a crazy fan. The police had been called in and launched an investigation, but so far, there'd been no arrest. Fear and looking over her shoulder had taken their toll on her. She truly needed a vacation.

"You're not joking?"

"I wouldn't do that to you. I could use a break. Not sure how this cruising the high seas works, but I'm willing to give it a try.

However," she said, "not a long cruise. One week max. I'm clueless how I'll react, so that's all I'll commit to. And you have to swear on your life that you'll be extra watchful. Christina still has no clue about all this insanity."

"I'll guard her with my life — you know that. You've spent most of your life around water when you lived in Corpus Christi, so you'll be fine. I'm going to book this cruise before you change your mind. It's Wednesday, and the *Splendor of the Sea* departs this Friday. That should be enough time to pack a few things," Mandy said. "Leave the details to me."

If Anna didn't know better, she would swear Mandy had an ulterior motive, but she'd always been up-front with her since day one, so she pushed the thought aside. She needed to rest and recharge, and this was as good an opportunity as any. She would relax and try to catch up on all the books piled up by her bedside. "I would say thanks, but I'll wait until I'm back."

"Anna, you don't *have* to go," Mandy said. "You work so hard, and we're way ahead of schedule. Though I kind of promised Christina I'd take her to SeaWorld."

"I knew it!" Anna laughed. "You two sneaking behind my back again?"

19

"Not really; it just came up in conversation a couple of weeks ago."

"And what about Mr. Waffles?" Anna asked.

"SeaWorld has a pet-sitting service. I checked."

"Looks like you've thought of everything."

"My cousin has a time-share in Orlando. She's not using it, so she offered it to me, and the idea blossomed from there. I checked the airlines, and there is a flight out of Lubbock on Friday."

"Then, yes, you can take Christina and Mr. Waffles while I . . . do whatever I'm supposed to do." She'd feel better knowing Mandy and Christina were out of town.

"I promise, you'll have a good time. You know I've been on more than a dozen cruises, and I had a blast every time. You'll be surprised at all the activities on and off the ship. Maybe you could vlog. No, forget I said that. This is a vacation from vlogging. Though you could take pictures."

"I'll hold you to that. If it's too awful, you're in for it, big-time," Anna teased. "And no pictures."

"Right. So, I can call the travel agency?" Mandy asked. "They've kept a room on the upper deck open for you; it's the best they have. We can fly to Orlando together. I don't think the flight was completely booked."

"Make the call."

"Consider it done," Mandy singsonged, taking her cell phone from her pocket. Mandy was the ultimate vacationer, being single and gorgeous. They'd hit it off right away when she'd applied for the assistant position, and they'd been best friends ever since.

Anna shook her head, amazed that she'd so readily agreed to Mandy's plans. She really did need some time away from work. As much as she enjoyed working, a few days to herself would be nice. Factor in the fear she'd been living with for the past few weeks, and Mandy's cruise plans couldn't have happened at a better time.

Since Wade's death, she had dated a few guys, but there was nothing serious with any of them. Except one. Sort of. James Banks. She wasn't really *that* serious about him, but he had been more than serious about her. He was a photographer she'd met while on location shooting a video for her YouTube channel. A true charmer. Blond, blue-eyed, and sexy as hell. She'd enjoyed spending time with him; he made her laugh and forget about the past. They'd already been seeing one another for three months when she learned he was still married. Feeling like a total fool, she'd broken it off immediately. He tried to convince her that he was in the process of getting a divorce. Anna adamantly told him no, see you later, have a nice life. She didn't need or want anyone's excess baggage. He'd called her numerous times, pleading for a second chance, but she'd politely told him he wasn't the one for her. He'd been hurt, but she knew he'd get over her, as he was quite handsome and outgoing. No doubt, women would line up just to have a date with him. She didn't need a man in her life. She and Christina had gotten along just fine without one in their lives, and she was positive she would continue to do just that.

Though late at night, when she was alone with her thoughts, she questioned her choices and how they would affect her daughter's future. Anna hoped that the absence of a male role model in Christina's life would not have any serious negative effects on her. She tried her best to be both mother and father, and so far, she hadn't heard any alarm bells ringing. Yet the issue was always present in her mind, especially now that Christina was a teenager. Hormones and peer pressure were very real. She didn't want her daughter to feel like she couldn't come to her if she had problems with school, her friends, or anything she wasn't sure of or comfortable with. So far, they'd shared a super mother-daughter relationship, and she prayed it would continue.

Anna had been raised in most part by her mother, her father having died from pancreatic cancer when she was only seven. She'd loved her dad so much, missed his big, booming voice when he'd come home from work, and for a while, it had been difficult for her to understand why he never came home again. With time and maturity, she understood, but she had never stopping missing him. He was the kind of man who walked into a room and people noticed him. He was movie-star handsome, with thick auburn hair and the same aqua-blue eyes she had, his smile as bright as the stars. People chartered his deep-sea fishing boat, the *Miss Ellie,* and he always had a story to tell at the dinner table. Her mother would laugh at his stories, telling him she knew a fish story when she heard one. They were a happy, fun-loving family. Then her father changed. Almost overnight. He lost weight, his bronzed skin became sallow, washed-out. His energy fizzled out like a deflated balloon. For months, her mother insisted that he go to the doctor for a checkup. And when he finally did, the news had devastated them. He hung on for nine months after his diagnosis. He died in her mother's arms late one night while Anna was sleeping. She remembered waking up that morning and seeing her mother, her eyes swollen from crying, and she knew her daddy was gone. Their sadness seemed to last forever after he died. Mom sold the fishing boat and their house. Then they'd moved to a small condo on Padre Island. While her mother tried her best, their lives were never the same. Holidays were lackluster, forced. In Anna's senior year of high school, her mother died of a massive heart attack at the young age of forty-two, and, once again, life for Anna drastically changed. With no family to speak of, she'd stayed with Elizabeth Callahan, her best friend in high school. As soon as she graduated, she moved to Lubbock to attend Texas Tech University. With three part-time jobs and a few scholarships, she managed to earn a bachelor's degree in marketing. She found a job with a small, family-owned ad agency in which she earned enough to rent an efficiency apartment and buy a secondhand Honda. Anna had many friends during her time in college, but none were so close that she shared with them the tragic story of how she'd lost her parents. It was still painful and raw, especially the loss of her mother and the nightmare of the panic attacks her death had caused. Those attacks almost crippled her as she blamed herself for her mother's death even though she knew it was impossible for her to have caused her mother to have a heart attack. It just seemed that everyone she loved died.

If she learned anything from her parents, it was to move forward and make each day count, to never live in the past. Positive to a fault, Anna did her very best to stay upbeat, but there were times when she thought she might fall apart. One lonely weekend, beyond homesick, she drove to Corpus Christi to check out her old house and all the places that were once so familiar to her. She'd purchased a sub sandwich from Heavenly Hoagies, taking it down to the docks at Red Dot Pier, where her father had anchored his fishing boat, and her life changed. Almost instantly.

She'd been lost in memories when a giant of a man caught her attention. For a moment, she'd thought it was her father, then realized how ridiculous that was. Her father was gone, but from a distance this guy reminded her of him. Tall, broad-shouldered, with light brown hair streaked from too much time in the sun. There was a worn leather tool belt hanging loosely around his hips, his muscular legs were encased in faded denim, and a too-tight, faded Houston Oilers shirt clung to his chest. Mesmerized, she'd watched him as he carefully sanded what appeared to be a piece of delicate wood. She wasn't sure of the type. Whatever it was, his long fingers touched it as though it were the most delicate object in the world. She was unsure how long she'd been sitting staring at him. Apparently it had been too long because he'd suddenly stopped and looked up, his eyes settling on her. He was the most beautiful male specimen she'd ever seen.

He tilted his head, as if in question, and she nodded, unsure why. She remembered the sound of the ocean slapping against the boat's hull, the briny smell, seagulls plunging down into the water, their high-pitched squeal piercing the air as they swooped down for their catch of the day.

It was as though time stopped. Anna had no memory of walking down the pier to the boat, though she did recall that his eyes never left hers. Time was endless. Without invitation, she'd reached for the hand he held out to her and stepped onto the deck. "I'm Wade Campbell."

26

"Anna Ross," she'd said, taking his hand. She'd never experienced such physicality from a single touch.

After that moment, her life was a whirlwind of change. She returned to Lubbock, gave a two-week notice at the ad agency. Luckily, she didn't have a lease on her small apartment. She packed what little she owned into the trunk of her Honda and, two and a half weeks later, she'd rented a dingy but cheap apartment in Corpus Christi. She wasn't so lucky finding work in her chosen field, so she'd taken a job as a desk clerk at the exclusive Omni Hotel. Eight months later, she and Wade were married in a small ceremony on the beach. Her life was almost perfect, and not a day passed that she didn't thank her lucky stars for her spur-of-the-moment trip to Corpus Christi.

For the next few years, Anna and Wade lived an ideal life. He finally saved enough money to purchase the shop he'd worked for, Woodworks. He specialized in restoring boats, yachts, and any water vessel that had any kind of wood. Though his was only a one-man operation, he made enough money for Anna to quit her job at the hotel. She'd saved enough for a down payment on a small house in Corpus Christi's Bay Area. The location was safe, family-oriented, and they both loved the neighborhood.

Anna had a knack for decorating, and she'd turned their average little home into a stylish yet comfortable living space. With so much time on her hands since she'd stopped working, she discovered she had a special flair in the kitchen. Her mother had been an excellent cook, too, so she assumed she'd inherited this skill from her. Wade was only too happy to be her taste tester. She fashioned new recipes for desserts and special drink concoctions, smoothies and a variety of drinks using Texas's famed Dr. Pepper as a base. She grew her own vegetables, herbs, and spices, another new skill she enjoyed. She relished entertaining in her tastefully decorated home and did so often, and the small group of friends they shared told her that an invitation to her dinner parties was in high demand from others in their neighborhood, neighbors whom Anna and Wade didn't know as well as they did Joyce, Robert, Ashley, and her husband, Bryan.

Once a month, she hosted a cookout for the neighborhood. They made more friends, and Anna looked forward to planning and preparing new and different meals for them.

Wade and Bryan both became motorcycle enthusiasts. Anna wasn't thrilled about it, but Wade enjoyed it immensely, and she was grateful he had a hobby that wasn't related to his work. After a few months of riding a second-hand motorcycle, he'd invested in a Harley, and this became his only mode of transportation during all but the rainy season. Then Anna insisted he drive his old pickup truck that had been on its last mile when they'd met. He was due for a new set of wheels, but until they saved up, he'd made do with his old truck and new Harley.

They had been married over two years when she discovered she was pregnant. Wade had been ecstatic when she'd told him the news. Unlike many new parents, they chose to wait until the birth to find out their child's gender. To Anna, this was part of the thrill of being pregnant. Their friends were astonished at this news but understood their desire to keep the excitement buzzing until the actual delivery.

As typical first-time births went, Anna was in labor for eighteen hours, Wade with her through every cry, every scream, then every push. He'd cut the cord, placed a tiny baby on her chest, and announced with tear-filled eyes, "We've got ourselves a little girl." She'd been over the moon, seeing her little bundle of joy, and only now would admit that she'd secretly hoped for a daughter the first time around. Andrew Wade Campbell would have a big sister whenever he arrived, if at all. Or not — because another girl would be just fine, too. They'd wanted at least two, maybe three children. Gender really didn't matter. Her love for Christina was enormous, so complete that she knew her heart would swell with love for each child she gave birth to.

The first few weeks were tough, but Anna was competent, patient, and madly in love with her daughter, so the loss of sleep and routine in their lives was worth it. She hadn't suffered from any dark moments after the birth and for that she was grateful.

Soon enough, they would be on a better schedule. Until then, she made the best of their new lifestyle. Wade took a month off work to stay home with her. She cherished the time but realized that one of them had to earn a living. Her first day alone with her daughter had been uneventful, and for that she was glad. As the weeks turned into months, her days and nights became more routine. Time flew, and suddenly, one day Christina was four months old, sleeping through most nights.

When Christina turned two, they decided to try for a brother or sister. Months went by and nothing happened. After a year of trying, they both visited their doctors to see if either had developed any medical issues that would prevent them from conceiving. Both were given a clean bill of health and were told to stop thinking about getting pregnant, and most likely they would easily have a second child.

On the fifth anniversary of their daughter's birth, Anna decided she would not have another child. It wasn't happening, and after many tears, anger at her own body, numerous crazy how-to-conceive concoctions, she told Wade she wasn't going to think about having another child. One was enough. Both were content with this decision. Secretly, though, Anna hoped that after having made the decision, she would get pregnant.

During Christina's first semester of second grade, her life, *their* lives changed forever. Anna couldn't forget that horrible day. She would never get over the loss though she'd learned to live with it.

She'd just put her daughter down for the night and settled on the sofa to read an article Wade had recently been featured in. Wade had a big job he'd had to finish, so she knew he wouldn't be in until late. Around midnight she'd gone to bed, knowing she'd see her husband in the morning.

Around four in the morning, she'd been woken from a sound sleep by the shrill sound of the telephone ringing. Thinking it was Wade, she answered with a sleepy-sounding hello.

"Mrs. Campbell?" a stern, businesslike voice asked.

She remembered sitting up, switching the bedside light on. "Yes, this is she."

From there, she always drew a blank. Her memory had completely blocked out the events of that early-morning tragedy. He'd been in a fatal motorcycle accident. All she needed to remember was that Wade was dead.

Her life would never be the same. The darkness overwhelmed her.

CHAPTER 2

"This is unbelievable," Anna said to the cabin steward.

"Yes, ma'am. This is the largest cabin on the ship," he said. "Your suite is the best we have to offer. No other compares."

She nodded. "It's more than I expected." It was like a luxurious apartment. There were two bedrooms, two and a half baths, and two private balconies.

"You'll have the entire fourteen hundred square feet of space all to yourself," the steward continued. "Unless . . . well, this *is* a singles cruise, ma'am." He added the last sentence with a wink.

"Call me Anna." She knew from the brochure she'd read on the plane that she was assigned a personal steward/butler. She didn't want to be called "ma'am" for seven days. Might as well get that out of the way.

"My pleasure. And you may call me

George," he said in a lovely Jamaican accent.

Extending her hand, she said, "We could be besties at the end of this cruise."

He laughed and shook her hand. "Besties?"

George appeared to be in his mid- to late-twenties. Tall and broad-shouldered, he was a good-looking guy. With his coffee-colored eyes, dark, closely clipped hair, and warm brown skin, he probably had women falling at his feet. "It's what my daughter calls her best friend, Tiffany. Besties."

"Of course. Then we will be 'besties,' Anna," he said, his smile friendly and a bit flirty in a teasing sort of way.

Some women might've been offended. She wasn't at all. Having the ability to read people, she suspected George was just as friendly to everyone he met.

Spying a silver bucket on the kitchen counter, she removed a bottle of Veuve Clicquot champagne. "Nice," she said.

"Allow me," George said, taking the chilled bottle of champagne from her.

"Thank you," she said, heading out to the balcony. Excited to have such a luxurious space all to herself, she settled onto a lounge chair. The summer air was thick with humidity, but there was just enough breeze from the Gulf for it to be tolerable. Glad she'd packed shorts and several sleeveless sundresses, she decided then and there she was going to do just as Mandy suggested. Rest, relax, and allow herself to be waited on. According to the brochure, that was the main point of cruising on the *Splendor of the Sea.*

George stepped onto the balcony, a glass of the Veuve Clicquot on a tray. "I'll leave the bottle to chill," he said. "If you need anything, Anna, please push the button labeled STEWARD. I'm available around the clock."

They really did wait on one hand and foot, she thought. "Thank you, George. I'm going to enjoy this" — she held up the crystal flute of champagne — "then I plan to unpack and get settled in."

George held up his free hand. "No, no you may not! I will unpack for you now."

"That's okay. I can do it myself."

"Anna, this is what I'm here for. Please allow me to do my job," he insisted.

She wasn't comfortable with him handling her lingerie and personal items. "I insist. I'm a bit OCD and have my own system, so please, let me take care of that later. I'll have another glass," she added, holding the flute out to him. If she continued to drink this fast, she'd be totally inebriated by dinner; she already felt a bit light-headed from just one glass. Not much of a drinker since she'd had Christina, she reminded herself to take it easy. She didn't want George to think she was heavy-handed with the booze. He whirled away and, within seconds, was back with a fresh flute of the bubbly.

"Thank you," she said. "I'm going to enjoy this." Once again, she held her flute up high as if she were proposing a toast. "And maybe a nap."

"As you wish," he said, standing in the doorway. "I'm only a button away if there is anything you need."

She nodded. "Thanks." This would go on forever if she didn't send him on his merry way. Feigning a yawn, she said, "That nap is calling."

Finally she had the place to herself and decided to explore her temporary home for the next seven days and six nights. The master suite was much larger than she'd anticipated. A king-size bed with a magnificent view looking out over the Gulf of Mexico would, she hoped, lull her to sleep at night. In addition to the bed and the view, there was a luxurious whirlpool tub on one balcony, and a flat-screen TV. Guerlain bath products and plush robes and slippers ensured a spalike experience. When Mandy said the accommodations were top-of-the-line, she wasn't kidding. Double sinks steeped in marble, a telephone, and a second flat-screen TV were just a few of the luxuries the ship provided. Tonight, she would take a bath, a much-loved pleasure, which she did most nights if her schedule allowed. Most of her free time was devoted to her daughter.

She wandered into the kitchen area and saw an espresso coffeemaker, her favorite brand of coffee, Kaya Kopi — no doubt Mandy's doing — plus a large assortment of the Norman Love chocolates she adored. From what she could see, Mandy had all the bases covered. Speaking of which, she was supposed to call Mandy when she had settled in.

Thankful for the satellite phone, she dialed Mandy's cell. Mandy must have been waiting for her because she answered on the first ring.

"I take it you like your room?" Mandy didn't bother with "hello."

"More than like," Anna said. "It's the size of an apartment. I don't even want to ask how much it cost because it might ruin the trip."

"Right. You could rent the entire ship and

not worry about pricing," Mandy teased.

She could, it was true, but she did not go around advertising her wealth. She'd always thought that doing so was a little on the tacky side. "This is perfect. I'm glad you decided I needed time away. I didn't realize I needed this until I saw the tub overlooking the Gulf."

"Pretty ritzy then?" Mandy asked.

"Let's just put it this way. If this were an apartment in New York City, it would sell for millions."

"I am always happy to help out," Mandy informed her. "Let me tear Christina away from Mr. Waffles. Hang on."

Anna smiled. Mr. Waffles had been a fantastic birthday present.

"Hey, Mom," Christina said. "How's the deep-sea stuff?"

"So far, so good. How's Orlando?"

"Hot but awesome. Disney is everywhere. They have Mickey Mouse telephone lines. Mandy cussed a few times in the traffic, I've had fast food all day, so it's totally off the charts."

Typical thirteen-year-old speak, Anna thought. She was not happy about the fast food, but it was her vacation, too.

"Sounds fun. How's Mr. Waffles?"

"Awesome as ever. I'm glad we didn't have

to give him that sedative. He's super nosy right now. I took him out of his carrier once we got the rental car, and he slept on my lap the entire time we were in traffic. It was like he knew he had to behave."

"He's a charmer, no doubt. What's on tomorrow's agenda?"

"SeaWorld, then Typhoon Lagoon, and Epcot the day after. Mom, seriously, you should think about coming here next trip; of course, I'll come along. It's gonna take us weeks to see all Orlando has to offer. Can we do this again next year?"

Anna heard the excitement in her daughter's voice. She knew Christina might have a totally different opinion on hanging out with her mom next summer, so she said, "Yes, we'll definitely do Disney together."

"Promise?"

"You've only been there for a day!"

"I know, but I want to come back," Christina said in her whiny voice.

"Tell you what. Spend the next six days seeing all the sights, and we'll plan a trip when we're both at home. How's that sound?"

"You'll love it here."

"I'm sure I will; now put Mandy back on," she said, then added, "Love you, sweetie."

"Love you, too." Christina returned the

sentiment.

"Sounds like she's having the time of her life. Just go easy on the junk food. I'm afraid she'll refuse to be my taste tester," Anna joshed. "Mr. Waffles digging the condo? No marking his territory?" The first week home, the cat peed all over the house, letting them know it was his place, too. Thankfully, it'd been on the tile flooring.

"Nope, at least not yet. I think he's inspecting the place," Mandy told her. "We've got all of his toys and his bed set out for him. He nosed around when we arrived, but no peeing. Speaking of peeing, how many guys have made a mark with you?"

Anna laughed. "That's gross! And I haven't had a chance to mingle. We had to go through all the safety regulations first. When we finished, I came straight to my cabin."

"Exciting, Anna. Promise me you're not going to hole up in that luxurious cabin for the entire cruise."

"My steward is hot," Anna said, just to get a rise out of Mandy.

"Tell me all about him," Mandy encouraged.

"His name is George. He's tall, broad-shouldered, very handsome. Sexy brown eyes. I think he's Jamaican. He's well-spoken, courteous. All that a steward should be; at least I think he is."

"Then go for it," Mandy practically yelled into the phone.

"Mandy, if I had to guess, I would say he's all of twenty-eight at the most."

"So what? Age is simply a number."

Anna rolled her eyes. "Stop! I'm not going to hit on George. He's cute but not my type." *Whatever that is,* she thought. "I don't plan to sit in the cabin for the rest of the week. I'd truly have cabin fever. There's a welcome-aboard dinner tonight at eight. I plan to attend. And mingle."

"Wear that Prada dress. You look drop-dead gorgeous in that," Mandy said. "And don't tell me otherwise."

The Prada dress was very expensive; she had bought it for a special YouTube event in Dallas but never wore it. "I'm wearing that on the last night. The itinerary says that's dinner-with-the-captain night. Surf and turf. Listen, you and Christina enjoy Orlando. I'll call you tomorrow at ten, just to say hi. Take care of my baby, and be careful."

"Absolutely, Anna. Enjoy yourself," Mandy said.

Grinning, Anna returned to the kitchen and made herself a cup of espresso. If she was going to mingle at dinner tonight, she'd need the caffeine. Two glasses of champagne were one over her limit. Without the coffee, she would fall asleep on that tempting bed.

Wanting to soak in the tub but knowing she was a goner if she did, she opted for a cool shower. All the glass made her feel exposed. Afterward, she wrapped herself in the plush robe and took her cup of coffee out to the balcony.

The cruise would take her to the Cayman Islands. For years, Mandy had been telling her about her trips to the Caribbean, Mexico, and the Panama Canal. She'd been to Spain and Italy, places Anna had only read about. She would never tell Mandy, but she had been envious of her faraway trips. She and Wade hadn't been on a honeymoon. They'd agreed when they decided to go, it would be the trip of a lifetime. Sadly, that was old news, and Anna doubted she'd ever have a honeymoon because she knew in her heart she would never replace her husband. She could have grieved her loss forever, but fortunately, she had a child to care for. In a sense, it was what had saved her from drowning in her own sorrow. In the beginning, it was her grief that had saved her, and now, looking back, she knew she wouldn't have been nearly as successful had she not started her vlog on the subject. Life had a strange way of giving back, she thought. She'd seen so much death. First her father, then her mother, and, finally, her husband. Would anyone be interested in someone like her? Would they see her as some sort of bad luck, a dark omen if she were to reveal this?

She tried to clear her mind, but her thoughts kept returning to her fear of death. Everyone she'd ever loved had died. Suddenly, she felt the familiar gnawing sensation in her stomach. Her mouth went dry, and her hands started to shake. Anna felt the familiar tightness in her throat and painful stomach cramps. She tried to take a deep breath, easing it out slowly, just as she'd been taught all those years ago. In and out. She closed her eyes and listened to the sounds. Focus. Laughter. Music. She took another deep breath.

Voices. Glass breaking. Seagulls. The ship's engines.

Opening her eyes once again, she had calmed down. She returned to the kitchen, took a bottle of water from the refrigerator, and gulped down the entire bottle. She closed her eyes and went to her happy place, a technique she'd learned when she was in therapy. It had been so long since she'd had an attack. Why now? If she had to speculate, she blamed the person who had been stalking her. Now that she was on her own, with no one covering her back, she felt vulnerable.

She should have gone to Orlando with the girls. If she did that now, then she would most likely ruin Christina's vacation since she adored being alone with Mandy. At this precise moment, she couldn't care less about her own trip.

Just thinking about why she had panic attacks caused her heart rate to triple and her palms to go damp. "No!" she shouted. "Christina is fine!

"I am not going through this shit again."

The physical act of talking calmed her down. She didn't care if anyone was outside her door listening. And who would be, anyway? George? The captain? No, she was letting her thoughts drive her back into that dark place.

She'd spent too much time in therapy to have it all go down the drain over her first vacation alone. All the skills were within her; she hadn't forgotten them. What she had forgotten, though, was that she might need to use them again.

Calm down, she told herself.

In the middle of the Gulf of Mexico,

alone, knowing no one, as much as she didn't want to, she went to the bathroom, opened her cosmetic case, and took out the bottle of pills she had brought with her. They were always with her. A security blanket of sorts. Yes, she'd dipped into the amber bottle a few times when she really needed them, but if ever there was an appropriate time, it was now. Before she could change her mind, she swallowed the yellow pill. Hating herself for being weak, she knew that if she was going to get through this evening, she didn't have much of a choice.

Xanax. Her dirty little secret. Not even Mandy knew of the stash she kept in that little bottle. Christina had found it once when she'd asked for some cash, and Anna told her to look in her purse. Her daughter asked her what the medication was for, and she'd lied to her, telling her it was for cramps. She felt horrible for lying to her daughter, but she couldn't tell her daughter about her hang-up.

If she did, who knew what kind of harm it might cause her? She was thirteen and vulnerable. She didn't know her like this, the old Anna. The Anna that for years had lived in constant fear of losing her daughter because she blamed herself for her family's dying and feared it could happen to her

45

child. And the current Anna, who had been looking over her shoulder for weeks. The phone calls. The letters. The e-mails. The constant feeling of being watched. She didn't want Christina to learn about this side of her.

How quickly she'd reverted back to her old ways, believing she was a jinx because all of her loved ones had died. She knew it sounded insane, but she had felt that way, and been forced to deal with it. When she started therapy, she'd learned there was no way she could have caused their deaths. In time, she was able to put the bad thoughts away and focus on Christina and her own career. She'd never been away from Christina for more than two or three days at a time. The separations were always work-related, and she had managed just fine.

Until now. She was allowing her thoughts to get the best of her.

Being out here in the middle of nowhere, away from her daughter, her work, and all things familiar, had caused her to panic. She was out of her comfort zone, out of control. This, and the crazy jinx she believed herself to have.

Fifteen minutes later, the Xanax started to take effect, more so than normal as she'd had those two glasses of champagne.

She knew better. She wasn't thinking clearly. Knowing she was in no shape to mingle, or do anything else, Anna gave in to the alcohol and the effects of the anti-anxiety medication.

CHAPTER 3

Anna woke to the sound of a symphony. At first, she thought they'd gathered outside her door, performing solely for her. Lying flat on her back, it took a few seconds before she remembered where she was.

The cruise ship.

She opened one eye, then the other. Sunlight attacked her eyes. Quickly closing them, she moaned as she recalled the events of the night before. She'd had only two glasses of champagne. And a Xanax. Shit, she'd mixed an anti-anxiety drug with alcohol. A definite no-no. With her eyes closed, she inched her way upright into a reclining position, slowly, so as not to encourage her brain or her stomach to react to her stupidity.

Carefully, she opened her eyes again, and this time, the sunlight streaming in wasn't so harsh. She realized that the symphony she thought was playing outside her door was in her head. A soft tempo pulsed against her temples. Knowing it wasn't going to go away on its own, she forced herself out of the bed and into the bathroom. Part of her wanted to heave the vestiges of last night's stupidity, but another part couldn't deal with the idea of hanging her head down in order to accomplish the deed. What she considered the sane part of her reached inside the shower. Adjusting the temperature to icy cold, she stripped out of the heavy robe, amazed that she'd actually slept in something so bulky. Of course, she was still in the robe because she had passed out. And without overthinking the situation, she forced herself to stand beneath the icy jets of water.

Lucky for her, there was a seat built into the shower. She directed the waterfall toward her face, then sat down, letting the cool water wash away her brain fog. When she felt stable, she stood, adjusted the temperature to hot, and washed with the Guerlain body wash, and shampooed her hair with shampoo that smelled like orange blossoms. She quite liked it, and squinted to see the brand. Maybe they'd have it available for purchase. She would ask George.

George.

Rinsing the shampoo from her hair, she

grabbed a thick towel and wrapped it around her hair and another around herself. On the marble counter, there was a toothbrush and toothpaste, not hers. But it would do until she unpacked. She looked at her image in the mirror. Her eyes were bloodshot and puffy. She really felt awful, but knew she'd feel better as soon as she had a cup of coffee and downed a couple of Advil. She'd never been much of a drinker, but there were quite a few times she remembered having more than two glasses of champagne. And she had never felt this crappy the next day. It had to be the Xanax on top of the bubbly. Anna was positive she'd never mixed the two before, and there was no way she would ever mix them again. Lesson learned.

She made a cup of coffee, thankful for the upscale espresso machine. As soon as the last drop filled the small white china cup, she brought it to her lips, inhaled the heady aroma, and took a sip of the rich, dark brew. "This is heaven," she said aloud just to hear some sound in the room. Standing in the compact kitchen with nothing but the taste of premium coffee and her thoughts, she remembered she had told George that she would attend the welcome dinner. Had he sneaked into her room and seen her sprawled across the bed, passed out? She hoped not, but it was his job to tend to her. He probably thought she was an old drunk, looking for a man. She'd certainly understand if that *was* what he thought. She brewed a second cup of coffee and stepped out onto the balcony without the whirlpool. She didn't remember closing the heavy drapes, so George must have come into her room at some point. She sat on the chaise lounge, not caring that she wasn't dressed. She would enjoy this while she had the opportunity. That's why Mandy insisted she take a vacation. To do what she wanted, when she wanted, without fear. Last night had put paid to that theory.

A light knock on her door sent her flying out of the lounge chair.

"Just a sec," she called. Hurrying to the bedroom, she took a fresh robe from the closet, slipped her arms through the sleeves, then returned to the door. "Who's there?" she asked, feeling like an idiot for even asking.

"Ma'am, it's George. I've brought a tray for you," he answered in that sexy Jamaican accent.

She adjusted the belt on her robe, planted a smile on her face, and opened the door. "Come in," she said, feeling completely washed-out.

George was all smiles. He was wearing a crisp white jacket and matching pants creased to the nines. It was obvious that, unlike her, he had not awakened with a hangover. He was very easy on the eyes. She stood aside and allowed him to enter her suite with the rolling cart of what she guessed was breakfast.

"You were not well last night, Anna?" he asked, as he removed silver covers from several plates.

That was putting it mildly, but he didn't need to know more than that. "I was a bit seasick, I think. I took Dramamine and slept like a log." She hated lying to him but told herself sometimes a little white lie was necessary.

"Quite common," he said, placing the plates on the dining table. "This is what we call 'the morning after' brunch. It should perk you up in no time."

Food was the last thing on her mind, but he was right. She'd feel better with something in her stomach.

"This is enough for a family of four," she said, eyeing all the food.

"This is a small feast, yes, but a bite of each and you'll feel brand-new," he said, a smile on his face and a twinkle in his eyes.

He pulled a chair out for her. Sitting down, she assumed that he was going to stand beside her and watch her eat. "Why don't you join me?" she asked, certain that he would decline her invitation.

"Thank you. It will be my pleasure," he said, and seated himself in the chair opposite her.

Did he think she was coming on to him?

She nodded and took another sip of her now-cold coffee.

"The green tea and honey are especially good for . . . your health." He placed a tea bag inside a fresh cup, added a huge dollop of honey, then poured boiling water from a carafe over the tea bag.

"True, but I'm going to have another cup of this," she replied, holding her cup in the air. Once in the kitchen, with her back to him, she asked, "Is this part of your duties? Having breakfast with me?" She waited for the dark brown liquid to fill the cup.

"Yes, it is, if required," he answered.

Fair enough, she thought. Turning to face him, she leaned against the countertop, sipping the much-needed caffeine for the extra jolt it provided. "So how do you determine if this is required?" she asked, a smile on her face. She couldn't help it. He was so handsome, so proper. Had he been twenty years older, she might be in trouble.

"I have my ways," he said, filling her plate with scrambled eggs and slices of avocado.

"Look, I know what you're thinking, and I'd think the same thing if I were in your position, but I only had two glasses of that champagne last night. What's the alcohol content of that stuff anyway?" she asked, pretty sure of the answer but needing to say something in her own defense.

"Ah, the Veuve Clicquot. No more than any other quality champagne. Around twelve or thirteen percent, I believe, but I'm no Philippe Clicquot, the founder of the French champagne house, one of the largest in the world. After he died, his wife — they called her the Grande Dame of Champagne — took over for him. Very successful. I believe she was in her late twenties when she was widowed. Quite the businesswoman for her generation, she invented the first-known rosé champagne by blending red and white champagne wines, a process still used to this very day. Very brilliant woman, as most are."

"I'm impressed," Anna said. "You're quite the sommelier and teacher."

He took a bite of egg, then a sip of tea. "Some would say it's part of my job to know these things."

54

"Again, you've impressed me."

"Eat, Anna. Please," he implored, not bothering to acknowledge her compliment.

She sat down, feeling more like herself after her third cup of coffee.

"What time is it, anyway?" she asked. "I wanted to attend the cooking class." She took a forkful of eggs and a slice of avocado. Chewing, she realized she was hungry and hadn't eaten since yesterday afternoon. She took a slice of watermelon from the plate, a banana, and a few strawberries. All good hangover foods, she knew.

"It's after two," he said.

"In the afternoon?" She waved her hand in front of her. "Never mind. Of course, it's afternoon," she replied, answering her own question. Glancing outside to the balcony, she could tell by the sun's position that it was midafternoon.

"You missed the class, but they will have another on the return trip. Tonight, there is a dancing contest. It's always one of the most attended events. You should go."

"I'm not much of a dancer," she said. The only rhythm she possessed was in the kitchen.

"As you'll find, most of the guests aren't. However, many will lose all inhibition when a bit of alcohol is consumed."

"That's not going to be me. I am a teetotaler from here on in," she said, then realized her mistake. "Possibly a fruity cocktail. I'll have to get my sea legs before I indulge." She almost added *anymore* but caught herself.

"Then I'll leave you to finish and prepare yourself for tonight. The fun starts at seven o'clock. If there is anything you need," he said, as he returned his chair beneath the table, "all you have to do is push a button. Enjoy your afternoon, Anna." He nodded, then returned to wherever he was supposed to be.

"That was fast," she said to no one.

Her first day at sea was a total flop. Literally. What to do until seven? She left the table, food and all, and returned to the chaise lounge. Unsure if George's behavior was normal, she reached for the satellite phone extension and dialed Mandy's cell.

"Hey," Mandy said, sounding out of breath.

"Hey, back. You okay?" Anna asked.

"Out of shape is what I am. Hang on," Mandy told her. "Okay, that's better. I had to sit down. Christina is on a roller coaster. No way was I going with her. She's fine. I had to trek across the park to the first-aid center. I've got blisters the size of golf balls."

Typical Mandy. "Please tell me you're not wearing those espadrilles? The ones with the four-inch platforms?"

Mandy didn't answer.

"You are, aren't you?"

"I didn't realize SeaWorld was so . . . hilly."

"Then go buy yourself a pair of sandals! I'm sure there has to be some sort of gift shop there that sells shoes. I can't believe you," Anna said, and laughed. "Looks before comfort, I know." Those were the words Mandy lived by. "Hilly? Isn't Florida as flat as West Texas?"

"Even more, if that's humanly possible."

"I have a question. . . ."

"I'm sure you do. Shoot," Mandy said.

"My steward, George. Super nice guy, but I'm wondering exactly what his duties consist of. I slept in" — another lie — "and he knocked on my door, had enough food for a family, set the table, then I casually asked him to join me, and I wasn't remotely serious. And he did. Is that normal?"

"Normally, no. I've never stayed in a cabin as luxurious as yours, but I'm sure the travel agent mentioned something about a personal butler. Did you ask him?"

"Yes, and he basically said the same thing. I just thought it a little strange. I'm not used

57

to being catered to." She'd never get used to it because she liked her privacy too much.

"I know what you're thinking. Don't read more into this. All I can say is, enjoy it while it lasts. We've a heavy-duty filming session for the upcoming fall season. Speaking of which, I'd give anything for a bit of cool weather. It's humid as hell today. What about you?"

"I'm in the middle of nowhere, Mandy. The weather is" — she paused — "warm and sunny. Tell Christina I called. I'll check in sometime tomorrow. "Remember, don't let her out of your sight, and make sure you're there when she exits the ride."

"She's fine. Tell me about the captain's dinner. Did you meet anyone worth mentioning?"

She knew Mandy wouldn't be satisfied without getting every detail she could. "I slept through the entire evening. I think I was . . . overtired. Plus, I had a Dramamine. So, no, I didn't meet anyone worth mentioning."

"Anna, please get your rear end out of that room and mingle. You can sleep later. Do you know how many women would love to trade places with you? You're out of your mind if you don't take advantage of all those single guys."

She rolled her eyes, glad that she was alone. "I'm going to the dancing contest tonight. I have to be there at seven, so give my girl kisses, and I'll talk to her tomorrow." Before Mandy could say another word, Anna disconnected the call. Now wasn't the time for a sermon. She felt bad enough as it was, wasting the entire evening, embarrassed that George had to deliver breakfast — rather . . . *brunch* — to her room. With that in mind, she returned to her room and unpacked. She hung all her dresses in the closet, put her lingerie in a drawer, and used another for her shorts and T-shirts. Before she did anything else, she took the bottle of Xanax out of her cosmetic bag and placed the bottle in the small safe in the back of the closet. She followed the instructions and assured herself the medication was secure, out of temptation for her or anyone else who entered her suite. Not that she didn't trust George. Worse, she didn't trust herself not to toss a couple pills in her bag, and at the first sign of a panic attack, pop them into her mouth.

Not wanting to go there, she decided she'd have a bath before the evening's big event. She filled the tub with hot water and lowered herself into the sweet warmth. This was perfect. She used the Guerlain bath

59

salts, the scent reminding her of a perfume her mother had worn. She knew it was still around but couldn't recall its exact name. Later, she might research it, but now, all she wanted to do was soak her worries away, get all glammed up for the evening, and just enjoy being here. Mandy had taken the time to make all these arrangements with the travel agency. Her special coffee and the Norman Love chocolates she was so fond of. She was right; anyone in their right mind would envy such a luxurious vacation.

Anna was about to drift off when she heard a noise. Unsure if George would wait for her permission to enter, she eased out of the tub, wrapping herself in a towel, and went to the cabin's main entrance. She waited but didn't hear anything else. Deciding it was some sort of normal ship noise that she wasn't aware of, she turned away and headed for her room and she heard the noise again. She stopped and waited.

Metal jiggling. Like keys in a pocket.

Could my stalker have followed me to the Caribbean?

It was probably someone passing her room who just happened to have keys in their pocket. Anna made a mental note to tell George not to enter her rooms when she was there unless she called for him or there was an emergency. While she appreciated the personal touch, she didn't want to have him just walking in whenever he wanted. Sure, this wasn't the cruise line's policy, but she still needed him to know she had boundaries.

Back in her room, she picked out a lemon-yellow dress, a leftover from last summer but still stylish enough to wear that evening. She spent the next twenty minutes drying her hair, then twisted it into a sophisticated topknot. She added a powder foundation and a bit of blush and mascara. A touch of sheer lip gloss was enough. She wore so much makeup when they were filming, it would be good for her and her skin to have a break from all the heavy-duty stuff. This was her glam for the night.

Anna took out a small silver clutch and added her cell phone, just in case, the lip gloss, and her room key. No need for cash, a credit card, or an ID since her room key would be scanned, and all charges added to her final bill at the end of the cruise. She couldn't imagine what damage she'd allowed Mandy to do to her bank account for this trip, but she'd live with whatever it was. With a smart financial advisor, Anna had secured not only her future but Christina's, too. Her daughter would be able to attend the college of her choice provided her grades were up to par. Anna would never allow herself to become dependent on Christina or anyone else for that matter. She'd worked her ass off to be in this position, and no one would ever take it away from her.

A bit proud of her own success, she left her cabin, and decided that, come hell or high water, she was going to enjoy the evening.

CHAPTER 4

The *Splendor of the Sea* was beyond magnificent. The brochure didn't do it justice. Glass elevators, giant chandeliers, and large, cushy sofas and plush chairs invited one to lounge in sumptuous comfort.

Anna didn't remember the stats of the ship, but surely, it could easily house a few thousand people. How in the world would she or anyone else find that *one* special person in such a large pool of singles?

Exiting the glass elevator, she was amazed at the quiet, especially knowing this wasn't just some deep-sea fishing boat of the kind, with only a few passengers, that her father had captained. She'd expected to be bombarded by crowds.

There was still an hour before the contest, so she decided to have dinner before the festivities. The main dining room, the Compass Royale, accommodated all guests in the more luxurious cabins, without them having to bother to make a reservation. Delicious scents guided her to a stunning room overlooking the water. There were round tables scattered throughout the room, adorned with crisp, white-linen tablecloths, and surrounded by lush gold-and-maroon seats that appeared as cushy as those in the main atrium. Not sure of the procedure since she'd spent her first night at sea passed out, she spied a giant lectern with two men dressed like George. She approached the pair, smiling. "Uh, hello. Am I too early for dinner?" She looked around, seeing only a sprinkling of guests seated sporadically throughout the large dining space.

"Not at all, ma'am," said one of the men in a heavy Spanish accent. "Please, follow me."

Anna followed him to a table overlooking the aquamarine Caribbean Sea. "This is stunning," she said, sitting down in the chair he pulled out for her. "I had no idea," she added, more to herself than him. She knew the waters of the Caribbean were much different from those of the Gulf of Mexico, but until actually seeing them, she hadn't realized how dazzling they were. Obviously, she'd slept through their arrival to the Caribbean.

"Excuse me," a deep male voice said, interrupting her reverie.

Anna turned her gaze from the blue water to a pair of striking sapphire eyes. Momentarily taken aback, she couldn't help herself. This man was gorgeous. With thick black hair a bit long, he reminded her of a Viking. He was tall — at least six-three — with a with broad and muscular chest, obvious given the tight white dress shirt he wore. He was so handsome, it disturbed her in ways she'd long forgotten.

"Yes?" she asked, feeling slightly embarrassed for staring but thinking he was probably used to it, given his good looks and body.

He smiled, and again, she felt physical sensations that'd been dormant for years.

"Forgive me for staring, but aren't you *the* Anna Campbell?" he asked. "From Lubbock?"

Relief surged through her, though she was unsure why. "I am, indeed," she said, in her best vlogging voice.

"I thought so," he said. "I'm a big fan."

Warning lights blared.

You're safe on this ship.

She knew she had thousands of fans but hadn't really thought about their physical characteristics. Many fans were men, and those she'd met did not look like the male specimen before her. "Thank you," was all she could come up with.

He gestured to the empty seat. "May I?" he asked.

So, this is how it works!

Hesitating for a few seconds, she replied, "Of course."

Seated across from her, she observed lines etched around his eyes and a smattering of gray hair at his temples. His skin was tanned, and a dark shadow of stubble outlined a chiseled jaw and square chin. Early- to mid-forties, she would guess.

He held a hand out to her. "Ryan Robertson from Lubbock, as you might've guessed. I'm just a groupie, and when I saw you, I had to introduce myself, make sure you're the real deal. I watch *The Simple Life* every Tuesday night, eight o'clock sharp."

Anna laughed. "I didn't realize I had any 'groupies,' Ryan Robertson from Lubbock." *And if I do,* she thought, *it never would have occurred to me that they'd look like you,* she wanted to add but kept to herself.

"Maybe that's not the right word, but I recognized you when I saw you sit down. So," he said, "I take it you're here alone?"

More alarm bells. Anna thought this was obvious since this was a singles cruise, and said, "If you're asking if I'm here with other singles, the answer is no."

"I'm sorry. I shouldn't have intruded on your privacy. When I saw you, I just . . . well, here I am. An overexcited fan," he said.

She wasn't sure if she should invite him to have dinner with her; she didn't want to seem desperate, however, this *was* a singles cruise. She needed to move forward, forget what happened at home. This man was gorgeous. Mandy would kill her if she missed this opportunity. "Please, stay," she said. "Have dinner with me?" Anna couldn't believe she was so bold.

Ryan appeared surprised.

"Are you sure?" He smiled, sending her pulse racing.

"Absolutely," she said. "I want to have dinner before the contest tonight," she added.

He nodded. "Ah, the dancing contest."

"Yes, but I'm only an observer. I'm not much of a dancer," she said, wanting to make it clear that in no way would she participate.

"Me, too," he agreed. "Though my daughter is an excellent dancer."

"You have a daughter?" she asked, relief flooding through her.

He swallowed, clearing his throat. "She's

thirteen. Need I say more? But she is the love of my life."

The tenderness in his words found their way straight to her heart. "I understand completely. I have a daughter, too." She didn't want to give out too many details about herself yet, as he was a stranger, no matter that she'd just invited him to sit at her table and have dinner with her. But she felt safe with dozens of people running around the dining room.

"Then we have two things in common."

She raised her brows in question. "Lubbock and single parenting?"

He nodded in agreement. "It has its moments, I have to say. I have a son as well. He just graduated from high school. I don't know what I'll do when it's just me and Renée in the house all by ourselves."

Anna could've interpreted his words a dozen ways but chose not to. "I don't even want to think about that yet. My daughter starts high school this year. I've been dreading it, though I shouldn't. She's a great girl." She missed her daughter at that moment and made a mental note not to forget to call her later.

"Patrick, that's my son, is a bit shy, which made high school a bit tough for him at times, but he did manage to graduate,"

Ryan said, in an offhanded way.

Before she had a chance to reply, their waiter came to the table. "Good evening, I'm Donal, and it will be my pleasure to take care of your dining needs during the cruise." A short man, maybe in his mid-fifties, with an unmistakable Irish accent, stood by their table. He had the reddish brown hair to match her image of an Irishman. Anna thought he had kind eyes.

"I'm Anna," she introduced herself, and held out her hand, not sure if this was appropriate etiquette for the staff, but manners were important to her, no matter the setting. She was a true Southerner, and these minute details were a part of her. Donal took her hand, brought it to his mouth, and gave it a light, friendly kiss. She blushed, then grinned. Apparently, he *was* a true Irishman. "And a beautiful lass, too." He winked.

"I'm not sure that's called for," Ryan said. Anna detected a trace of disapproval in his tone.

Anna spoke up, saying, "It's perfectly fine." She shot Ryan a warning look. She'd just met this guy five minutes ago, and he had no say over what she or anyone connected to her said.

He held both hands up. "I'm so sorry, I

don't know what came over me. Talk of my daughter, I guess. Donal, accept my apology."

"Of course, sir," Donal replied, then focused his attention on Anna. "What about drinks? We have every imaginable drink in the world."

"Just ginger ale for me," Anna said.

"I'll have the same," Ryan said, not looking at Donal.

Dismissive, Anna thought now, wishing she'd been more discerning when it came to inviting this stranger to dinner. It wasn't like she had a lot of experience in this area.

Unsure of what to say, she said nothing. Good advice from her mother.

"I seem to have offended you, Anna. I am so very sorry. I confess that Renée was on my mind. She's become boy-crazy, and I'm having a hard time dealing with it and took my insecurities out on poor Donal."

"I've yet to go through the boy phase with my daughter, but I'm sure it's right around the corner. I gave her a kitten for her thirteenth birthday. Most of her energy is focused on him, so I guess I'm lucky." Briefly, Anna wondered how Mr. Waffles was adapting to vacation life.

"Renée is allergic to cats," Ryan said.

"I'm sorry" was all she could think to say

70

though she knew it was a fairly common allergy.

"She did have a bird once. A parakeet she called Mrs. Peck. Poor bird died after three weeks. She's never wanted an animal since."

Donal returned with their ginger ale and two small menus. "Whenever you're ready," he said, then left them alone.

"That's too bad," Anna continued. "Poor girl. We've always had animals, though this is the first animal that she has complete responsibility for. So far, it's been good for her. I imagine that when school starts, we'll have to make an adjustment."

"How so?" Ryan asked.

Anna did her best to keep from stating the obvious without appearing rude. "I'll have to take care of Mr. Waffles while she's at school," she explained. "It's no problem since I work from home."

"You work from home? I thought *The Simple Life* was recorded in a studio?"

She smiled. "Lucky for me, I have a studio at home." She thought all her fans knew this. "The best of both worlds. It can get hectic at times, trying to balance work and home, but it's working, and I'm sure it will continue for as long as I need it to." Hearing her stomach growl, she took a sip of ginger ale, somehow managing to knock her

71

flatware onto the floor. She bent down to retrieve it, knowing Donal would provide another set. "I think we should order now. I don't know about you, but I'm famished."

Ryan tossed his head back, laughing. "No one is famished on a cruise," he said. He felt around for something in his shirt pocket, yet Anna saw nothing in his hand. Maybe a former smoker, feeling for a pack of cigarettes in his pocket.

She couldn't help but laugh. Mandy told her she'd probably gain five pounds on this cruise. So far, she had only eaten the eggs and avocados and a couple of bites of fruit. He didn't need to know that. "I'm afraid I spent my time on the balcony, relaxing and drinking coffee from that super fancy espresso machine in my cabin."

"You're staying in one of *those* rooms?"

Anna was sure she heard a note of criticism in his voice. "Lucky me," she replied again.

"I guess so," he replied. "I'm on a lower deck." He stopped as if considering his next words. "I was told there wasn't anything available on the upper deck, though I admit this was a last-minute trip. A birthday gift from my coworkers."

"Nice gift, and happy birthday," she said, then took a sip of her ginger ale. "My cabin is more like an apartment. Really more space than one person needs, but it's there, and I'll just rotate the bedrooms at night." She chuckled. "Keep my cabin stewards on their toes with all the bed changes."

"Maybe you'll show it to me sometime," he said.

Anna felt her cheeks flush, her heart quickening. Unsure what to say, again, she took her mother's advice again and said nothing.

He stared at her, his royal blue eyes darkening as he held her gaze. "I've done it again," he said, breaking the uncomfortable silence. "It's been a very long while since I've done . . . this." He placed a hand on his chest, then held it out in her direction. "I'll leave you alone, now."

When he pushed out his chair, preparing to leave, Anna spoke, "No, don't. I understand what you're trying to say. I'm in the same boat." She shook her head. "Not sure if that pun was intended, but don't leave. Stay. Have dinner with me," she added, hoping she didn't sound desperate. She didn't want to be alone then. She suddenly didn't feel well but kept quiet.

"If I put my foot in my mouth again, please give me a good kick under the table. As I said, it's been a while."

Part of her liked the fact he hadn't been on the dating scene, had been busy caring for his children instead. Without knowing the circumstances in which he became a single parent, from her own experience, it wasn't easy being both mother and father. This was why they had singles cruises — it wasn't easy to put oneself out there, especially when you're a certain age. "It's fine," she said.

Once again, Donal returned to the table. The dining room had started to fill up, the din of voices serving as a reminder that there were others Donal had to serve.

"Are you all ready to order?" he asked.

"I'm going with the poached salmon and the spinach-mango salad," Anna said slowly. That was light and healthy. She wasn't sure how much more food her stomach would handle as she'd only had a few bites of the eggs, avocados, and fruit earlier.

Donal smiled. "Excellent choice."

"I'll have what she's having," Ryan told Donal.

"Very well," Donal said.

"Wasn't that a line in a movie?" Anna asked as soon as Donal stepped away from the table. She felt dizzy; there was a definite buzz in her head.

Ryan laughed. "I think so, but the title

escapes me."

"So, tell me about your children," Anna said, forcing herself to pay attention.

He took a sip of his drink and said, "Where to start? Patrick is eighteen going on three, and Renée is a good kid, other than this new boy-crazy phase she's going through."

She didn't want to pry, but wondered why he compared his son to a three-year-old? Unless he had mental disabilities. But surely a parent wouldn't be so crass as to make such a comparison? "Kids certainly keep us on our toes, don't they?" Generic enough, thinking kids were supposed to keep them on their toes. If they didn't, then something was wrong.

"I wouldn't have them any other way," he agreed, then went on, "though Patrick has been a challenge. But he has a big heart. Sometimes too big."

Not wanting to ask what he meant by that statement, she knew that if she didn't, it would be too obvious, so she asked in a singsong tone, grinning, "Can anyone ever have too big a heart?" She took another sip of her ginger ale. She was so thirsty. And tired. But she had promised Mandy she'd mingle.

"No, you're right. Patrick is testing the

waters and, at times, does things without thinking of the consequences."

Anna found herself nodding. "As do most teenagers, according to what I hear. I'm sure my days are coming, but I've always told my daughter she can come to me with anything, even if she believes it's something I'll disapprove of."

He nodded. "Same here. Renée is very open with me. Patrick, as I said, he's shy and keeps to himself, so it's tough to get him to say or do much of anything. I'm hoping when he goes to college in the fall, he'll open up and make new friends. Find himself, I guess."

"That is an entirely different world. I'm sure once he gets used to being on his own, he'll adapt. College life is completely different from high school," she said, struggling to keep her composure.

"Don't I know it. I'm a math professor at Texas Tech," he said, shaking his head from side to side. "Though I have a different opinion. I spend most of my days with college kids. Some adjust quite well, some don't. It's a tough adjustment period for any kid. I'm just hoping Patrick can handle it."

"Some young adults need time before starting college. I think it's called a gap year.

Going from high school to college is a big change, especially if they're attending college in another state." She took another sip of her ginger ale. "Will he be staying in Texas?"

Ryan followed her moves, taking a sip from his glass. "Yes, he's going to Texas Tech, though I'm not sure it's the right fit for him. It'll be great for me, financially, but I have reservations."

Would he think she was prying if she asked exactly what those reservations were?

He must've read her mind. "Patrick has never been very outgoing; he's spent most of his teenage years holed up in his room. I've sent him to several therapists, yet none have been able to correctly diagnose him with a specific mental or physical disorder. He goes to school, comes home, then we usually don't see him until breakfast the next day. It's gotten so bad, I actually put a mini fridge in his room and stocked it with snacks. He's so thin, it worries me." Ryan's blue eyes darkened. "I'm betting this is not what you wanted to hear."

"No, it's fine," she said. "I don't mean your situation, just that it's okay to tell me."

Donal returned with their salads, putting a stop to their conversation. "Thank you," Anna said, then dug into her salad as soon as he stepped away.

Ryan seemed to mimic her movements. After several bites, he said, "It's not an easy topic for a first date."

Did he think of this as a first date?

She decided to let that comment slide. Maybe he simply needed someone to discuss his son's problems with. Being in the public eye, Anna found that it was not uncommon that strangers felt like they knew her and would often reveal personal issues because they felt at ease. She had also had moments when she needed a shoulder to lean on, someone to take over the parenting when Christina's behavior pushed her to the brink of a nervous breakdown. Fortunately, it didn't happen all that often, as she was a pretty easygoing kid. Thankful for Mandy's friendship during those times, she briefly wondered where she'd be without her, as Anna thought of her as family and couldn't imagine a life that didn't include her. Then there was Mona and Jeb, housekeeper, gardener, and as close to a mother and father as she had. She'd met them at the diner they owned when she was in college, before they sold it and came to work for her.

Once again, Donal arrived at their table in time to prevent further discussion. "They tell me this is fresh from Alaska," he said, placing the plates on the table. "You'll tell me if this is accurate?" He grinned, letting them know he was teasing.

"Absolutely," Anna said, wanting to ask for another drink.

Ryan took a bite of his salmon, dropping his fork. "This is cold." He forced himself to swallow the rest of the salmon.

"Yes, the menu said it was served chilled," she reminded him.

"Well, I guess this is on me since I was distracted," he indicated.

"It's not for everyone. Why don't you ask Donal for something else?" Anna pointed at his plate.

He shook his head. "I'm not really hungry. The salad was enough."

Feeling silly sitting there with him watching her eat, she took a few more bites of the salmon, then pushed her plate aside. "A shame you don't like this, as it's excellent, just as Donal said."

The bubbly waiter returned to the table, offering a variety of desserts, but neither indulged. "Thanks, Donal. You can tell the chef the salmon was fantastic. And the salad was, too," Anna said. The waiter removed their plates and gave a slight bow.

"So, you want to watch the dancing contest? Together?" Ryan asked, as they left the main dining room.

"As long as we're just watching. Like I said, I'm not much of a dancer."

"I haven't danced since" — he paused — "my wedding day."

Anna didn't know how he expected her to respond, so she said, "I think that's the dance one always remembers most."

"That was a very long time ago, and I'm here with you now," he said, then took her hand in his, as though it were the most natural thing in the world to do. She didn't mind either.

"What do you think about skipping the contest and going to my cabin for an espresso?" she asked, feeling so light-headed that she wondered if she'd manage to make it to her room.

"I think it's the best idea I've heard all evening," Ryan answered.

CHAPTER 5

When Anna awoke, her legs were twisted in the bedding. Struggling to untangle herself, a sharp, piercing pain in her head forced her to lie still. Taking a deep breath, she slowly exhaled, hoping to ride through the intense throbbing in her temples. Careful, so as not to worsen the pounding radiating throughout her skull, she maneuvered herself just enough to free up her legs. Fearful of further movement, as the pain seemed to worsen, she lay completely still until she felt she could move without intense pain. She opened her eyes, then immediately closed them. Light filtering in through the drapes felt like hot irons poking her eyes.

What is wrong with me?

Struggling through the pain, she forced herself upright to recline against the pillows, their softness odd against her skin. Her heart was beating so fast, she thought it would burst through her chest. Deep breath in, deep breath out, Anna was able to control her pulse to a tolerable level. Hands shaking, she fumbled for her cell phone on the night table beside the bed. Moving her hand side to side, she felt nothing. Hadn't she left her phone on the charging station?

Wait . . .

Opening her eyes, Anna was shocked to discover she was not in her bedroom at home. Though it was painful, she glanced at her surroundings, moving her head left to right, and was overwhelmed with relief when she remembered she was in her cabin. The cruise ship. Pulse pounding, she forced herself to the edge of the bed. She was completely undressed, though she almost always slept in a nightshirt.

Wait . . .

She spied a puddle of bright yellow on the floor beside the bed. A small wad of cream-colored lingerie lay next to it. Straining to identify the material, she had a flash of wearing a bright yellow dress.

She needed a shower and caffeine. Using laser-like effort, Anna managed to stand for a few seconds before her muscles decided not to cooperate. On the floor, she pushed herself upright, leaning against the bed frame. Heart thumping, intent on avoiding a full-on panic attack, she went through her deep-breathing exercises. In and out, she slowly lowered her pounding heart rate a second time. Had she really invited Ryan back to her room with her? Had he invited himself? He must have slipped out already, left her alone. More deep breaths, and Anna was finally able to stand, and, though wobbly on her feet, she made it to the bathroom. Her stomach roiled, and she emptied its contents into the toilet bowl. She had been sick before. Did she have some kind of bug? One of those viruses that cruise ships were known for? Deciding that's exactly what must be happening, she adjusted the taps in the shower and, with shaking legs, stood beneath its spray, hot water easing the cramps in her leg muscles, inner thighs, and, oddly, her buttocks. She eased down on the built-in seat, letting the water soothe her aches while she struggled to soothe her mind.

The pulsating sensation in her head eased enough for her to step out of the shower. Wrapping a towel around her, she made her way to the small kitchen. Spying the espresso maker, she made fast work of brewing a cup of coffee. Sipping the hot brew, she went into the living area, then reclined on the sofa, her thoughts a kaleidoscope of images. The yellow dress, the dining room, and Ryan. What was she missing? Remembering the night before, undressing, she felt her face flush. She zoomed in on her private parts, feeling a tinge of a familiar soreness. One she hadn't experienced in many years. She hadn't been with a man since Wade, and she felt as if she'd betrayed him, betrayed Christina.

"Shit!" she said out loud. "What have I done?"

She suddenly felt an urge to get off the ship and leave it — and Ryan — behind.

"Yes, that's exactly what I'm going to do." She did not feel safe aboard the ship anymore.

Uncaring that she was still weak from vomiting, and her head still throbbing, she returned to the bedroom and easily located her clothes in the drawers and closet. She slipped into a pink lace bra with matching panties, a bon voyage gift from Mandy, and found the jeans she'd worn on the flight. Donning a light blue T-shirt and sneakers, and without bothering to organize her packing, as she would advise her viewers, she crammed her clothes into the open luggage she'd placed on the bed. Returning to the bathroom, she brushed her teeth, pinned her hair up in a clip, and tossed her toiletry bag in her luggage. Grabbing the yellow dress and lingerie off the floor, she threw that into her bag, then spied the silver clutch purse under the raised night table. Opening it, she saw her cruise card, a lip gloss, and her cell phone. She ran her finger across the screen. Nothing. The battery was dead. Scanning the room for her charger, she caught a glimpse of a long white charging cord on the built-in dresser. Plugging her phone in, she returned to the kitchen and brewed a second cup of coffee. She leaned against the counter while she sipped it, knowing it would take a good ten minutes for her to get a decent charge on the phone. Hoping she wasn't going to be sick again but knowing her body needed fluids other than caffeine, she took a bottle of water from the refrigerator and gulped it down. Bringing her coffee into the bedroom, she saw that her phone was charged, with twenty-two percent power. Enough to make a phone call.

"She's fine," Mandy answered without saying hello. Caller ID.

"I'm not. Listen, I can't go into it now, but I need to get off this ship." Anna could hear the anxiety in her voice.

"What? You're joking, right —"

"No! Just listen to me!"

"Okay, calm down. What's going on?" Mandy asked, concern in her voice.

"Find out where this ship is now and do whatever you have to do to get me off it. I don't care how much it costs, whom you have to bribe. Just do it. I'll call you back in fifteen minutes." Before Mandy could bombard her with more questions, she hung up. She plugged the phone in again, needing to charge it as much as she could before leaving. Who knew when or where she'd get a chance to charge it again?

It was 9:37 — surely Mandy would have enough time to work the kind of magic she was known for. It was one of the reasons Anna had hired her. The woman was a dynamo, could work circles around anyone and anything.

She waited until ten o'clock, then hit redial on the phone. "So?" she asked, not bothering with niceties.

"Write this down," Mandy instructed.

"Hang on." Anna took a pen and pad with the cruise line's name on it from the night-table drawer, having no clue how she'd known it was there. "Shoot."

"You're in Georgetown, in the Cayman Islands. United Airlines has a flight that leaves out of Owen Roberts International at one-thirty. It's a direct flight to Houston.

All you'll have to do is figure out a way to get there. I'm sure your steward, George, can help you with that. An Uber or a taxi. That's the best I can do. I wish to hell you would tell me what's going on. Do I need to come home, too, Anna? This is really scaring me."

"No, stay where you are. There's no need to ruin your trip. Thanks for doing this. Listen, I know I sound crazy, but I have to get off this ship. I'll fill you in as soon as I land in Houston."

"I didn't arrange for any transportation from Houston to Lubbock. There wasn't time."

"That's fine. I'll rent a car or catch a commuter flight. Now, keep this quiet. Don't mention it to Christina because I don't want her worrying. She's okay?" Anna asked, knowing that she was but needing to ask anyway.

"She's in the shower. Mr. Waffles has a girlfriend, and I have scabs on my heels. We're all fine. Just do what you need to do and get on that plane. Sunday is the only flight out, and it's weekly, so do whatever you have to do to make sure you're on time."

"I will, and thanks, Mandy. I owe you one," Anna said, and ended the call.

Scanning the room one last time to make sure she had not left anything behind, she closed the luggage and tucked the charging cord and her phone inside the silver clutch purse.

Pulling the luggage alongside her, purse tucked beneath her arm, she opened the main door and stepped into the hallway. It wasn't locked. Had she been distracted the night before so that she'd forgotten to lock her door? This was not the person she was. If one-night stands were her thing, no judgment here; it just wasn't hers. At this point she just wanted to leave this ship immediately.

"Hey, I was starting to get worried about you," a male voice said as he approached her.

Stunned, she stared at Ryan, standing in front of her, blocking her exit. The hallway was quite narrow, making it practically impossible for her to walk past him.

"Anna! What's wrong?" he asked.

Now more confused than ever, she shook her head. "Listen, I have to go. Please, step away from me." She knew she was being irrational, even cruel, but it was all too much.

He held his hands high in the air. "You sure as hell didn't feel that way last night."

She stopped. And asked, "What did you

say?" Though she heard exactly what he said.

"I'm sorry. You know, last night. I don't think either of us planned on anything happening, but it did, and I'm not sorry. We were supposed to meet on the upper deck for breakfast at nine. When you didn't show, I started to worry."

"I'm sorry" was all she could say.

Anna felt that she had no other choice but to return to her cabin. With trembling hands, she removed the room card from her purse, held it up to the doorknob to scan. As soon as the light turned green, she practically ran inside, her luggage banging against her heels as she hurried into the room. Locking the door behind her, she crumbled to the floor, shock and shame consuming her.

Damn! What had she been thinking?

This was totally out of character, yet it had happened. She needed to get out of here. Immediately. Standing, she peered through the peephole and didn't see him, but that didn't mean he wasn't lurking on either side of her door where she didn't have a clear view. Carefully, she unlocked the door, easing it open just enough so she could stick her head out. Seeing the long hallway was empty, she released the breath she'd been holding.

She closed the door, locked it, and returned to the master bedroom. She felt like there was something she was missing yet she couldn't place exactly what it was. Anna retrieved her luggage, brought it back to the bedroom, and opened it. She went through her clothes and her cosmetics case.

Anna stooped, feeling the residual weakness in her muscles. Following the directions on the safe, she opened the door and saw a bottle of pills. The Xanax. Now she remembered. She'd put it there the first night of the cruise after taking one when she had consumed a couple of glasses of champagne. Fearing she'd need it more than normal, given she was out in the middle of nowhere, alone, she'd locked it up so it wouldn't be easy to get to, since she needed to be in control. Relief washed over her. Not because she had the pills but because she remembered doing this. Stuffing the bottle in her jeans pocket, she checked the bathroom and found nothing unusual. No nagging feelings.

Anna had to hurry because she did not want to miss her flight. She used the phone to call the steward. A familiar voice asked, "How may I help you?"

"George?" Sure, this was his name. She

remembered that now, too.

"Anna."

"Yes, listen, I have an emergency. I have to leave the cruise and fly home. I've made arrangements for my flight, but I'll need a lift to the airport. Can you help me?"

"Yes, yes, of course. I do hope your emergency is not life-threatening?"

"It's vital, though no one's life is at stake." She hoped she was right.

"Good. Can you meet me at the main atrium in fifteen minutes?" George asked.

"Yes, I'll be right there. Thanks, George." She wanted to add "You're a lifesaver" but didn't.

She zipped the luggage shut, then went to the door, being careful when she opened it that the man was nowhere in sight. Scanning the hall, she didn't see him, so she took that as her signal to leave.

Anna ran into several groups of passengers, none paying attention to her as she headed to the enclosed glass elevators that led to the main atrium. She spied George as soon as she stepped out. She hurried to meet him.

"I am so sorry you have to leave," he said, taking her luggage. "I have a private car that will take you to the airport."

"Thank you. I really do appreciate this."

"Let's see the purser, then I'll take you to the car."

"Of course." She had to formally check out.

She removed her keycard from her clutch purse, then it took all of five minutes to certify that her leaving was because of an emergency. She left George a beyond-generous gratuity and assured the purser she would cruise with them in the future. Never again, but they didn't need to know that.

Anna had to practically run to keep up with George's long strides, but she didn't care. She couldn't dispel her feelings that this cruise had been a huge mistake. No matter how good Mandy's intentions were, there was no way, come hell or high water, she would ever put herself in a situation like this again.

"So, we say good-bye, Anna. It's been my pleasure serving you, if only for a short time. Now" — he pointed to a sleek white Jaguar idling by the embarkment bridge — "that is Marshall. He will take care of all your needs. Anna, I will keep watching your program." He winked at her, and she smiled. "No matter that you left my ship."

Sly George had never let on he knew who she was until now.

"Thank you. For everything." She gave him a quick hug, then ran to the waiting car.

CHAPTER 6

Anna wasn't a fan of flying, but as soon as the Boeing 737 was airborne, she relaxed as much as she could. Remembering the Xanax in her pocket, she broke one in half and swallowed it without water, then put the bottle inside her clutch. After she checked to make sure her phone was still inside, she tucked the silver clutch beneath her legs since she did not want to put it under the seat in front of her. She had taken only half a pill because she did not want to get too loopy since she had to plan the rest of the journey home. After what she'd been through, she told herself, she deserved a bit of medically induced calm.

Once they reached thirty thousand feet, she closed her eyes, hoping she'd remember what had happened. She dozed off and on, then was jarred awake when they hit a bit of turbulence. Trying to relax, as her flight didn't land for another half hour, she did her best to focus on her future, the busy fall schedule, Christina's prep for high school, then Thanksgiving and Christmas.

The captain's voice came across the intercom with the usual spiel, saying they were about to begin their descent into Houston International and would land in approximately fifteen minutes. Anna almost stood and cheered as she could not wait to put as much distance between her and the Cayman Islands as humanly possible.

Having sat through the longest fifteen minutes of her life, Anna stood up as soon as the seat belt light was off. Thankful she only had a carry-on, she stepped out into the aisle as soon as she could.

"Thank you for flying with United today," said a cheery flight attendant.

Anna nodded, then heard whispering behind her. She'd been recognized. She hurried to escape before someone spoke to her because just the thought of having to put on her vlogging face made her feel sick.

Familiar with the Houston airport, she found the airline that flew into Lubbock. She'd lucked out because the flight was preparing to board, and she was able to purchase a ticket before the cutoff time. Racing to her gate, which thankfully wasn't all that far, she breathed a sigh of relief when she saw people still waiting in line. Glancing at her seat assignment, she grinned. First class.

Once she was on the plane, it only took a few minutes for the flight attendants to make sure all passengers were secure in their seat belts and prepare for takeoff.

Anna wanted to scream, cuss, and stomp her feet in frustration. This must be what a two-year-old felt like when they tried to express their frustration and didn't know the correct way to do it. She would be much more understanding the next time she heard a child throwing a temper tantrum in public. *Just go already,* she thought. *Surely, everyone on this plane has heard the flight instructions at least once in their lifetime.*

When the plane was finally off the ground, the passengers were almost immediately served drinks since the flight was less than an hour. Anna asked for a ginger ale, then froze.

"Ma'am, are you all right?"

She suddenly remembered that she had ordered ginger ale at dinner last night and so had he.

"Ma'am?" the flight attendant persisted. "Are you ill?"

"Uh, no. I'm . . . my stomach," she said hoping the woman would get her the drink and leave her alone.

"Yes, the ginger ale. Right away."

The flight attendant handed her a small plastic cup of ice, along with a can of ginger ale. "Thanks," Anna said, then filled the cup, drinking the soda slowly. Her stomach knotted with anxiety; she prayed that she wasn't about to have another panic attack. Deep breath in and deep breath out.

The man sitting beside her in the aisle seat hadn't spoken a word since boarding, yet chose to now. "A panic attack?" he asked.

She nodded. "Yes, sorry." She took another sip of her drink.

"My wife has them. I recognized your breathing technique."

Anna turned away from the window to look at the man. He had light brown hair, graying at the sides, with friendly-looking, clear blue eyes. She guessed him to be in his early fifties. "I don't like flying," she told him, knowing this was a common reason for panic in a lot of people.

"It's a natural fear," he said. "I see it in a lot of my patients."

"You're a doctor?" she asked.

"Yes, a general practitioner."

"I was on a cruise in the Cayman Islands. I left because I was sick."

"Not uncommon. Were any other pas-

97

sengers ill? It could be norovirus."

Anna had heard of it. "I don't know. What are the symptoms?"

"Gastrointestinal upset, headache, fatigue, muscle aches."

She was unsure if she should tell him she'd had these specific symptoms because she knew if she did, it was highly possible *that man* had them as well.

"No, I'm recovering from sinus surgery." An incredible lie, but if asked, she could give specifics since Mandy had gone through the surgery last year. She would see her doctor as soon as she got home.

"That's an uncomfortable surgery, I hear," he said.

Anna nodded. "Yes, very." Mandy had been miserable for several weeks following the operation.

Though she appreciated his concern, she wished he would stop talking to her. Not wanting to be rude, she leaned back in her seat, closed her eyes, and relaxed as much as she could. She would get an Uber as soon as she landed and head home. A dozen thoughts ran through her mind, and none of them were good. Sure, this was common on singles cruises, but she felt so ashamed of herself for being gullible and weak. Nothing would ease some of the guilt she now felt.

A tap on the shoulder from the flight attendant who'd given her the ginger ale brought her back to the present. "Ma'am, we're preparing to land. I need you to put your seat up."

"Sure," she said, adjusting her seat, eager to end this nightmare of a trip.

When they finally landed at Lubbock's Preston Smith International Airport, Anna felt the urge to cheer and stomp her feet, this time, though, in excitement. Checking her clutch for her cell and the bottle of pills that had caused her so many problems, Anna tightened the laces on her sneakers and prepared to exit the plane. The doctor was kind enough to grab her luggage from the storage compartment. She thanked him and was the third person to step off the plane. Taking her cell from her purse, thankful she still had a charge, she tapped the Uber app, saw there were several drivers near the airport, typed her info into the app, and exited the airport.

Outside, it was hot, but, unlike Florida with its intense humidity, the air was dry. As promised, she called Mandy.

"I take it you made your flight?" Mandy asked.

"Yes, and lucked out getting a quick flight home. Hang on." She spotted the red Ford Flex. Waving a hand, she stepped off the curb, pulling her luggage behind her.

"Anna," Mandy said.

"Just a sec."

The Uber driver took her luggage, then opened the door for her. She mouthed, "Thanks."

Relieved to be in the car with the air-conditioning on, she fastened her seat belt, reclining in her seat. "Okay, I'm in Lubbock. Mandy, you didn't tell Christina I left the cruise, I hope."

"I didn't. She and Mr. Waffles are catnapping. We spent the day at Typhoon Lagoon, he spent the day with Bell."

"I assume she's his new love interest?"

"Yes, but forget that. What is going on with you? I've been worried," Mandy added. "Were you followed?"

"I'm pretty sure I wasn't, and I apologize for worrying you. I don't have much power left on this phone. I'll tell you everything when you're home. Promise me you'll enjoy the rest of the trip and not worry," Anna begged. "I'm really fine. I don't think cruising is my thing, a bit too isolated, so let's leave it at that for now, okay?"

"I hate when you do this," Mandy responded. "But I get it."

"Hate when I do what?"

"Leave me dangling off a cliff, but as long as you're safe and sound, that's all that matters. Why don't you call Christina tonight? We're going to Epcot later, so we'll be up."

"I will. Give her my love, and I'll call this evening," Anna said, just before her phone gave up the ghost.

Enjoying the ride, as it was cool and quiet inside the SUV, Anna knew that, as soon as she returned to the house, there would be a million and one tasks that would need her immediate attention. Closing off her mind was another technique she'd learned in therapy all those years ago. She'd been so panicked and frightened the past twenty-four hours, she hadn't even considered this. Maybe she would be able to use this method to relax so much so that she would recall last night and what had led her to be in this insane position now. Anna could only hope.

As soon as the Uber pulled through the gates of her house, she got out of the car, stretching her muscles, discovering they weren't as sore as they'd been earlier, which was odd since she'd been sitting on an airplane for half the day. She'd just accept the small amount of relief she had now and enjoy it, however long it lasted. The driver brought her bag from the rear of the vehicle, placing it next to her. "Is there anything else?" he asked.

"No, nothing, but thanks for the lift."

"My job." He grinned, gave a hasty wave, and returned to his SUV.

Taking a deep breath, one of sheer joy just to be standing near her house, then releasing it, energized her. She looked out through the gates at the sweeping fields of bluebonnets that surrounded her house. Nothing made her feel more at home than those bluish purple flowers stretching out for miles. A uniquely Texan sight.

She saw that Mona and Jeb, her housekeeper and groundskeeper, were home, since she could see their ancient white Subaru parked next to the small guesthouse where they lived. She'd met them when she was in college; they'd owned and operated a small family diner close to the college. When she returned to Lubbock after Wade's death, she had looked them up, found out that they had sold their diner, and retired. When she built this new home, with her studio, she'd added a guesthouse almost as an afterthought. Needing a housekeeper because her house was much too large for two people, another crazy indulgence, she'd contacted Mona, and the rest was history.

They'd kept their small home in Idalou just outside Lubbock, but most nights they were here. Tonight, she was grateful because she knew Mona would make an appearance to find out why she was home from vacation so soon.

Dragging the luggage to the side of the garage, she punched in the code on the new alarm system she'd had installed, opened the side door, and stepped into her ultra-modern mudroom. Knowing Mona would be here shortly, she didn't bother to reset the alarm. She kicked off her sneakers and left the luggage by the washing machine. A second door led to her gourmet kitchen. She smiled. This is where she felt the happiest. The kitchen she filmed in was quite similar to her personal kitchen, but smaller. She had a studio that served the purposes of her vlogging. A living area to film in, a kitchen, a small bathroom when she was sharing beauty items, and, of course, the main studio, where she sometimes did voice-overs for her channel. Anna knew she was blessed to have such a perfect workspace, but she'd worked very, very hard to earn this.

Anna hit a control switch that illuminated the kitchen in soft light while she opened the plantation blinds. There were still a few hours of daylight left, and she planned to take advantage of them. Opening her custom-made refrigerator, she took a can of Coke, flipped the metal tab, and its fizzy foam spilled over the side of the can onto her hand. Wiping her hand across her jeans, she sat on one of the stools at the island she'd had built specially for this kitchen. She had every gadget one could ever need, all of them built-in. Phone chargers, flash drives, notebook charging. Anna was a neat freak; dangling cords had always been a pet peeve of hers. This way, all the electronics when charging were out of sight. Most modern homes addressed these issues in today's high-tech world. She placed her phone on the charger for now. She'd call Mandy and Christina from the house phone tonight.

As predicted, she heard a light rap on the mudroom door, then another.

"Mona, the door's open," Anna called out.

Mona entered the kitchen. "That was a right quick vacation, Miss Anna." Mona's Southern twang made each word sound as if it had at least two extra syllables.

Anna couldn't help but laugh. "Yes, it was."

"Why'd you lit out like a bat outta hell? If ya don't mind me askin'."

A true Texan, Mona. Anna knew she wouldn't relent until she explained why she'd come home. "I was sick. I spent most of the time in bed, and honestly, I didn't like being on that ship. Cruising is fine for some, but it's not for me."

Mona slid onto the stool beside her. As always, she wore faded Levi's, the old dark blue kind, stiff, that took hundreds of washes before they were comfortable. She wore a floral-pattern blouse, faded, and a pack of Camel nonfiltered cigarettes was in her breast pocket. What was so odd about that was that Mona had never smoked a day in her life. Both of her parents had died of lung cancer when she'd been in her early twenties. She told Anna this was her way of remembering them. Personally, Anna thought it was a bit morbid, but Mona wasn't your average seventy-one-year-old. She competed in Lubbock's annual rodeo and most of her friends were old college students she'd befriended at the diner years ago. Jeb once told her that this was her way of caring for the children they'd never had. It made sense, and Anna adored her for her quirky ways. Mona was tall, slim, and wore her long silver hair in a braid that almost reached her knees. In essence, she was stunningly beautiful and couldn't care less.

"Me neither, though I ain't ever been on one. I'll stay right here, where I can walk outside without havin' to swim. You didn't see that stalker, did ya?"

Anna laughed despite the seriousness of her question. "No, nothing like that." She hoped. Taking the focus away from a topic she did not want to get into, she went on. "The ship was like a floating city, really. Though I admit I didn't explore all they had to offer, it's just not my thing," she said, wanting to tell Mona more but unsure if she should burden her with her problem.

"Okay, Miss Anna, now tell me the real reason you left," Mona ordered in that distinctive tone, the one where she meant business.

"You can't tell Christina," she said, then downed the rest of her Coke.

"Anna Marie Campbell, I ought to turn you over my knee and bust your britches. Have I ever wagged my tongue when you asked me not to?"

"Of course not. It's just this is a very *sensitive* situation."

"I figured as much. Go on," Mona said, "and tell me what caused you to lit out o' that ship so dang quick." Having said this, she got off the stool, went to the refrigerator, and extracted two more Cokes. She removed two glasses from the cabinet and filled them with ice. "Here," she said, then flipped the metal pop top and filled their glasses with the sweet brown soda.

"Start talking," Mona demanded.

Anna raked a hand through her hair, sighing. "Where to start," she said, more to herself than to Mona. "The first night on the ship, the steward poured me a couple of glasses of champagne. I'm guessing this is the typical bon voyage experience, specifically for guests in the upscale cabins. Mandy really outdid herself this time; the cabin was like a small luxury apartment." Pausing, she took a drink of soda. Her mouth was so dry, she thought she might be dehydrated.

"I'm listening," Mona said.

"I was going to attend a welcome-aboard dinner that evening." Had it been only seventy-two hours ago? "I became very anxious, panicky, and I took a Xanax." Mona knew she'd had to take these at times, and never once made her feel as though she were crazy.

"Mixed with champagne, I passed out."

"Sweetie, that ain't the worst thing in the world, but you gotta watch them pills these days. People eatin' 'em like candy and all, it's dangerous."

Anna nodded. "Long story. I didn't make

the dinner that night, but Saturday I decided to get out and mingle, as Mandy puts it. There was a dancing contest I wanted to watch later that evening. I knew I needed to eat — I had felt like garbage earlier that morning — so I went to the dining room to have dinner before the contest. This man" — she stopped before saying his name — "Ryan. Robertson." Her jaw slackened.

"What?" Mona asked.

Anna literally felt the color drain from her face. "I had dinner with him."

"Ain't nothing wrong with that," Mona said.

"I know, I know," Anna said, taking another sip of her Coke. "Mona, can we discuss this later? Just trust that I had good reason," though now she wasn't so sure that she did, "to come home. I'm wiped out. All I want to do is take a hot bath and relax." Her thoughts raced while she tried to make sense of what she'd just recalled.

Mona grimaced, shaking her head. "I don't get it, but go on up, get a good soak, and I'll clean up this mess."

Two glasses and three cans constituted a mess in Mona's world.

"Thank you. If you don't mind locking up, I'll see you in the morning. We can talk more then."

"Just so you're all right." Mona got off the stool, gave her a quick hug, and took the glasses and cans to the sink.

"I'm okay, just wiped out," Anna said. "I'll make breakfast for you and Jeb in the morning."

"Nope, ain't happening. You let me know when you're up, and I'll take care of breakfast."

"You're right. I'll see you then," Anna said. She took her cell phone from the charger, to bring it up to her master suite, in which she'd had the same hidden chargers and flash drive ports installed. She put her phone on to charge again and checked for any text messages from Mandy or Christina. None, just as she'd expected. Anna glanced at the clock, saw there was plenty of time to relax in the bath before making her call to Christina.

She walked into the master bath, or en suite as they were called now. She preferred *master bath.* She'd had thousands of viewers ask this on her channel, and they'd pretty much agreed that *master bath* sounded better.

She filled the giant Jacuzzi tub with the hottest water she could stand and threw in a full bag of lavender-scented Epsom salts. Anna stripped, tossed her clothes into a hamper, then placed a foot into the hot water.

"Dang," she mumbled when she put her other foot in the water. Gradually lowering the rest of her body into the water, she reclined against the back of the tub. She clicked a button, and the jets turned on, instantly providing relief to her sore muscles. Knowing she was doing all that she could to avoid thinking about the cruise, Anna gave in, surrendering to the images of Ryan Robertson.

He was extraordinarily handsome. If he had been unkind, she didn't remember. Closing her mind to all negative thoughts, she pulled up her ability to calm herself by visualizing the flow of a stream — smooth, clear, and constant. Sounds of water gently lapping against stones, the sweet scent of honeysuckle, the light touch of a breeze against her bare skin.

"Forgive me for staring, but aren't you the Anna Campbell?"

"I am, indeed."

"I'm a big fan."

"Thank you."

Anna sat up so fast that she knocked a small candle off the edge of the tub, sending it shattering to the floor. She grabbed a towel from a decorative wire basket she kept beside the Jacuzzi and stood, wrapping the towel around her, and stepped out of the deep water, careful to avoid the shards of glass.

Her hands shook as she sidestepped around the sharp objects. She dropped the towel on the floor, removed her robe off a hook, slipped it on, and secured the belt. "Just what I need," she said aloud. She hurried downstairs to the kitchen for a broom and a handheld mini vacuum. Quickly, Anna cleaned up the mess, going over it several times, hoping she hadn't missed any tiny shards. Mr. Waffles roamed the house, and it would only take a tiny sliver of glass to cut his tender paws.

Ryan Robertson. His name had a nice ring to it.

His name!

Given how tech-savvy she had to be in her profession, she sure as hell had missed the boat here. Before she changed her mind, she went to the small writing desk in her room and booted up her laptop, the one she used for personal business.

Anna brought up the search engine and typed in his name, then added "Lubbock, Texas."

One million two hundred thirty thousand hits. Knowing what he looked like, though she couldn't remember if he'd said what his profession was, she clicked on the first one. She clicked for the next hour, finding no image of the Ryan Robertson she'd met. Next, she went to Facebook and brought up her private page, the one in which she only used her surname and her initials in order to keep it private. She'd opted to use a stock photo image in place of a legitimate picture. In the search bar, again, she typed in his name. Several hits. She scrolled through the dozens of Ryan Robertsons until she finally hit pay dirt!

Anna recognized him immediately. She clicked on his page. *TO SEE WHAT HE SHARES WITH FRIENDS, SEND A RE-QUEST.*

No way, she thought. She went through the tabs at the top of the page. TIMELINE ABOUT FRIENDS' PHOTOS.

Anna couldn't stop herself. She clicked on the ABOUT tab. Two red capital *T*'s, one imposed over the other, the college she'd attended, her alma mater. The good old Red Raiders. Texas Tech.

Then she remembered.

"I'm a professor at Texas Tech."

CHAPTER 7

There'd been more to his statement, but it didn't matter. After debating with herself for a few minutes whether or not to send him a friend request or e-mail him through his public e-mail address at the college, she decided against both. She glanced at the clock on her nightstand.

It was time to call Christina; then she'd hash this situation out with Mandy.

Using the landline, she punched in Mandy's cell, and, as expected, she picked up without saying hello. "You're all snug in bed with a mug of hot tea and the latest murder mystery," Mandy stated, amusement in her voice. "And the alarm is set."

Anna chuckled. "No, no, no, and yes. Let me talk to my daughter. I miss that girl — then if you can, I need to talk without Christina around, if you can manage."

"Sure," Mandy said, then called Christina to the phone without bothering to place her hand over the receiver. Anna held the phone away from her ear.

"Mom, how are the high seas? Are you eating a lot? Mandy says that's all people do on cruises, and drink, too. Have you been drunk yet?"

Anna burst out laughing. "Christina, you little rat! I think I'm going to have a talk with Mandy. To answer your questions" — she hated lying to her but didn't want her knowing what an idiot her mother was — "the seas are high, normal food intake and" — here she goes — "no, I have not been drunk." What was one more lie in a small hill that would soon become a mountain of lies if her daughter continued with these kinds of questions?

"You're having fun, I hope. It is so freaking awesome here, I can't wait to come back next summer. I'll probably want to bring Tiffany if her parents will let her go with us. You'll talk to them, right?"

"Christina, slow down. You're still there. Of course, we'll try to go next summer, and yes, I'll ask Barb if Tiffany can go with us. Now tell me what you two did today, and I want to know all about Mr. Waffles' new love."

"It's so cute. SeaWorld pet-sitting service is so awesome. Bell is staying there, duh, but Lisa, she's one of the pet keepers, she said that Mr. Waffles followed Bell around all day the first day. Then when we picked him up, he hissed at us. Lisa brought Bell to him, and he kept rubbing against her, and she was rubbing all over him, and he stopped hissing. They're totally in love; Lisa thinks so, too. She said Bell's parents wanted to meet before we left, so maybe we can hook them up later. He's neutered, right?"

"Yes, he is. Take pictures of Bell if you can; I'd love to see her. So other than manipulating Mr. Waffles and Bell's romance, what parks did you visit today?" Anna knew perfectly well where her daughter had spent the day, but the joy in Christina's voice was so intense, Anna needed to hear all about her day, at least her version of it. *This call could last all night,* Anna thought.

"Typhoon Lagoon was a blast. I'll send you some pictures. Mandy and me look like two tomatoes, though. We forgot the sunscreen, but we did use the after-sun cream once we came back to the condo. We both took naps; and then we went to Epcot. That place is a total blast, and we're going back tomorrow because we didn't get to see a lot, just the fireworks and laser lights. We're going to the Magic Kingdom the day after that. Mandy's taking me to swim with the dolphins, at Discovery Cove. Can you believe it? I am so stoked I could scream. It wasn't easy to get reservations, but she did, and I am going to swim with a real live dolphin. Mom, I wish you were here, but I know you're having fun. Have you started to tan yet? I'm hoping this sunburn turns into a tan."

Anna laughed. "I am sure I packed sunscreen for you both. Use it, or you'll get wrinkles and skin cancer. No, I'm not tanning. I'm good using the fake stuff. I miss you, kiddo, but I want you to enjoy yourself, okay? Give Mr. Waffles a good scratch on his belly for me, and put Mandy back on. Love you, baby," Anna added.

"Love ya, Mom. Hang on." Christina gave the phone to Mandy.

"Sounds like she's having the time of her life," Anna said to Mandy. "Make her use that sunscreen. And you, too."

"I will. Okay, she's just taken the cat to her room. What did you want to talk about?"

"The ship thing . . . maybe it wasn't so bad after all. It would take all night to explain what happened, and yes, it involves me and a handsome guy. I may have left too soon." For the next half hour, Anna gave

116

Mandy the footnote version of what'd happened the two and a half days she'd spent on the cruise, ending with her illness.

"Are you one hundred percent sure you had norovirus? You saw the ship's doctor?"

"Not exactly, but on the flight home, I sat next to a doctor. I just told him I'd gotten ill on the cruise and had to leave. He asked me if I'd been throwing up, and all."

"As smart as you are, I can't believe you didn't inform the ship's doctor. People can die from that. It spreads like wildfire. How are you feeling now?"

"A thousand percent better. Do you think I should call the travel agent, tell her I had that virus? Maybe she could check to see if anyone else is sick?" Anna realized the rash decision she'd made might have dire consequences, especially knowing the Center for Disease Control would have to get involved.

"Get your ass to the emergency room tonight. Tell them what you think you have, but don't tell them you were on a cruise ship. I've been on enough cruises to know that virus is contagious for several days even if you feel better. If you don't, no harm, no foul. If you do, I'll call the cruise line myself. Now, hang up. I'm going to have Mona spy for me, so if you don't go, she'll tell me. Now what else did you want to tell me?"

"Nothing; that was it. I'm going to the emergency room. I'll send you a text when I get back, though I don't know if they'll be able to figure this out or not, but you're right. It was stupid of me not to report to the ship's doctor."

"Text me the minute you can," Mandy said, then hung up.

Before Anna made the trip to the emergency room, she Googled norovirus. Sure that she had it, even though she felt better now, Mandy was right. If this was true, the cruise line needed to be made aware of it. She put on a fresh pair of navy capris with a white top. She ran a brush through her hair, took her normal Louis Vuitton bag out of the closet, and checked her wallet to make sure her insurance card was there. She'd been such a slacker when she'd packed for the cruise, she hadn't even bothered to bring it with her, though she did have a photo of the card saved on her cell phone. Still, she was not up to par.

Thirty minutes later, she pulled into the emergency-room parking area for Lubbock's University Medical Center. It was late, so Anna hoped this would be quick, but had her doubts. It was a large facility, but she'd been there a few times in the past and knew that the wait could be brutal.

As soon as she entered the waiting area, she was greeted by a male nurse who wore a mask to prevent him from inhaling the millions of germs that he encountered on the job; at least that's what she thought it was for.

"Can I help you?" he asked, his voice muffled by the light blue mask.

"I'd like to see a doctor. I was on a cruise ship, and had to leave early because I got sick. I didn't see the ship's doctor, so I thought I'd better get checked out." So much for not mentioning she'd been on a cruise.

"How long ago?" he asked.

"I returned late afternoon, earlier today," she said.

"Follow me," he instructed her.

Anna followed him to a bank of windows where at least half a dozen hospital employees were seated behind a large glass window. "They'll take your information."

"Thanks," she said.

"Miss," said a woman from behind the glass. She sounded like the people at the bank. "Please put on a mask and gloves," she said, and pointed to boxes on the counter. Anna did as she was told.

"I'll need your identification and insurance card. You can slide them under here." She pointed to a metal, cuplike indentation in the counter. Anna placed her license and insurance card inside, and the woman looked them over and began typing. She slid them back through the metal cup area when she finished.

"Please step around the corner, and a nurse will see you now," the woman told her. "Keep the mask on."

Anna walked around glass windows where a female nurse in hot pink scrubs waited. She had a paper in her hand. "If you'll follow me, Mrs. Campbell."

She wasn't a missus, though Anna didn't feel like correcting the nurse.

After they weighed her, took her temperature, and checked her blood pressure, they put an ID band around her wrist, and she was taken to a room. "The doctor will be in as soon as possible. First, we need to do some bloodwork. Are you okay with needles?" the cute nurse asked. Though she was smiling when she said this, Anna wondered what she would do if she'd told her they terrified her and that she passed out at the sight of them. "I'm fine with them," she answered.

"Sit tight. We'll draw the blood first."

Anna waited for an hour before the phlebotomist came in to draw blood. "Sorry you had to wait so long," said the young man who appeared not a day over twenty-one.

"It's fine," she replied.

Within minutes, he took a sample of her blood, then asked her to relax, and said the doctor would be in soon.

Another hour passed, and Anna was starting to get a bit impatient. She was tired and hungry. All she wanted to do was, go to bed. It'd been a very long day.

"I am so sorry, Ms." — the male doctor looked at her chart — "Campbell. We've been swamped. Now, it says here you were on a cruise, became ill, and left. Tell me your symptoms."

Again, she explained how sick she'd been, with vomiting and weak muscles.

"That's normal then. Probably from the fever. Did you check your temperature?"

"No. As I said, I immediately made arrangements to fly home. I didn't think of it." She knew she sounded ignorant, but at this ungodly hour, she didn't care.

"Okay, one more test, then you can go."

He explained that she needed to provide a urine sample, which required a trip to the bathroom. "How long before I get the results?" she inquired.

"Probably a week at most; if they come in sooner, we'll let you know. I see you have your GP listed, so we'll let her know as well."

Anna went to the restroom and did as instructed, then returned with her sample. The hot pink nurse was waiting. "Okay, we'll get you out of here now. There are just a few things for you to sign."

She handed her a clipboard with several papers, and Anna signed them and handed them to the nurse. "I'm free to go?" she asked, just to make sure. She was so tired, she didn't know if she'd be able to keep her eyes open long enough to drive home.

"You are. Here is a list of instructions the doctor would like you to follow. If you're not feeling one hundred percent in a couple of days, he wants you to make an appointment with your GP. If your tests are positive, we'll contact the authorities, and they'll decide what to do then."

Anna thought it sounded like she was on trial, awaiting a verdict. "Thanks," she said, then rushed out the door before the nurse bombarded her with anything else.

As soon as she returned to her car, her cell phone chimed. As promised, pictures of Christina and Mandy showed them having a fantastic time. Wet hair stuck to grinning faces, Christina making a peace sign for the camera, a photo of the two of them flying down a wicked-looking slide, obviously taken by the park's camera. She laughed. If only she'd listened to her heart, she'd be in Orlando with them now. Her old adage, "It is what it is," came to mind. "Deal with it, Anna," she said out loud. She responded with a smiley face, placed the phone on the passenger seat, then remembered she'd promised Mandy she'd text her as soon as she left the hospital. A hasty message, no news, and she'd report if and when. Mandy instantly replied with a heart emoji.

Overly tired, her senses were heightened, and her thoughts returned to the man on the ship, Ryan Robertson. It was still hard to process, but she'd been intimate with the guy even though she knew almost nothing about him other than that he worked as a professor at Texas Tech. Maybe when she got home, she'd shoot him an e-mail. If he was like the rest of the world, he checked his e-mail account daily if not hourly as some did. She felt like she owed him an explanation. She ran from the guy, hiding in her cabin, because she couldn't handle the situation. Would he understand if she explained the effects of the virus? If he was a decent guy, yes. If he was just a scumbag out for a one-night stand, he wouldn't. Sadly, she didn't know him well enough to pin either label on him. She could only hope that since she'd taken a major leap with him, hopping into bed just hours after meeting, she must have had some instinct that he was a good guy and seen possibilities in him. Maybe he felt the same? Or not? The only way for her to find out was to do her best to stop obsessing over it. If she'd made a mistake, then she would move on.

When she pulled into the long drive, she turned the lights off on her Nissan so they wouldn't shine in the guesthouse windows though she saw the kitchen lights were on and knew Mona was waiting up for her. Mandy must've called her just as she said she would.

She pulled inside the garage and was not the least bit surprised when she heard her name.

"Anna, what did the doctors say? Jeb and me ain't goin' to sleep till we know you're safe and sound." Mona wore a white nightgown that covered her from head to toe.

Anna pushed the button to close the garage door. Mona followed her inside.

"They think I'm just fine. Though they did check me for that virus, the doctor didn't seem to think it was anything serious. They won't have the test results for a week or so, according to the ER doctor." Anna went to the kitchen, Mona trailing behind her like a dog with a bone.

"That's it? You sure?" she asked.

"Mona, why would I lie to you?" She wanted to take the words back because she'd been telling lies for the past three days. "I'm sorry. Don't pay any attention to me. I'm overtired and starved."

"I can remedy the starvin' part right now. Sit." Mona pointed to the barstools they'd sat on just a few hours ago.

Anna rolled her eyes. "You don't need to fix me anything. I was going to have a piece of fruit and call it a night."

"Bull, you're gonna have something solid if I have to spoon-feed you. Now sit," Mona said, in her you-better-do-as-I-say-or-else tone.

Calling on her years of experience in the diner, Mona whipped up eggs, bacon, three slices of wheat toast, and a sliced tomato, a true Texas breakfast in portions large enough to feed a family of four.

"Thanks," Anna said, and realized she was truly famished. Digging into the plate, she ate three fried eggs, two slices of the toast, then added three slices of bacon on the third piece of toast with the tomatoes on top.

"A piece of fruit, huh?" Mona said when she saw Anna's empty plate.

"So, you were right. I was hungry. Now I'm stuffed, and I'm going to bed. Good night, Mona." Anna knew if she asked her not to clean the kitchen, to leave it until tomorrow, she would make enough noise to wake the dead, so she left her alone to do her thing.

Upstairs, she saw that her laptop was still on and decided to poke around online before she went to bed. She went to the Texas Tech website and clicked on the FAC-ULTY tab. She scrolled through a long list of names, with their photos, and when she came to the *R*'s, she went through them very slowly. She recognized him instantly. She clicked on his name and read through his bio.

Ryan Robertson, Professor of Mathematical Studies.

His bio was quite impressive. He'd attended Texas Tech, then earned a doctorate at Harvard. Listed was his office number and e-mail.

She debated sending an e-mail. Maybe he wouldn't remember her. No, that was stupid. Men might be jerks at times, as well as some women, but when a guy had sex, especially on a singles cruise, it was highly probable he would remember it. She looked at the time on the top right of the computer screen.

It read 4:18 A.M. Either she would appear desperate, an early riser, or just plain nuts. Would he look at the time stamp on the e-mail? Did he even check his work e-mail over the summer? Did he use a different e-mail address for personal friends? Anna knew she could go on and on with these stupid, childish questions all night if she allowed herself to continue. She was beat, so she closed the laptop, but not before writing down both his e-mail address and work number. She had a few days ahead of her, plenty of time to decide. And then she would make the call. Or not.

CHAPTER 8

Anna slept until noon on Monday. She almost fainted when she looked at her bedside clock, then remembered she hadn't gone to bed until the wee hours of the morning. She stretched, enjoying the fact that, technically, she was still on vacation. Knowing she had a dozen items that required her attention, she would spend the day taking care of them, then maybe she'd spend a few hours in the gardens with Jeb. Gardening was such a stress reliever, she almost wished Jeb would leave the work to her, but it wasn't possible, given her chosen profession, and how hectic her schedule would be. As soon as Mandy returned, they would plan their fall programs and start filming.

The bluebonnets were blooming, and now the black-eyed susans' bold yellow leaves dotted the garden, as though rays of sunshine had dropped from the sky. In the evenings, the pink evening primroses gifted her their soft yet aromatic scent. The crimson cedar sage, an edible plant she often added to recipes, gave a warm and sweet flavor to stews and desserts. While this was one of her many passions, she knew that she had to leave most of the work to Jeb. But whenever she could, Anna tried to help out as she truly enjoyed digging with her fingers in the dirt.

Anna showered and dressed in a pair of cutoff jean shorts and an old red, faded Texas Tech T-shirt from her college days. She tied her hair up in a ponytail and headed downstairs. In the kitchen, she made herself a cup of coffee, her favorite, Kaya Kopi from Indonesia, the same brand that Mandy had arranged for her to have on the ship. When the brewing had finished, Anna took her cup outside, going through the French doors from her formal dining room that led to the covered patio. The Texas sun blazed this time of day. Hot, and dry. She'd spent her entire life in Texas and was used to the high temps. Reclining on a chaise lounge, she relaxed, enjoying the solitude of being at home. Giant pots of greenery were scattered strategically, and baskets of Southern wood ferns hung in bright yellow pots in every corner of the patio, which was really an extension of the house, just screened in. Anna loved this area, and if she weren't so concerned with privacy issues, she would film here. So, when the opportunity presented itself, she spent as much time as she could in this very spot, enjoying the gardens and all the fruits of her labor.

"I knew I'd find you here," Mona called, as she stepped out of the small cottage behind the main house. "I let you sleep in, told Jeb if he even acted like he was going to run one of his damned contraptions, I'd divorce him."

"Damned contraptions" was Mona's way of saying either Weedwacker or lawn mower.

"That's a bit drastic, don't you think?" she asked. "Sit," she said, and pointed to the lounge chair beside her.

Mona sat down. She was wearing her Levi's and floral blouse, and Anna checked for the pack of cigarettes. Yep. Still there. She smiled.

"What's so funny?" Mona asked.

"Nothing. Just a thought I had," Anna said.

"You ain't very good at tellin' lies, Miss Anna. You know that, right?"

If only, she thought. Normally Anna was a stickler for the whole truth and nothing but. She'd instilled this trait in her daughter, and fortunately, she was an honest young girl.

"If you say so" was all she was going to agree with. "Where's Jeb? I thought I might help him out today, putter around in the gardens a bit." She deftly changed the subject because she had no clue where Mona was headed with the "lying" conversation.

"Jeb's waitin' for me to give him the go-ahead to start up the contraptions. I've just decided it'll have to keep till tomorrow. You need some peace and quiet today."

Mona was definitely the boss, Anna thought. A second mother of sorts. She'd met her and Jeb at the diner all those years ago when she was broke and doing her best to earn her degree. She'd bring her books to the diner, order a cup of twenty-five-cent coffee, and cram for hours. And more often than not, a meal was included with that twenty-five-cent cup of coffee. She would never forget their kindness and how they'd made sure she'd had a full stomach when money was short, which back then was most of the time. When she'd moved to Corpus Christi, they'd visited her a time or two. Then, she and Wade were so busy being a married couple that they lost contact, except for the occasional Christmas card or a phone call. When she'd returned to Lubbock, much wealthier than when she'd left, Mona and Jeb were the first people from her former life she contacted. They knew Wade had died in a motorcycle accident and sent flowers, but she'd been so lost in her grief while trying to maintain some sense of normalcy for Christina, she'd never acknowledged the card with as much as a simple thank-you note.

"What's Jeb have to say about that?" Anna asked, taking a sip of her lukewarm coffee.

"He ain't got no choice in the matter, Missy. He does as I say," Mona said, a grin as wide as the state of Texas displaying her pearly-white teeth. Her own, she would tell anyone who commented on them. Then she'd go into the history of her family genetics, telling anyone who'd listen how no one in her family had ever had a single cavity. How she knew this was beyond the scope of Anna's knowledge, but she still had a smile most people would pay big bucks for.

"Mona, can I ask you a hypothetical question?" Anna asked.

"What's that?" Mona probed.

"You mean the question, or what is a hypothetical question?"

"Missy, if you was a young'un, I'd swipe your little ass with a branch from that wee-

132

pin' willow tree. I may not have your college degree, but I ain't stupid."

"I never said you were. What I meant to say is can I ask *you* a hypothetical question."

"Oh, well, sure. Go on, ask me," Mona stated.

Anna knew Mona had a vested interest in the psychic world, as she swore that her grandmother "had the gift" and always told stories that Anna found quite believable. Knowing this, she chose to ask her before hitting Google up for a recommendation.

"Do you believe feelings can be . . . helped through hypnotism?"

Mona patted her pocket of smokes, almost as though she were a true smoker and was preparing to light up. "I do. Why do you ask? You got some childhood nightmares you wanna deal with?"

Anna shook her head. "No, and if I did, I don't think I'd want to relive them. I'm talking about coping," Anna explained.

"I see," Mona said. "Clara Bennet. She's the one you'll want to see if you're lookin' for . . . She's downtown, next to that fancy soap shop that just opened. You wanna see her, I'll give her a holler. She's got a German shepherd, Rover. He protects her, so she'll have to know that you're gonna be there at a certain time. Else he'll make sure you never return."

"That's lovely," Anna snarked. "I wouldn't want to be attacked, but yes, call her. Set up an appointment. I'm free until Mandy and Christina come home."

"You're serious, ain'tcha?"

"I am," Anna said. "Just for fun, in a way."

"If you say so, I'll call her now." Mona stood and stretched, bending backward, her silver braid almost touching the floor.

"Okay, I'm going to have another cup of coffee. I'll be right here."

"Give me a couple of minutes, and I'll see if she's got any openings."

Anna went inside and made another cup of coffee. Still full from the giant meal Mona had prepared in the wee hours, she would drink lunch and enjoy the much-needed caffeine this exclusive brew provided.

She hoped this Clara woman could help her. It truly wasn't a life-or-death situation. She knew her feelings of shame and distress were exaggerated, perhaps by what physical illness had hit her around the same time. But she felt she needed a push to help her get over it. It wasn't easy for her to ask for help, but she knew she needed it.

Mona came running to the patio as soon

as Anna returned with her coffee.

"She can see you this evening at seven if you're serious."

"I am. Seven is perfect."

"Good, I told her you'd be there. On time. Remember, Rover? Plus, I said I was coming with you. Just in case," Mona informed her.

"Just in case? Of what?" Anna asked, but truly didn't mind if Mona came along for the ride.

"I don't know," Mona said. "Just in case whatever it is you're tryin' to remember bites you on the butt, I'll be there."

"Thanks, Mona. Really. One more thing," Anna said. "Don't mention this to Mandy, and certainly not to Christina. They'll think I've lost my mind."

"You don't have to keep asking me to keep your business to myself. I ain't no gossip. You ought to know that by now."

"I do, Mona. I'm just a bit . . . confused right now. I'll make sure to be ready to leave by six; that way we can allow for traffic," Anna told her. "Maybe we can grab a Whataburger on the way home?" she asked. A well-known Texas hamburger chain — Anna had craved Whataburgers when she was pregnant with Christina, and to this day, it was her favorite guilty-pleasure food, along with the Norman Love chocolates.

"You got yourself a deal," Mona said. "I'm gonna scrub up the kitchen floors now, so if there's anything you need, you better get it now. I didn't stock that pretend kitchen of yours 'cause you ain't workin', so don't go lookin' for food down there." The entire lower house consisted of her studio, office, bathroom, and on-set kitchen.

"I promise I won't get in your way. I'll be ready to go at six," Anna said, then went back inside for one final cup of coffee before Mona started on the floors, which already sparkled like the Hope Diamond. Cleaning was Mona's gig, and she loved it, so Anna let her do whatever her heart desired.

Once Anna was upstairs, she spent the next three hours responding to comments and questions from her viewers. While it was virtually impossible to answer every question, she did as best she could. Sometimes the comments were hateful, downright filthy. She had the power through YouTube to block them. She didn't like doing this, but she had an audience ranging from age eleven to ninety-eight. *The Simple Life* was just that. Ways to make life easier, ways to prepare quick, nutritious meals. She worked hard to be unique, yet not so much that ingredients, materials, or whatever products she used were hard to come by. She remembered how, back in the days of neighborhood barbecues, she'd had a neighbor comment on why she didn't use fancy ingredients like Martha Stewart, and her answer had been, "I like to keep it simple." And to this day, that was her practice. Yes, she could whip up a gourmet meal in less than an hour, she could design clothes and sew them as well as any fancy designer, but her passion was food, and decorating her house, and sharing these passions with her viewers.

When she finished with her comments, she returned to the Texas Tech website. She pulled up Ryan's bio and read through it again. She skimmed through a few other professors' bios just out of curiosity.

"I'm not sure if it's a good fit for Patrick."

She remembered his telling her that his son was headed for college, and . . . Texas Tech might not be right for him.

With Clara's help, she hoped she could better understand what had caused her to shed her inhibitions as fast as she'd obviously shed her clothes that night; at least she'd have some understanding of her actions.

It was so out of character for her that he surely had to be one in a million for her to get intimately involved so soon. There hadn't been any alcohol; she was sure of that, because when she'd been sick on the ship, she'd been full of coffee. If Christina learned of this, she would be mortified. Some example she was. They'd had the sex talk last summer, when Christina started having periods. She wasn't bashful about discussing sex with her mother, either. Kids in Christina's generation had sex before they were in high school. Some even earlier. While she wanted her daughter to have a normal and healthy attitude about sex, she did not want her learning that dear old mom made a habit of sleeping with the first date, if you wanted to call it that.

First date . . .

There was something about those two words. He'd said them, though in what context? Unsure, she forced herself to stop obsessing over her one indiscretion. This was the twenty-first century. If anyone found out, Anna doubted they'd pin a scarlet letter on her lapel. It was her and her old-fashioned upbringing that was the problem. She wouldn't stray from her beliefs anytime soon. She was forty-one. At this late date, she highly doubted she was going to revert to some kind of street slut. She laughed at the thought.

138

Her cell phone rang, and she took it from the bedside table and looked at a number that she didn't recognize. "Hello," she said.

Nothing.

"Hello? Mandy, Christina? I can't hear you."

The line went dead.

Probably a wrong number, as she would've recognized Mandy's and her daughter's cell numbers. Or her stalker back at work? Debating whether to call the police, she decided not to. Could it be Ryan? Had she given him her cell number? Another possible action that she didn't recall. No, she would not give her private cell number to a strange man.

But you will sleep with one.

Her guilty conscious was killing her.

Forcing herself to think of something other than this insane topic, she went downstairs to the mudroom and unpacked her luggage. The yellow dress was wadded up and would have to go to the cleaners. The black Prada she'd told Mandy she would be wearing to the captain's dinner on the last night of the cruise, was crumpled in a corner beside the other dresses she'd packed. This would definitely need special care. She put it on top of the washing machine, then dumped the rest of the luggage's contents on the floor. Her cosmetic bag was there. She searched inside, hoping to find something, anything to prove . . . Stop!

Anna was driving herself nuts with all this crap. Taking her lingerie and the rest of the sundresses and shorts she'd packed, she dumped them all into the washing machine, not caring that some were delicate and others were bright colors that would bleed. She adjusted the temperature to cold, threw in a Tide Pod, and hit START.

Taking her luggage upstairs to her room, she put it in the back of the closet and put the cosmetic case in the bathroom. She'd left the shoes in the mudroom.

But her thoughts kept drifting back to Ryan. The more she obsessed over it, the worse she felt. What if she'd gotten pregnant?

"Son of a bitch!" She wasn't on birth control, and as far as she knew, she could get pregnant. Just because she and Wade didn't have that second child didn't mean she was infertile. If Mandy were here right now, Anna was sure she'd kill her for sending her on the frigging cruise.

Not only could she not remember screwing some guy; for all she knew she could be pregnant! At forty-one. Unmarried. Quickly,

140

she calculated when she'd had her last period. She should've been safe according to the calendar, but who took that chance at her age? And with a stranger?

The words *sexually transmitted disease* came to mind. What in the heck was she thinking? She'd have to make an appointment with her gynecologist and have a test. At least if she was pregnant she figured they would have likely detected it during her visit to the ER. She rested a bit easier after realizing this.

This so-called vacation of hers was getting worse by the minute. She crossed her fingers that Mona's recommending Clara would be her solution to getting a handle on these feelings. She had time before she needed to leave but couldn't force herself away from the laptop. She searched for various diseases, the symptoms and treatments. It would take weeks, according to the articles she read, for any symptoms to appear.

Headaches. Fever. Nausea. Delirium. Vomiting. She'd experienced all of those symptoms but knew it had to be the virus. Even as naïve as she was, Anna knew the symptoms of STDs didn't kick in that quickly. What a mess she had made of things.

A glance at the time. She had an hour before she had to get ready for her appointment. Needing to keep busy, knowing she'd continue this path of craziness, she went downstairs. The washing-machine cycle had finished, so she removed the clothes, and, luckily, none of the darker colors had bled into her lingerie. She hung the sundresses on a hanger and placed the rest of her delicate items on the rack she had for this purpose. Still having a half hour to spare, she returned to the patio with her watering can and clippers. Anna watered the ferns and clipped the brown leaves, tossing them in her compost bin.

"Jeb won't like your doin' his work, Missy," Mona said.

Startled, Anna jerked around. "You scared the daylights out of me! Don't sneak up on me like that," Anna said, her heartbeat having kicked up several notches.

"You're losing your hearing. I've been in the kitchen."

No, Anna knew that she wasn't losing her hearing. She was just trying her best to focus on the simple tasks and wasn't listening for footsteps or noises coming from the kitchen. Really, she was thinking about what she'd learn with Clara.

"Whatever, you startled me," she said,

resuming her clipping. "Jeb knows I take care of the patio plants whenever I can. His job is safe," she added, a slight grin on her face. She adored Mona and Jeb, but there were times when Mona's hovering was too much. Now was one of those times.

"You wearing that?" Mona asked, giving a wide sweep of her hand.

"Not hardly. I was about to finish up here and go change."

"Then get your hiney upstairs," Mona said. "You want to drive, or you want me to?"

Anna's eyes doubled in size. Mona drove like a NASCAR driver. "No, I'll drive. Meet me in the garage at six."

"You got it," Mona said, and disappeared.

Anna disposed of her clippings, took her gardening tools back to the mudroom, and headed upstairs to dress for her meeting with Clara.

She was going to find out what she could; then she would put the past few days out of her mind. Or else.

CHAPTER 9

Clara's office was the complete opposite of what Anna had expected. Thinking of someone as a hypnotist brought to her mind images of a dark, shadowy room with crystals and patchouli incense, eerie music playing in the background. Completely opposite, the office was warm, decorated in soft cream colors, with a few small potted plants and two comfortable celery-green recliners facing one another, with a small glass table in between. Rover, the full-grown German shepherd, didn't so much as growl at her when she entered. He stayed with his master and didn't seem the least bit intimidating.

After Mona made the introductions, she said, "I'm gonna visit that soap shop. I'll be waitin' for you."

Again, Anna's images of a hypnotist were totally askew. Clara wore a pair of khaki slacks with a peach-colored shell top. On her feet were matching Tieks, which went perfectly with her casual attire. Her steel-colored hair, mixed with streaks of black, was cut into a perfect bob. She had dazzling sky-blue eyes, and when she smiled, her entire face glowed. Anna guessed her to be in her mid-sixties.

"Mona said you were struggling with some tough emotions," Clara said. "Let's see if I can be of any help. Please, have a seat." She directed her gaze to the recliners, then Rover. "Sit," she directed, and the dog obeyed instantly.

Anna sat down and waited. Clara sat in the opposite recliner. "Have you ever been hypnotized?"

"No," Anna said.

"First, let me dispel a few myths about hypnotism. Most of the stories you might have heard are false. I'm not going to make you quack like a duck or stand on your head." Clara smiled. "I can't make you do anything that is out of character."

"I wondered about that. You see all these stage productions of people doing all kinds of silly things. I'm glad to know that's fake."

"It's not necessarily feigned; it's simply a state of mind. Some people can't really hypnotize anyone and perform for entertainment purposes only, which gives legitimate hypnotists a bad rap. Why don't you tell me a bit about yourself? That is, if it's something you're comfortable sharing. I'll need to start somewhere," Clara explained.

An unwelcome blush spread across her cheeks. She didn't realize she was expected to reveal details since it was the details of her experience that she was there to remember. "I was on a cruise. I left early because I was ill. I'm not sure exactly what I had, but I went to the emergency room last night, and they checked me for the norovirus. I think — no, I know, I did something totally uncharacteristic. I'd . . . I'd done something crazy, at least for me." Here goes the part she'd been dreading. "I slept with a man I'd just met. It's not something I would normally do. I'm trying to understand why I acted so out of character, just so I can, I don't know, justify what I did." There, it was out. Her blush deepened. She hoped their conversation would stay between them, and asked, "This is confidential? What I tell you?"

"My lips are sealed; it's a requirement, just like the confidentiality you share with your medical doctor."

She sighed with relief. "My best friend insisted I go on this singles cruise while she and my daughter spent a week in Orlando, doing all the Disney things. It never felt right to me. I've had a history of panic attacks, which is an entirely different issue, but I felt isolated on the cruise and a little frightened, being out in the middle of the water like that. I didn't know anyone, and I panicked when I let my thoughts get the best of me. I had two glasses of champagne on the first night of the cruise in my room, and one thing led to another, so I took a Xanax to calm myself.

"I know it's dangerous to mix the two. I'm ashamed of myself. I fell asleep, spent the first night zonked out, passed out, whatever you want to call it. The next morning, I felt under the weather and spent the day pampering myself a bit. A hot bath, lots of coffee, ashamed of myself for drinking, taking the pills. So I wanted to, I guess, start over. I'd made such a mess of things the first night of the cruise. There was a dancing contest that evening I wanted to watch, so I went down to dinner early, and this man came up to my table. He said he was a fan" — no way was she going into the story of her career — "and we had dinner together."

"I see," Clara said.

Anna was surprised that she didn't take notes.

"Well, then let us see what we can do to

help soothe you a bit. Are you ready, or do you want to talk a little more? Clear your head?" Clara suggested.

"I think I'm ready unless you want to ask more questions," Anna said, thinking she probably wouldn't have the answers if she did. That's what she was here to find out.

"I'm ready as long as you are," Clara said. "First, let me explain exactly what we're going to do."

"Of course."

"This may not matter to you, but I always tell my clients I'm a member, in good standing, of the American Psychological Association. I've trained extensively, and I've been doing this for twenty-eight years." She paused. "So I am quite experienced at what we're about to do. Also, you should know that not everyone can be hypnotized, or I like to use the word *hypnotherapy* since we're in a therapeutic setting."

"Meaning, I'm not onstage," Anna stated.

"Yes, I'll instruct you to a certain level of awareness, different from your ordinary state of consciousness. You'll be aware of what I say and, of course, what you say. Your focus and concentration will be very heightened."

"So no swinging a pendulum back and forth?"

"No, but I will ask you to focus on an object and close off your thoughts. We only want to work on retrieving those lost memories. So, if you're ready, we can get started."

Anna nodded. As soon as she was comfortable, Clara began speaking.

"Anna, I want you to relax, release all negativity. Imagine a bubble as a negative thought, and focus on it gently moving away, taking all your negative thoughts with it as it drifts away. I want you to look at this blue pen in my hand and nothing else. Focus your sight on this pen. Relax your shoulders as you continue to focus on this pen."

Clara was soft-spoken, her words soothing. "Don't take your eyes off the pen. You were on a cruise ship, a relaxing place to be. The water gently flows beneath the ship, the waves are relaxing, constant. We are relaxed, our bodies content to be surrounded by calming waters. It's time for an event, and you take steps to prepare. What are those steps?"

"A bath, it overlooks the Gulf, the smell of the body wash is fragrant, my mother's scent. I heard a sound and stepped out of the tub. I heard keys jangling, but no one was there. I wore a yellow dress, and I had a silver purse."

"You wore the dress to dinner," Clara coaxed in her soft voice.

Anna smiled. "The man came to my table; he was so striking, handsome. Tall and broad, a Viking," she said.

"You spoke to him," Clara said.

"Yes, I invited him to have dinner with me," Anna said.

"And after dinner, you went to the dancing contest."

"No. I changed my mind, and invited Ryan to my cabin. He made coffee, and we were on the balcony." Anna paused. "I felt strange; he kissed me. It had been so long since I'd been kissed that way. Intense, the air around me felt electrical, a shudder went through me." Her breath quickened. "Ryan's kiss was unlike anything I've ever experienced."

For the next half hour, Clara guided Anna's feelings about that night. Her guilt, her shame, and her more positive feelings underlying them. When Anna returned her attention to her surroundings, she could feel a slow burn, from the pit of her stomach, up her neck, and up to her cheeks.

"Wow" was all she could say.

"Here." Clara handed her a small cup of water. She hadn't realized the woman had even moved, she was still so focused on what she'd remembered. She drank the water, then set the cup on the glass table. "I can't believe this happened."

"The mind is a very powerful tool when we know how to use it. How do you feel?"

Anna struggled for the right words. "Content but incomplete. Does that make sense?"

"It does."

"So where to go from here?" she asked.

"That's up to you. We can schedule another session later if you'd like to," Clara said. "It's your choice."

"No, not yet. I need to think about things; maybe later," Anna said. She felt so relaxed, as if she'd had a Xanax without the sleepy side effects. "Do you work with clients who have panic attacks?"

"All the time. Some say it's helpful, that they no longer need to use anti-anxiety medications; others have said it didn't help at all. I believe that its success or failure depends on the individual and is impossible to predict in advance. We can try a session or two if you'd like," Clara said.

"I might, later," Anna said.

"Whenever you're ready."

"I'll see," Anna said. "Guess I'd better get Mona out of that shop next door. Who knows what she'll come home with?"

Anna paid for her session, then headed to the soap shop. Mona was outside sitting on a bench, a huge pink decorative bag clutched in her hands.

"Looks like a lot of soap," Anna said.

"They got other stuff besides soap. You finished up?" Mona asked.

"I am."

Anna spent the next half hour listening to Mona explain in great detail the process of making the soaps *and* the candles she'd purchased. She'd agreed to think about doing a segment on the topic in the future as soon as she'd researched the process.

Back at home, after she had settled in, and Mona had said her good nights, Anna returned to her laptop, this time with a plan. She remembered most of what had taken place in her cabin, and she'd really given Ryan Robertson a raw deal.

She used his e-mail address from the university, hoping he'd check in sooner rather than later. Before she changed her mind, she wrote a short e-mail. She left him her cellphone number, and the option to reply to her e-mail or call. As soon as she clicked SEND, she had second thoughts. What if he thought she was looking for something he wasn't? As in a permanent relationship? That was the farthest thing from her mind. She didn't know Ryan very well, though she knew that if she were given a second opportunity, she would give him another go-around. And it was not because his kiss was so . . . *perfect.*

Closing her computer for the night — it was after nine, and the breakfast she'd consumed was long gone — she went downstairs to the kitchen and made herself a turkey sandwich and a glass of sweet tea.

Satisfied with herself and not so mortified now, she rinsed her glass, placed it in the dishwasher, and returned upstairs. Knowing it was probably too soon to check her e-mail, she did anyway.

She opened her e-mail account and was amazed when she saw a reply:

Hi, Anna,

My wish has been granted! Was hoping you'd look me up. So sorry you were ill. I haven't heard of any illnesses among the passengers, so you probably had a bad bug! I'm so sorry you left early. I'll call you as soon as I return.

XOXO,
RR

"That was fast," she said out loud.

In her e-mail to him, she'd explained how

153

she'd been sick and had gone to the emergency room. Knowing what she knew now, she felt silly. Ryan was a nice, decent man, and like her, he was a single parent trying to fill the role of not just a father but a mother as well. She knew from her own experience that it was an enormous undertaking, but for her, it was also her greatest accomplishment.

Before she could change her mind, she replied to his e-mail:

I'm happy to grant your wish! I'm so relieved to hear the passengers are healthy. I was worried. I'll look forward to hearing about your trip when you call.

Anna

She read the e-mail a couple of times before sending it, hoping she didn't sound too childish. Too late now. Anna closed out her e-mail, then logged off the Internet. She was not going to be one of those women who sat around waiting for *her man.*

It was late, so she sent Mandy a text message.

Anna: R U up?

Mandy: Yep, what's up?

Anna: I'm pretty sure I don't have a virus

Mandy: Results in?

Anna: No
Mandy: ???
Anna: Long story
Mandy: Call me

She brought up Mandy's name and hit SEND.

"You're sure you don't have the norovirus? How?" Mandy said with her usual candor.

"I didn't say that, but I sent Ryan an e-mail, and he said he hadn't heard of any passengers being ill."

"I'm not even going to ask how this came about. Spill it," Mandy said.

Anna explained her therapeutic hypnotherapy session, giving her the bullet points. "It helped me sort through my thoughts, the panic attacks. You know how I can overreact." Mandy knew about her panic attacks, but Anna had never told her about the anti-anxiety medication. It made her feel weak. Mandy was such a strong woman, Anna didn't want her knowing about her weakness, as she saw it. Yes, they were best friends, but even best friends had secrets.

"Okay, sounds plausible. So what's next? Want me to arrange a flight so you can meet him at the next port?"

Anna laughed. "No! I'm not that crazy or desperate. He said he'd call me; that's enough. I do feel a bit embarrassed, though.

That incident in the hall, when I ran into him. I can't forget those words. But at least I know I'm not carrying around that virus."

"No, you won't know that until it's confirmed by the doctor. Don't jump the gun."

"Ryan said no one was sick on the ship. Doesn't that count?"

"Did he take a survey of all the passengers? Or is he assuming, just as you are?"

Anna thought she had a point. "I'm sure he didn't go to such extremes, but wouldn't you think if there was an outbreak, he would know?" Anna asked.

"I do."

Typical Mandy.

"Then I think it's safe for me to assume I'm not contagious. I feel just fine. Mona made breakfast when I returned from the ER this morning. You know how that goes."

"I do. So, you're gonna see this guy when he returns? Or what?"

"I think so, yes. He's a nice guy, plus he's an incredible kisser." Anna smiled, imagining the look of shock on Mandy's face because she rarely talked this way.

"Score two points for kissing. That's always at the top of my dating list. If they can kiss, they zoom right to the top," Mandy teased. "I'm glad the cruise wasn't completely in vain. At least you didn't come home empty-handed. Exactly how long has it been since you've had a real date?"

"Too long. I haven't actually been putting myself out there," Anna reminded her. "I have obligations that are more of a priority. Christina, my work. You," she added. "How is my daughter and Mr. Waffles? I miss those two."

"Fine."

"Mandy!"

"If you want me to say they're homesick, they're not. Christina is having the time of her life, and Mr. Waffles is head over heels in love. Me, on the other hand, my feet are ruined, and I can say good-bye to my Jimmy Choos for the rest of the summer. I have blisters on my blisters."

Anna chuckled. "If you're looking for sympathy, you're not getting any from me."

"I didn't expect to, but still, you know how heels always make my legs look hotter than they are."

"Gawd, you're so conceited." Anna was laughing so hard, tears filled her eyes. "And that's just one of the many qualities I love about you."

Mandy burst out laughing. "I'm going to bed; this shit is too mushy for me. I'll have Christina call sometime tomorrow."

" 'Night," Anna said, ending the call.

The call hadn't accomplished much, but it felt good just to shoot the bull like they did most of the time when they weren't working. Mandy was like a little sister to her, and Christina had told her more than once that if she could handpick a favorite aunt, it was Mandy. They were a hodge-podge family, if you added Mona and Jeb into the mix, which she did. They were her people, and she knew they felt the same.

Anna felt as though the love gods were shining down on her now. In a few days, she was going to see Ryan again. And she knew he would play an important role in her life.

■ ■ ■ ■

PART TWO

■ ■ ■ ■

CHAPTER 10

Three months later

"How do I look?" Anna asked Mandy, twirling around like a teenager about to go to her first prom. She wore the black Prada dress she'd brought on the cruise yet hadn't had a chance to wear since.

"Spectacular, but I don't see why you're making such a fuss of going out to dinner. It's not like you and Ryan haven't been glued at the hip the past couple of months."

As soon as he'd returned from the cruise, they had started dating. Relieved when he found out she didn't have the norovirus, Ryan told her no one had been sick on the cruise. She'd felt bad at first, not reporting to the ship's doctor, but thankfully she'd only had a simple bug.

Anna smoothed her hair. "I'm meeting his kids tonight. It's a big deal to me. I want to make a good impression, that's all."

"I feel sure they've seen you online and

know exactly what you look like," Mandy shot back. "I'm wondering when you're going to introduce *me* to Ryan."

"I said I would when the time was right, and as far as the kids, they only see my online persona, Mandy. I'd like for Patrick and Renée to like me for me, not a YouTube sensation."

"Aha! So you do think you're hot stuff! I knew that poor-me-humble attitude was just an act."

Anna rolled her eyes. "You know what I mean. I want them to like me, for who I am, not what I do professionally."

"If I recollect, you didn't make such a fuss when Ryan met Christina," Mandy reminded her.

"This is different," Anna said.

Mandy plopped down on the bed. "How so?"

Though he'd never gone into much detail, Anna gathered Ryan's son was somewhat of a loner. They hadn't really discussed his children seriously since they'd started dating; it was all about getting to know one another. He'd hinted they wanted to meet her, and she was honestly excited to meet them. Ryan was taking them to The Shallows, an elite restaurant where it usually took months to get a reservation. They'd been there a few times already. Anna thought it a bit fancy for their age, but Ryan said Renée had chosen this place because she knew it was special to her and Ryan, which Anna thought extremely sweet.

"I can't really say. It's just different, I guess. Christina is an easygoing kid, she likes Ryan, knows we enjoy one another's company. Ryan hasn't said a lot about how his kids are reacting to his spending so much time with me. Ryan says Renée really wants to meet Christina, the two being the same age. That's certainly a great starter for them when they do meet. Teenage girls, they'll find something in common, I'm sure. Though Ryan did tell me Renée is allergic to cats. That could be a problem, what with Mr. Waffles."

Anna looked in the mirror, blotted her lipstick, then turned to face Mandy. "There you go. A Brady Bunch, minus the cat," Mandy teased.

"Don't let Christina hear you say that. Besides, we're not there yet," Anna said, but she knew that her feelings for Ryan were more than those of a casual friendship or friend with benefits, and his were as well. He'd told her as much. And his kisses were to die for, and the sex was mind-blowing, but they were talking kids now, his and hers.

163

"I'm taking this one day at a time. I don't want to rush into anything, and neither does Ryan. We have three teenagers between us," Anna said. "Now, if I don't get out of here, I'll be late. I'm meeting them at the restaurant."

"I'll keep a watch over Christina and the cat, so enjoy your time with Ryan and his family," Mandy told her.

Anna heard something more in her tone, a sharpness, more so than her usual cynical remarks, which always held a trace of humor. Even though Mandy hadn't met Ryan, Anna got the feeling her best friend wasn't too high on her newly budding relationship. She hadn't actually put that into words, but she knew Mandy. Now wasn't the time to question her, but later, when it was just the two of them, and they had more time, she would ask her. If her best friend didn't approve of Ryan, was she missing something? No, Mandy was beyond outspoken. If she had concerns about Ryan, she would have told her. Why look for trouble where none existed?

Pushing aside her doubts, Anna said, "I won't be late. Just make sure Christina cleans out Mr. Waffles' litter box. I've asked her to take care of this all day, and she's always too busy." Anna had struggled trying not to throw up this morning when she saw it hadn't been emptied. "I wouldn't want to either, but it was part of our deal when Mr. Waffles became part of the family."

"Ugh. I'll see what I can do, but don't hold your breath. I'm with Christina on this one."

"I'll see you later," Anna said.

"Yep, I'll be waiting to hear all the gory details," Mandy said.

Anna rolled her eyes. "Right."

As soon as she pulled out of the garage, Anna felt a shiver of panic. What if his kids didn't like her? Would Ryan call it quits? Hoping she would hit it off with both Patrick and Renée, she swallowed the lump of doubt, focusing on the upside of their situation. They were Ryan's children, and he was a fantastic guy, a great father, she was sure. So what if he'd hinted that Patrick had issues? It certainly wasn't out of the ordinary for a teenager who had lost his mother at a young age to show some type of rebellion. Teenagers in two-parent homes rebelled. It was part of being a teenager. Christina was already showing a bit of defiance when she'd refused to clean the litter box when Anna had asked her to. It was a normal part of their development. Though if she were being truly honest, she didn't blame Christina for her lack of enthusiasm. That was the downside of having a cat.

Anna spied the turn for The Shallows and pulled her Nissan into the first available parking space. She pulled the vanity mirror down, touched up her lipstick, and fluffed her hair. She hoped that she wasn't over-dressed, but it was too late now. She'd added a Chanel bag to complete her evening dress, trying her best to look professional yet approachable. As savvy as she was with most topics, she hadn't broached what to do when meeting your boyfriend's children for the first time.

Taking a deep breath, she opened the door, muttering to herself, "You're about to find out."

The Shallows was one of Lubbock's most exclusive restaurants. Reservations were booked months in advance, yet Ryan had no trouble booking a table. Anna was greeted by a young waiter wearing a tuxedo. "Ms. Campbell," he said in a professional voice. "You're with the Robertson party." He placed a hand on her elbow, guiding her to a table in the far corner of the restaurant.

Ryan stood when she arrived at the table. "Anna," he said, taking her hand.

"Ryan."

The waiter pulled out her chair, and she

sat down, placing her bag on her lap. "Thank you," she said.

Ryan sat down. He seemed nervous. "So, this is Renée," he said. "And Patrick."

She shot them her best smile, the one she reserved for vlogging. "I'm so excited we're finally meeting," she said, expecting a simple return of sentiments. Neither of them said a word.

The familiar surge of panic churned in her stomach as the two young people stared at her, through her. Patrick had long, dark hair like Ryan, though it was hard to tell his eye color in the dim lighting. With an elbow on the table, he cupped his chin in his hand, staring at her.

"Patrick," Ryan said, his voice stern. "Where are your manners? Renée? You, too."

"Hey," Patrick said, acknowledging her at last. "Glad you could make it." The words held no sincerity whatsoever.

She cleared her throat. "I wouldn't have missed this. Renée, your dad tells me you picked tonight's venue." *Too rehearsed,* Anna thought, realizing that she sounded as though she were on camera. "I mean, I'm . . . it's good to finally meet you two."

Renée hadn't said a word and still didn't. She had watched Anna's response to Patrick, a slight grin on her face. Renée looked nothing like Ryan, or Patrick, so she assumed she took after her mother. She had hot pink hair, which, Anna knew, was a product of their generation. Both eyebrows were pierced, and a small diamond stud in her nose flickered in the light.

"Renée," Ryan warned.

"Oh, sorry," she added, a slight smile of defiance on her face.

Ryan's eyes hardened. When he spoke, his words were blunt and to the point. "What the hell is wrong with you?"

Poor kid seemed to be surprised at her father's language. "I'm sorry," Renée said. "I just, I dunno, kinda felt like speaking my truth."

Anna thought her reply made absolutely no sense at all, but remembered that she was only thirteen. Feeling like it was up to her to break the tension between Ryan and his kids, Anna reverted to her best role. Mother. "This is awkward for you both. I understand. If you don't want to be here, maybe we can do this another time?" She glanced at Ryan. Anger had hardened his handsome face. "Or maybe I can make dinner at my house. Christina has been dying to meet you both."

She was saying whatever she could to fill the silence, and if Ryan didn't pick up on

168

what she was trying to do soon, she did not see how she could sit through their behavior through dinner and dessert. This was not going as she'd imagined.

The tuxedo-clad waiter appeared then, filling their crystal glasses with ice water. "Have you looked at our wines tonight?" he asked.

Anna knew what they had, and so did Ryan. They'd shared a bottle of Cuvee d'Elme on their last visit. "I'll have a ginger ale," Anna said.

"I want a Coke with no ice," Renée said. "And in the biggest glass you have."

Ann watched Ryan, the corners of his mouth turned down. "She'll have a Coke, in whatever size glass it's served in." He cast a warning look at Renée, then directed his stare to Patrick. "Tell the man what you want. A Coke?"

"A Coke is good," Patrick mumbled, repeating what his dad suggested.

"Two Cokes and I'll have a ginger ale as well," Ryan told the waiter, his tone dismissive.

Anna waited for Ryan to do or say something, but all he did was give both kids the evil eye. She realized they'd embarrassed him but knew that if he lowered himself to their level, they would delight in his fury.

He was furious, too, and Anna could see it in his eyes as his hands strangled the white linen napkin on his lap. Definitely not a good sign.

"How about we start over?" Anna said. "Renée, aren't you starting high school this year?"

Apparently, Renée's attitude changed on the turn of a dime. "I am, and I can't wait. Dad says that Christina is going into ninth grade, too. I really would like to meet her. What school does she go to?"

This is more like it, Anna thought. She glanced at Ryan, seeing some of the tension ease, his death grip on the napkin loosen. "She's going to Bishop Coerver. She's been at St. Cecilia's since second grade. What about you?"

Renée chewed on her lip. "I don't know yet," she replied. "We're in that new school district change."

Anna hadn't been to Ryan's house but she knew where he lived. He'd been hesitant when she'd asked about stopping by one evening when she'd had free time on her hands, telling her the kids weren't quite ready for another woman to see the home he'd shared with their mother. Thinking this odd, given how long ago his wife had died and the fact Renée had never really known her mother, who had passed away when she was just a baby, she told Ryan it was fine, and she'd stop by another time.

"The school choice," Ryan explained. "Renée took a while to decide where she wanted to go. She's going to Lubbock High, her third option. Not too happy about it, but it's what happens when you aren't responsible."

"That's a tough choice to make when you haven't been to high school. Maybe you should consider Bishop Coerver?" Anna suggested.

"That's a private school. Dad can't afford it. He can barely afford Patrick's tuition at Tech. I can't see him shelling out anything for a *private* school. Right, Dad?" Renée asked.

Ryan looked down, his hands knotting the cloth napkin again. Anna felt incredibly sorry for him. It appeared as though Renée was trying her best to humiliate him. Never having been in this position, she didn't know what to say.

"Renée, why are you doing this? Is it because I wouldn't let you get a tattoo? Or another piercing? You're acting like an idiot, and I don't like it. You will apologize to Anna for being such a little brat."

"Ryan!" Anna said, stunned that he would

speak to his daughter so crudely, no matter how she was behaving. He was the adult.

"I'm sorry, okay?" she said to her dad. "I still think I'm old enough to get a sleeve tattoo. What do you care? It's not your body."

So, Ryan was right. Renée was deliberately trying to embarrass him into agreeing to a tattoo. Relief flooded through her, though she didn't approve of his name-calling. Though some parents didn't realize they were cussing, she wasn't one of them.

The waiter brought their drinks to the table. Grateful for the break in round one, she waited until the waiter left before speaking. "So, what kind of tattoo were you thinking of? I've seen some that are true works of art."

This got Renée's attention. *Easy enough,* Anna thought.

"I'm not sure yet. I just know that I want one," Renée said, finally speaking directly to Anna.

"So maybe you could search for something meaningful to you? Put some real thought into your choice before making a commitment," Anna suggested, feeling the tension ease.

"I suppose I should since it's gonna be like a forever thing." Renée took a drink of her Coke. "Do you have any tattoos, Anna?"

"No, I was always too afraid of the needles, though my dad had a tattoo, a blue marlin. It had a symbolic meaning for him."

"Really?" she piped up, then turned to her dad. "See, it's not just white trash who get tattoos."

Patrick laughed.

"Renée, you know what I meant when I said that. I think Anna is right. Maybe you should put a bit of effort in what you'll be living with for the rest of your life."

Finally, Anna relaxed. Renée was a belligerent teenager, pissed at her dad. Patrick seemed to enjoy watching them argue. Nothing that couldn't be worked out with a little bit of patience and common sense.

"Can we go this weekend? To the tattoo parlor?" Renée asked her dad. "Just to get an idea?"

Ryan laughed, the relief showing on his handsome face. "I suppose we could, but I want you to calm down. Let's enjoy dinner. You wanted to come here to meet Anna. I hope she'll consider going out with us a second time," he said, turning to her.

Would she? "Yes, I will. I think we should have dinner at my place. I'll barbecue Labor Day weekend if you want. We can swim in the pool and make a day of it."

"You've got a swimming pool?" Patrick asked.

Finally, she thought, *they're opening up to me.* "Yes, it is hardly ever used. I would love it if you all would come to the house. Christina will be thrilled, as well as Mona and Jeb." She hadn't talked too much about her hodge-podge family but felt it was time Ryan and his kids got to know them. They adored kids, especially teenagers. With the diner being so close to the college campus, it was only natural that they'd befriended all the strays who spent hours there. She should know. She had been one of them.

"Aren't they the couple that takes care of your lawn?" Ryan asked.

Slighted somewhat, she answered, "Jeb does, but they're like family. They live in the guesthouse most of the time. They have a home of their own in Idalou. I like having them nearby, especially when Mandy isn't around."

"Who's Mandy?" Renée asked.

"She's my best friend, and she works with me. You'll get to meet her, too," Anna said. "She's the brains behind *The Simple Life.*"

"Cool. So like, why did you start a YouTube channel? You're kind of old for that." Renée looked at her, then backpedaled. "I mean, most YouTubers are kids, younger

174

people."

Anna laughed. "It's okay. I do lifestyle videos, cooking, and decorating. Sometimes I do beauty videos, hair and makeup, which is truly not my area of expertise, but it's fun to break the mold once in a while. Do you have any favorites you watch?"

"I like Jaclyn Hill," Renée said. "She's a makeup guru."

"Yes, I know who you're talking about. She has quite the following. Christina watches her. She does amazing stuff with makeup." She smiled at Renée.

The waiter returned to the table and took their orders. Ryan hadn't said much, but she got the feeling he liked that she was able to carry on a conversation with his daughter. She had only been a baby when her mother died. It was natural that she would open up to a woman. Anna felt bad for her and made a mental note to see if Ryan would allow her to hang out with her and the girls, Christina and Mandy. Mona, too.

Out of the blue, Patrick asked, "How big is your pool?"

Anna took this as a good sign. Maybe he was a swimmer. "It's pretty big, not quite Olympic-sized, but large enough to get a good workout in, or just float around on a hot day. That's mostly what we use it for the few times we do. Are you a swimmer?" Anna asked.

"Patrick was on the swim team his freshman and sophomore years," Ryan answered for him.

Perplexed, because Ryan hadn't mentioned this before, she let it slide. "That's awesome. You're welcome to practice in the pool anytime. So, what was your specialty?"

"Two-hundred-yard freestyle and backstroke."

Anna wanted to ask why he hadn't competed in his junior and senior years but felt now wasn't the time. They'd just met, and this could have something to do with the issues Ryan said he had. In all honesty, he seemed normal enough. He didn't say much, but again, some teenagers didn't talk to adults about their everyday life unless you pulled it out of them. Maybe he'd gone through some weird antisocial stage and spent a lot of time holed up in his room.

"Patrick, I didn't realize you still had an interest in swimming," Ryan said, a surprised look on his face.

"I don't. Just curious about her pool, that's all," he said, dropping his head to stare at his lap.

Maybe he *did* have issues. Animated one minute, sullen the next. Anna wondered if he was depressed. Though she certainly wasn't an expert, she knew that this, too, wasn't uncommon with teenagers. She thought of school shooters and felt herself blush. She was labeling a young guy, and that wasn't her way. She wasn't going to figure out these two kids in one night, but she certainly knew they would be challenging if she and Ryan were to become more serious than they already were.

Finally, the tension eased up enough. They finished their dinners, and when the waiter returned to ask if they wanted dessert, Ryan spoke for all of them. "No, I think we've had enough. Right, kids? Anna?"

"Yes, thank you, I am beyond stuffed." She'd barely touched her chicken Caesar salad.

"Just bring the bill," Ryan told the waiter.

Abrupt, but he could be that way sometimes. Anna didn't care for that side of him. No one was perfect, but she'd always treated service staff with respect. It was a hard and often unrewarding job. Maybe she'd mention this in the future.

She said her good-byes to Patrick and Renée, with a promise to barbecue Labor Day weekend. Ryan gave her a kiss on the cheek and walked her to her car. "I'm sorry the kids were such little shits. It's been rough on them since their mom died. I hope you'll give them another chance?"

She smiled. "Of course. Let's do the barbecue, see how it goes. They're kids, Ryan. I get that. Remember, I have one, too. And there is something I need to discuss with you," she added, hoping he'd take the bait and give her a line to start a conversation she'd been dreading.

"We'll talk later. You're an angel. Anna," he said, this time leaning close to her, whispering in her ear, "you know I'm in love with you?"

Shocked, Anna just stood there, a million thoughts racing through her mind.

CHAPTER 11

Anna drove home almost in a state of shock. She cared for Ryan and knew that he cared for her, too. But to tell her that he was in love with her, at what she thought of as such an inappropriate setting, time, whatever, struck a chord with her, and it was not a pleasant one. While she didn't expect a fairy tale, she hadn't imagined he'd confess his feelings for her in the parking lot of a restaurant while his kids waited in the car. But then again, they were both older, and maybe this is how these things worked now, seizing the moment and all.

She remembered Wade proposing to her. It had been so romantic; he'd hired a limousine, taken her to the beach, they'd shared a glass of Dom Pérignon. Then he stooped, pulling her with him, and as they gazed at the stars above them, he'd asked her to share his life. It was perfect. She shouldn't be comparing Ryan's declaration of love to Wade's marriage proposal. They were two different people. And why was she thinking *marriage*? Ryan hadn't mentioned it, never even hinted that he was ready for such a lifelong commitment, and she wasn't either. Though she had to admit that she had thought about it in general terms, especially the past few weeks.

The phrase *It's complicated* came to mind. It was. She'd never really thought much about how her life would change if she were ever to remarry, but it would not be a simple step at this stage in life. Mixing two families would require skill and finesse if she and Ryan made it that far.

As she pulled into the drive she saw that the lights in the guesthouse were on. Her bedroom lights were burning brightly, which meant Mandy was waiting up for her. Anna entered the kitchen, where Christina and Mandy sat at the bar, an empty pizza box, soda cans, and an empty box of Twinkies between them.

"Gourmet delights, I see." She kissed Christina on the head. "Where's your side-kick?"

"He's in your bed," Christina said. "And, yes, I cleaned out the litter box. I saw one online I'd like to get. It cleans itself, sort of. Can we get one?"

Welcome home, Anna thought, and she was so relieved to be with her family that she grinned. "If it makes your job easier, go ahead and order one." Christina could have asked for the moon right then and there, and she'd do her best to give it to her.

Mandy did not look good. "Are you okay?" Anna asked, "You look like you're going to barf." It was something she totally understood. The smell of pepperoni pizza was so intense, she held her breath for a few seconds.

"I'm full of this." She gestured toward the empty boxes on the counter.

"I see," she said, slowly releasing her breath. She kicked off her heels and tossed her Chanel bag on the counter.

"Okay, spill it. I want to know details. I've spent the last three hours gorging myself, waiting to hear how your evening went."

"Me, too, Mom. Did you like Ryan's kids?" Christina asked, cutting straight to the point.

"I'm going to make myself a cup of peppermint tea first," Anna said, wanting something soothing to settle her stomach. As soon as she finished, she pulled out a chair and joined Mandy and Christina at the bar, their favorite place in the kitchen.

"Ryan's kids are totally unique," she said.

"You would love Renée's hot pink hair." She smiled when she saw Christina's reaction.

"To die for, I bet!" she said.

"No. Before you ask, you are not coloring your hair."

"Pink hair, huh?" Mandy singsonged. "All or partial?"

"All, but it's short."

"How about the son?" Mandy asked.

Anna found herself on the defensive for Ryan's children. They'd had a rough life, she suspected. She wanted Mandy to back off but didn't want to go into details in front of her daughter.

"Patrick was a swimmer for a couple of years in high school. He's tall, like Ryan, lean." On the thin side; she saw why Ryan had been concerned. But he didn't appear sickly at all. "I think he's shy, but he's a nice kid."

"And the girl? Was she nice?" Christina asked.

"Renée likes to test her dad, but all in all, they're normal kids."

"That's it? Just normal kids? No tattoos, strange body piercings?" Mandy was questioning Anna as if she were a suspect in a crime.

Anna took a deep breath. "Renée has a few piercings."

"Cool! Where?" Christina asked. "Not that I want one, because I know you won't allow it, except for my ears."

"Her nose and eyebrows are pierced." *At least that's all that was visible.* "Other than that, she's just a regular thirteen-year-old girl."

"Most thirteen-year-olds don't have their nose and eyebrows pierced. At least none that I've seen around Bishop Coerver," Mandy said.

"It's not allowed. If you have any, you can't wear rings in them unless it's your ears. Which is totally stupid if you want my opinion."

"When you're old enough, you can get as many body piercings as you want; until then, we'll stick to your ears," Anna explained, not wanting her daughter to get any ideas. Personally, she wasn't a huge fan, but kids will be kids. "I've invited them over for a barbecue and pool party Labor Day weekend. You will both get a chance to meet them and form your own opinions."

"Then dinner went smoothly?" Mandy asked.

"We had a few bumps. Renée is angry at Ryan because he won't let her get a tattoo. She was . . . defiant at dinner. I told her about my dad's tattoo, which seemed to clear the air. Ryan is going to take her 'tattoo shopping' to see what she likes. I explained that it was a lifelong commitment, so she had to be really sure of what she wanted. And no, you're not getting a tattoo, either." Anna smiled at her daughter.

"I never said I wanted one. Besides, I don't like needles. I'll be just fine with plain skin."

Mandy raised her brows. "Plain skin?"

"Free of tattoos. At least not yet. I might feel different when I'm eighteen."

"I don't think your aversion to needles is one of those things that suddenly changes when you become a legal adult. But when you are an *adult,* you can choose for yourself. Right now, since I'm your adult person, it's time for you to hoof it upstairs and call it a night. It's late, and I am tired."

"I can take a hint. 'Night, Mandy, I'll see you later. 'Night, Mom." Christina hugged Mandy and gave her mom a kiss.

" 'Night, sweetie," she said.

As soon as Christina was out of earshot, Mandy started in. "All right, tell me what you really think. Are the kids weird, or what?"

"Mandy! That's mean." She remembered her earlier thought about school shooters and forgave her friend's minor indiscretion.

"Well, are they? Just because you have the hots for the dad doesn't mean his kids are . . . lovable. I can tell by the look on your face that something happened. You don't want to tell me, that's fine."

"It's not that, really. Yes, the kids aren't as friendly as Christina, which I kind of expected. Ryan said he'd had 'issues' with Patrick in the past. Didn't say exactly what they were except that he'd been to several therapists, though they never diagnosed him with a physical or mental disorder. He told me that when we were on the cruise, that night at dinner."

"You never told me that."

"Mandy, I don't always tell you everything, and I know you sure as hell don't tell me everything you do. As is your right. We're adults; we don't have to explain or justify what we do in our personal lives. I just remembered that he said this, and he may not even remember telling me. When I met Patrick tonight, he was definitely aloof, quiet. He didn't speak until Ryan forced him to. Then, later, when he learned I had a pool, he perked up for all of four or five seconds. What's odd is that Ryan had told me on the ship that Patrick spent most of his high school years holed up in his room. At dinner, he told me Patrick was on the

185

swim team in his freshman and sophomore years."

"Why is that odd?"

"Why would you tell a total stranger your kid spent four years holed up in his room when he was on the swim team for two of those four years? I don't think it's a big deal, but it does conflict with what he said on the cruise."

"Did you ask Ryan about it? You know how we adults can exaggerate things. So what if he was or wasn't on the swim team? Why does that even matter?"

"It doesn't. It just makes me wonder about Ryan. Either he's confused or his years are off. I'm leaning toward confusion. He's been nothing but a perfect gentlemen to me. We enjoy one another. In and out of bed. Don't look surprised. You know I'm sleeping with him." The world might know, sooner rather than later.

"I don't care. As you said, that's your personal life. As long as you two aren't into any kinky shit that leaves marks on your body, you can do whatever you want. Just make sure you look good on film."

"You're crazy!" Anna said, then burst out laughing. "You're a slave driver."

"I can be. Look at all of this." She tossed her hands in the air. "You earned this, without me — well, most of it. I'm looking out for you. I don't want to have to call a damned makeup artist in if you two are into kinky shit." Mandy grinned.

"Be quiet — I don't want Christina to hear us. Trust that I'm not into anything weird."

"But something about tonight bothered you. I know you too well. It's up to you if you want to talk about it. And while I'm thinking about it, you haven't been yourself lately. Is there something I need to know?"

Anna wasn't sure if she wanted to voice what Ryan had told her in the parking lot to herself, let alone share it with Mandy, not to mention tell her what she suspected. Part of her was thrilled, yet another part of her was alarmed. She felt it was a bit too soon in their relationship to say the *L* word and definitely not the *M* word. But hadn't she admitted to herself that her feelings for him were more than those of simple friendship with benefits?

"I don't want to yet. I need to think things through. We care about one another, and yes, we sleep together, but I'm not so sure about taking our relationship to the next level."

"What's your idea of next level?"

She didn't know. It was different now. She

was forty-one years old. She had a teenager. He wasn't Wade, and that bothered her more than she cared to admit. She'd shared a child with him, and now, this. It might be nothing, but she hadn't decided anything at this point.

"I'm not sure. I haven't been in a serious relationship since forever. It's just different."

Mandy stood and started clearing away the boxes. "You can tell me when you're ready."

What to tell?

Ryan was in love with her. That was it, yet Anna couldn't say this aloud and wouldn't discuss it at all. She needed time to absorb his words, how she felt about her situation, the horrible timing. When she felt the need to unload, she'd talk to Mandy.

"Thanks. I need to think," she said.

"I understand. Eric asked me to move in with him," Mandy said.

"You're kidding?" Anna was surprised — and glad the conversation's focus was off her. Mandy and Eric were exclusive, but she hadn't known they had reached this stage in their relationship.

"I'm not, but I thought it was sweet of him to ask me."

"So, you two are really serious?" Anna

inquired, hoping to take the spotlight away from her evening with Ryan and his kids.

"Not really. And I can't see living with him. He's a slob for one, and you know how I am."

Mandy was the epitome of a neat freak.

"Ten strikes against him. That's the only reason?"

"No."

"And the other, or should I say *others*?" Anna coaxed.

"As if being a slob isn't enough? He's funny and kind, but he's a bit immature for me. He's thirty-five and still likes Disney movies."

"*I* like Disney movies."

"I don't see you wearing T-shirts or hanging posters on your walls."

"Hmm, well, to each his own. I can't see how that's a deal breaker."

Mandy sprayed the island counter with Lysol, then wiped it off with paper towels. "It's not just that. He has an ex-girlfriend who won't leave him alone. Personally, I think he still has feelings for her and won't admit it."

"Have you asked him about it?"

Mandy sprayed the counters a second time, then wiped them down with fresh paper towels. Three times was usually her limit. Anna didn't mind her obsessiveness. Her counters sparkled after one of their gab sessions.

"Not yet, but I am planning to. He always takes her phone calls, responds to her text messages, and, from what I can see, monitors her Facebook and Instagram accounts like a mother hen. Seems weird to me."

Anna raked a hand through her hair. "I don't know, Mandy. In today's world of social media, I don't think it's especially weird to give a like or view an old friend's social media pages."

"You would if your boyfriend did so while you were out on a date with him."

"What? That's rude, no matter who it is he's following. Did you tell him that it bothered you?"

"As I said, I haven't, but I plan to. We're going to watch *Toy Story* tomorrow." Mandy rolled her eyes. "I can't wait. I plan to tell him after the movie. If he doesn't like what I have to say, then so be it, it's his loss. To be honest, I'm getting bored with him. His Disney habit doesn't sit well with me, either."

"You know what's best, what makes you happy," Anna said, and then thought of Ryan. Was he what was best for her? Was she happy when she was with him? She'd always believed a relationship, a lasting one, enhanced your life. She was unsure if *enhanced* was the word she'd use to describe how the relationship with Ryan affected her life. Other than the sex, which was spectacular, Anna wasn't sure exactly what Ryan brought into her life. Certainly nothing like what Wade had. Still, it'd only been a couple of months. They'd had a strange start. Time would tell.

"I do, and I'm pretty sure Eric isn't my true love." Mandy laughed. "Heck, I know he isn't. This is good. I'm sure he's going to get the boot after the movie. Or maybe I should tell him before. Big, life-altering decision-making here."

"If you're joking about it, it's probably best to move on. You're in charge of your emotions." Anna felt stuck, her words a salve to a wound that wasn't real. Mandy would have to decide to heal herself in whatever way worked for her. Anna was the last person to be offering advice in the romance department.

After round three of spritzing and wiping, Mandy put the cleaner away, washed her hands, three times, then sat down. "I know, I hate starting all over again. Think I'll stay single for a while. I've decided to tell him before the movie. I don't think I can sit

191

through another Disney movie. Maybe someday, when I have *kids* of my own, I'll have a different opinion."

"Then that settles that." *Enough kid talk,* she thought.

"We've got a hectic schedule this week. We're doing Halloween treats, decor, and costumes. I've ordered most of the supplies you asked for. I think three videos will cover us for Halloween since we're only a weekly vlog. That covers all of October, early enough for your viewers to create their versions of your trick-or-treating month. In November, we'll focus on Thanksgiving. Mona said she'd assist with the grocery shopping for that, which is great, because Rebecca is headed up north to visit family for three weeks." Rebecca was Mandy's right-hand gal. "I've been contacted by Kraft. They want to sponsor a segment on holiday desserts. I think it's a cream cheese thing, so I need to know if you're up for that."

"Absolutely. Did they specify exactly what they'd like to see, or do I have free rein?" Sponsorships were a huge part of her income, but some wanted control over her presentation. Others allowed her to use her own creativity. As her YouTube channel had grown, she'd been flooded with offers of sponsorships by some of the biggest companies in the food business. If it was a product she liked, she would endorse it on her channel, and more often than not, she was asked to continue working with a brand. However, if she didn't agree with a company's ethics, or simply didn't like their product, she would decline a sponsorship.

"They said you had complete control."

"I like that," Anna said. "It makes it so much easier. I'm glad we've got our Labor Day filming behind us so we can enjoy the day here. I really want to make a splash when Ryan brings his kids over this weekend. I think I'll do a good old Texas brisket and ribs. Any special requests?"

"Your spicy barbecue rub, and the Mexican corn on the cob. The one with the lime juice."

"You think I should ask Ryan if his kids have any food allergies? What they like, dislike?" Anna wanted to make them feel comfortable, and knowing what kind of foods they liked would help, maybe let them know she'd thought of them beforehand.

"I would; these days, you can't be too careful. Peanut allergies, shellfish. The last thing we need is a lawsuit on our hands."

Anna shook her head. "Why would you even say that?"

"Because it's the truth. You're well-known, financially stable. People have been known to take advantage of people like you."

This was unlike Mandy. She'd always had Anna's best interests at heart, both professionally and personally. Anna felt like her concern was directed toward Ryan. Did Mandy know something she wasn't telling her? "I'm not worried about being taken advantage of." She paused, thinking before she continued. "This is about Ryan, isn't it?"

Mandy shrugged. "Maybe. I don't know the guy since I've never met him. I'm assuming you trust him?"

Not one hundred percent after Renée's reference to her dad's inability to afford a private school, and Patrick's tuition, since she was aware that a professor's family members received reduced tuition. Maybe Ryan *was* having financial problems. If he was financially strapped, then why all those dinners at The Shallows, the pricey Lone Star Inn? It didn't add up. "If you're talking money, Mandy, I don't have a reason not to trust him. He's always taken care of dinner and whatever else we do." She wasn't going to discuss the Lone Star Inn, though Ryan had paid for that, too.

"I'm probably overreacting. Forget I said

that, though I would check to see if his kids have any food allergies."

"I will. I'll e-mail him later. Speaking of later, I'm bushed. I'm going to call it a night. You staying over?" Mandy had her own bedroom at the house, but she also owned her own home across town. When they worked crazy hours, it was easier for her to stay over.

"Yeah, too tired to drive home. Get some rest. I'll see you in the morning."

" 'Night," Anna said. She took her Chanel bag and high heels upstairs. Mona would croak if she saw them where they shouldn't be. She was almost as bad as Mandy, minus the obsessive cleaning part. A place for everything, and everything in its place, Mona's mantra when Christina tossed her backpack, shoes, anything where it didn't belong.

When she entered her room, Mr. Waffles lay curled on her pillow, his fuzzy orange tail flipping side to side. "Hey, fella." She scratched him between the ears and received a slow, contented purr as her thanks. "Good kitty."

Tonight hadn't gone as she'd hoped. The kids were fine, possibly in need of extra attention, which wasn't abnormal. What bothered her most was Ryan and how he had spoken to them. He had been impatient and curt, and she didn't want Christina around him if that was how he was with kids. She knew that parents sometimes lost their cool — she had more than once — but she didn't call her daughter names. Wouldn't you want to be on your best behavior when you introduced your children to the woman you were dating? Agitated, Anna opened her laptop to send Ryan an e-mail. It was harmless to ask if the kids had food allergies, but how would he react if she asked him to control his cursing when he was with her daughter? And his kids, too. Simply put, she didn't like it, had felt extremely uncomfortable at dinner, and he hadn't really seemed to care that she witnessed his anger.

Tapping out a quick e-mail, she asked about the allergies and also that he watch his language around Christina. Her Labor Day barbecue was this weekend. If he had an issue with her request, she would handle whatever came up.

CHAPTER 12

"You would think you're havin' the Queen of England over," Mona observed. "I ain't seen you act like this since *The Today Show* was here." Last year, the popular morning show filmed a segment with her in her studio kitchen. She'd been a nervous wreck for weeks prior to filming.

"True," Mandy piped in. "She doesn't put this much effort into filming for her channel."

"I want tomorrow to be fun for everyone, that's all," Anna said. "This is my jam." She laughed, using Christina's favorite word.

"There's enough ribs here to serve the Dallas Cowboys. They big people?" Mona asked in her usual Texas twang.

"You mean tall?" Anna asked in a teasing tone.

"No, I mean big. As in heavy," Mona shot back. "Are they?"

"Not at all. I want to make sure there's

197

plenty of food for everyone. You know men and boys, they eat like they're starving," Anna said, as she gathered spices from the pantry for her dry rub mixture for the ribs.

"Did you find out if the kids have food allergies?" Mandy asked.

"Yes. Ryan said as far as he knew, they'd never had a reaction to any foods. I'm sure they're fine. Aren't food allergies something kids have when they're young, and grow out of?"

Mona, busy at the sink unwrapping the ribs, spoke. "Not all the time. Some young'uns develop allergies in their twenties and thirties."

"Geez, then I guess I'm still at risk, being a 'young'un' at thirty-five," Mandy added. "Right, Mona?"

"Yep, you're just a smart-ass. Maybe some extra hot sauce in your mouth might cure ya," Mona prodded, giving Mandy a hard time. "Little shit ass."

"Don't start, you two, and knock off the cussing. I don't want Christina hearing it." A bit ridiculous, she knew, because she'd accidentally dropped a few foul words in front of her more than once. The e-mail she'd sent Ryan asking him about his kids' allergies, and cussing had been noted, and he had apologized several times, promising he would be on his best behavior.

"She's outside with Jeb, doing work on your pool that your pool guys should be doing," Mandy told her. "Unless Christina has supersonic hearing, she didn't hear a word. You're too protective. If teenagers are like they were when I was in school, Christina's probably heard far worse."

"True; I just don't want to encourage it at home." Anna took a bowl from the cupboard, and said, "I'm sure the days of my being overprotective are numbered. I realize kids aren't perfect." She just wanted to keep her daughter safe as long as she could.

Soon enough, she'd be in college, on her own. Anna had wished her parents had been there for her during her college years. She planned to be there for Christina as much as she could without suffocating her. Her daughter would need her independence, but knowing someone had her back, a loving mother and friends to stand alongside her, was important.

"No, ain't none of 'em perfect. Just some has troubles. Bad upbringin' and all," Mona offered.

Anna measured the spices into the bowl. "I don't know if that's always the case. Some kids are" — she almost said "evil," but stopped herself — "easily influenced."

Mandy sat at the bar, shucking corn. "Whose kids? Ryan's maybe?" She ripped off a pale green husk, tossing it into a large brown bag for composting.

Sighing, Anna drew in a deep breath. "You really have it in for his kids, don't you? You've never even met them, Mandy. Why don't you just back off?"

"Bullshit. You've got issues with them; I know you too well. Since dinner the other night. Every time Christina mentions their names, you've done nothing except remind her that they're good kids. If they are, okay, but you're on the defensive, Anna, and you know you are." Mandy continued to pull the husks off the corn. "And you've met them only once," she added.

"Just back off. They'll be here tomorrow. You can form your own opinion. They're just kids. Nothing to worry over. I just want them to feel welcome while they're here. I don't think that's asking too much." She looked away from her spice mixing and directed her gaze at Mandy.

"I'm sorry. I didn't mean to insinuate that Ryan's two are anything other than two kids without a mom. I don't know what's wrong with me. Maybe I'm a little jealous? I've had you and Christina as my family all these years, and now you've got Ryan, his kids.

Don't pay any attention to my big mouth, okay?" Mandy got off the stool she was sitting on, walked across the kitchen where Anna was standing, and wrapped her arms around her. "I guess I'm afraid of losing my best friend, and my boss."

"Oh, Mandy, that's ridiculous! No one will ever replace you. You're the little sister I never had, plus I wouldn't be able to work without your smarts. I *am* on the defensive; you're spot-on. They're just pissed at their dad, I think. Tomorrow, you'll get to see them for yourself. You are family, okay? 'Nuff said," Anna quoted Mona.

Mandy's eyes pooled with tears. "Thanks. I needed to hear this. As I said, I'm a little jealous." She dabbed her eyes with the hem of her Pink Floyd T-shirt.

"Don't be."

"If you two don't stop your hootin' and hollerin', we ain't gonna get this mountain of food ready for tomorrow," Mona called over her shoulder. She was still at the sink, prepping the ribs for Anna's dry rub.

Anna grinned at Mandy.

"We're fine, Mona. Why don't you switch places with me? I want to get this rub on and let it marinate overnight," Anna said, glad they were finally focusing on the food prep.

"Gladly; this old woman needs a two-minute break," she said, taking a can of Coke from the refrigerator and sitting on a barstool to drink it.

Christina burst through the back door, the smell of chlorine clinging to her, her wet shorts and T-shirt dripping all over the floor. "You've been in the pool," Anna said.

"Duh, yeah. Jeb dropped the bag of mesquite chips in the pool. He tried to get them out with the net, and pushed them too far for me to reach, so I just jumped in and got them. No biggie." She plopped the wet plastic bag onto the bar. "You're supposed to soak these or something?" she added.

"Something like that. Thanks, sweetie. Why don't you run upstairs and change into dry clothes? You can help with the dessert later if you want."

Anna was going to make her mother's red devil's food cake for tomorrow. She liked it to sit overnight, as it always tasted better that way.

"Only if I get to lick the beater," Christina tossed over her shoulder, heading upstairs.

"Always," Anna called out. "They never outgrow the beater licking."

Mandy shot her a wry smile. "I could run with that, but I'll be kind and not. I'll leave it, but only till next time."

"You're such a pig." Anna tossed a mesquite chip at her. Back to their usual crazy banter, Anna hated that she'd made her feel even the slightest bit of jealousy. Certainly it wasn't her intention. She didn't understand why she felt so defensive, other than that she suspected Ryan might be a bit hard on his kids. She would see how the barbecue went tomorrow. For her, this was a test. If Ryan's mouth let loose, she would tell him they needed to sit down and discuss this habit of his. It was another slight problem, that she had recently learned needed attention, that was concerning her. She wanted to see how he interacted with Christina *and* his kids together, plus Mandy, Jeb, and Mona. If there was even a hint of his implying he was better than they were, something she'd picked up on a few times when she spoke of Mona and Jeb, she would seriously consider ending their relationship. Maybe. Regardless of that, the *slight* problem she had required both of their attention or there could be issues down the road. *How did I get myself into such a mess?*

Though she wasn't one hundred percent sure, she wasn't naïve. Having these suspicions should be a deal breaker. But she would give them all a chance to get to know one another, then make her decision accordingly.

"Deep thoughts?" Mandy asked, dumping the freshly shucked corn in a large bowl.

"I never have deep thoughts," Anna said, forcing a laugh. "My only deep thoughts consist of food and grocery lists."

"I know from personal knowledge that your grocery bills dig *deep* into your bank account."

"True, but that's part of the job, so I'll let my accountant worry about it," Anna quipped, finishing her spice mix and focusing her attention on the slabs of ribs. She smeared her dry rub across them on both sides, then took the baking sheets and placed them inside the refrigerator. "Remind me to set those out a couple of hours before putting them on the grill. They'll cook evenly when they start at room temperature."

"You're not filming," Mandy said.

"Habit. Just tune me out."

"Yep, it's what I always do," Mona said from her place at the bar. "Tune ya out. I wait to watch ya on the show each week. Me and Jeb have supper every Tuesday night in front of that smart TV you gave us for Christmas. I don't get why it's smart, 'cause I can't figure how to turn the darned channel. Jeb's good for it, though."

"I'll give you a lesson anytime. Just say the word," Mandy said.

"Nah, gives Jeb somethin' to do. Makes him feel smarter than me, and the TV."

"Men and their TVs," Anna said. She'd bought them a smart TV because they couldn't figure how to watch her YouTube channel on their computer, a desktop which was so old, it was a miracle they could log on to the Internet. She planned to get both new laptops for Christmas this year. Mandy could give them a crash course in how they operated.

"I wouldn't know, being single and all," Mandy tossed in. She'd broken off with Eric.

"You ain't got to be in no hurry to get unsingle. Someone'll find you when you're ready. Matter of fact, enjoy being alone for a while longer, 'cause I guarantee, when you do tie the knot, you ain't gonna get no TV time unless you beg. When Jeb ain't a-workin', that TV blares like a battle cry. He's addicted to that show about dead people that walk. Dumbest stuff I've ever heard of," Mona said.

"I know that show, and agree, it's a stretch of the imagination," Anna said. "Christina and Tiffany watch it. It's probably not very age-appropriate, but I can't control everything she does."

"She's knows it's not real. Anyone with a brain does," Mandy said.

"Then that leaves Jeb out," Mona said.

Anna burst out laughing. "You're so mean!"

"Nope, it's the truth. He thinks that stuff happens or it's gonna happen, not sure which, but you can't tell him it's malarkey. He'll argue with ya till the cows come home."

When Mona was on a roll, and had an audience, she was as entertaining as any stand-up comedian.

"Did I hear my name?" Jeb himself stood in the mudroom entry leading to the kitchen. He was a true Texan. He wore blue Levi's, one of his many Stetson hats, a pale blue, short-sleeved western shirt with snaps in place of buttons, and a worn leather belt, with a silver buckle in the shape of Texas with a brass star in the middle. A full head of white hair showed when he removed his hat, and the hatband had left a deep dent around his head. His bright blue eyes were as alert as those of a man half his age. "What lies you tellin' these kids now?" he asked his wife as he planted a kiss on her cheek.

"Nothing that ain't true," Mona said.

"What're you doin' in here? Thought you was cleaning that pool."

"I'm finished. No sweet tea in the little house." Jeb always referred to the guesthouse as the little house. "So I figure Miss Anna's got to have some here in the big house."

"Always," Anna said. She washed her hands, grabbed a glass, filled it with ice, then took the pitcher of tea from the refrigerator and filled the glass. "Here you go, Jeb. Thanks for taking care of the pool for me. The guys at Neptune are off the entire month of September."

"I'd be hirin' another company," Mona said, sipping her Coke. "It's hotter than a jalapeño in a baby's mouth right now. Why in the world would ya take this month off?"

"Wasn't a lick a trouble," Jeb said. "I'm gonna head out, get the grills ready for tomorrow. You need me for anything else, just holler." Jeb downed his glass of tea, gave a wave, put his Stetson on, and exited as fast as he'd entered.

"I swear that man makes my ankles swell," Mona said. "I'm gonna go make some sweet tea, so you girls behave yourselves." She went through the mudroom and out the back door.

Mandy waited until the door closed. "Are

you setting the alarm during the day? I was curious since they're running in and out like house flies, as Mona would say."

"No, I haven't. I don't think it's unsafe. If I did, I wouldn't let Christina run in and out. The gates are locked, the security cameras are on."

"I take it that you haven't heard any more news then?" Mandy asked.

Grateful for her concern, Anna answered. "No, it's been a while. I think whoever they are, maybe they decided I wasn't worth going to jail over. Whatever the reason, I don't have that creeped-out feeling I had when I was being watched. I know it's a possibility that they could start up again. I think we've got enough security and alarms to ensure we're all safe here at the house. Out in public, there isn't anything I can do about it except stay on high alert. And I have. I promise you." They hadn't discussed her stalker in a while, and Anna found that she could speak about it now without the fear she had once had.

"I worry about you." Mandy seemed to be struggling with whatever it was she wanted to say. "You seem, I don't know, different. Are you sure there isn't anything you want to tell me?"

Anna sat down at the bar on the stool

beside her best friend. "You know me that well, don't you?"

"I'd like to think I do."

Anna felt anxious, unsure whether she wanted to tell Mandy what she suspected. By all rights, Ryan should be the one she told first, but this felt right.

"Can you keep this to yourself for a while?" Anna asked, turning her stool so that they faced one another.

"I'm sure I can, whatever it is," Mandy said.

Closing her eyes and trying to visualize her next words, she couldn't see an easy way to say what she needed to other than spit it out as Mandy would tell her to do. "I think I might be pregnant."

Mandy stared at her, apparently at a loss for words.

CHAPTER 13

The front doorbell rang promptly at twelve
o'clock. Ryan, Patrick, and Renée were
standing at the door, each holding a package, though Ryan had a gorgeous bouquet
of Texas bluebonnets. Anna smiled. "I'm so
glad ya'll came. Come on in." She took the
flowers from Ryan. "These are a favorite of
mine, thanks." She inhaled their slight scent.
"How did you find these this time of year?"

"My best-kept secret," he intoned, his
dark blue eyes twinkling with amusement.

"Fine by me," Anna said. "Patrick, Renée,
glad you're here. Christina is already in the
pool. I want you all to meet her. Follow
me," she said. Neither of the kids spoke,
but Anna got that. This place could be a bit
intimidating, the size alone, not to mention
the two winding staircases that expanded to
three levels at the main entrance. Eight
bedrooms, five full-size bathrooms, all
equipped with Jacuzzi tubs, the same luxu-

ries she had in her master bath. She'd sunk several million dollars into the place, but in spite of its grandeur and size, she'd managed to make it homey and comfortable.

"Does YouTube make people rich?" Renée asked out of the blue, handing her the small package.

"Renée Robertson! Where are your manners?" Ryan said in a stern voice. "That's not very polite."

Anna stopped when they reached the kitchen. "It's okay, Ryan. Thanks for the gift. It's sweet of you both." Anna placed the package on the bar, and Patrick placed another matching gift beside hers. "Renée, lots of people make their fortunes in jobs that make them happy. I've been very blessed to do what I love and earn a living. It's always been my hope that one day this house will be full of kids and grandkids, and all their families. I was an only child, so some might think I've gone a bit overboard. But someday this will all go to Christina and her family. So" — she smiled at Ryan, who was listening intently — "that's my story.

"Come on, through here. Jeb and Christina worked on the pool yesterday to make sure it was fit to swim in. The pool company I use takes a vacation in September," Anna explained. She led them through the kitchen, to the mudroom and outside.

Christina was floating in the center of the pool on a giant pink flamingo, her latest float. Free-floating in the pool were a giant duck, a frog, and a doughnut, all picked out by Christina when she had learned of the pool party. Mandy had taken her to Paul's Plus, where they had the most unique, sturdy floats in town. Anna laughed but allowed her daughter to put her mark on whatever she thought she could do to add to the ambience, if you will, and most of the time, she was spot-on. Today was no different.

"Cool!" Renée said when she saw the pool. She ran ahead of them, stopping when she reached the raised ledge, an area Anna had had built for those who wanted to sun alongside the pool without being splashed. Most of the time it was a safe space. However, when Christina and her friends were in the mood, no one was safe around them as they splashed and jumped off the diving board. A total free-for-all.

"Patrick, what do you think?" Anna really wanted his opinion as he was a swimmer. They stood around the deck taking in the enormity of the pool and the areas surrounding it.

Anna continued. "It's about forty feet long, and sixteen in width. I had to check the specifics as I wasn't sure when you asked me at dinner. Eight feet deep, and the shallow end is about four foot deep."

Patrick stepped toward the pool, not saying a word as he stripped off his shirt, kicked off his flip-flops, walked around to the diving board, and slowly walked to the edge. He looked down, walked back, then took off in a run, bouncing high into the air, his lean body forming into a perfect dive, hitting the water with barely a splash.

"Holy cow!" Christina called. "That is totally the most perfect dive I've ever seen." She slid off her flamingo and swam across the pool to where they were standing. Without bothering to use the steps, Christina easily lifted herself out of the pool. She was wearing a fluorescent orange one-piece swimsuit. "Hey, I'm Christina. You must be Renée. And I know that's your brother. Mom said he was a swimmer, but didn't mention anything about being an expert diver." She held her hand out to Renée, but the girl just stood there. "Hey, Ryan." Christina focused her attention on him.

"How's it going, kiddo?" he said to her.

"Well, Patrick needs no encouragement,

but did you all bring swimsuits?" Anna asked.

"They did." Ryan answered. "They're in the car, with a change of clothes for all of us. Wasn't sure, so I told the kids to pack like they were going on a trip. Renée brought her entire bedroom," he said jokingly. He turned back to Christina. "Looks like you've been out in the sun for a while."

"Yeah, sorry, Mom. I forgot the sunscreen. I'll go inside and put some on." She stopped, turned to Renée, and asked, "You want to see my room?" That was so typical of her daughter, polite to a fault.

"Yeah, sure," Renée finally answered.

"Come on," Christina held her hand out, and shockingly, Renée placed her hand in Christina's. "We'll be back in a bit, Mom," she said.

"No worries. Take all the time you want."

"That's unusual," Ryan said. "She's not the most outgoing kid."

"She's great! Now why didn't you tell me that Patrick was such an expert on the diving board?" Patrick swam to the end of the pool and back so fast that Anna was truly amazed. "And that?" She pointed to his fast-moving figure in the pool. "Dang, he's good."

"Yeah," Ryan said, a note of disappointment in his voice. "He was."

"Was? I think he still *is,*" she countered, emphasizing the two verbs. "Want to talk about it?" she asked. Anna had been avoiding discussing Patrick and whatever his issues were, but now, being in the condition she was, she truly wanted, *needed* to know what had happened to take him away from a sport he obviously excelled at.

"It's not something I like to talk about. Maybe later?" He turned to her, a smile on his face. "I want today to be perfect, nothing negative to ruin it for me."

Anna sighed. "Okay, but I truly would like to learn more about your children, what made them become the people they are now. But if you'd rather wait, I understand."

Ryan pulled her close to him, his forehead touching hers, though he had to stoop down to do this as he was much taller than her. "That's what I love most about you, Anna. You're so understanding. Patrick doesn't like me to talk about this, but later, I . . . No, forget that. Step over here," he said, guiding her to one of the four tables with giant blue-and-white-striped umbrellas. They sat down and he pulled his chair as close to hers as he could. "This is between us, okay?"

"Of course," she replied.

"The summer before Patrick's junior year, he met this girl, Rosalee; they were inseparable, they were madly in love. You know how first love can be?" He paused, as if he needed her to answer.

"Sure," she said. Did she ever.

"One thing led to another, and Rosalee was pregnant by the end of the summer."

"Oh, I had . . . no idea." *Anything but that,* she thought, but she let him continue with this story before the rest of her hodgepodge family made their first appearance.

"Yeah, it wasn't a good time for either of them." He rubbed the bridge of his nose. "Her family went ballistic, as you would expect. I wasn't happy, but as a guy, I understood."

Would he be as understanding when she told him of her suspicions?

She nodded encouragingly.

"Patrick wanted to marry her, said he would quit school, get a job. He wanted to take care of Rosalee and their baby. While I admired him for accepting his responsibility, as his father, I couldn't allow him to ruin his life over one summer love, since, as we both know, first loves last like a paper to a flame. They're hot and exciting, then most die out as fast as they began. Logan, his swimming coach, got word of this, not sure

216

how, but he came to me, told me it was highly probable that if Patrick continued on the swim team, he'd get a full scholarship to a college of his choice. So, of course, I was thrilled to hear that, but I knew it wasn't possible if he dropped out of school and took a damn job selling hamburgers. He had a bright future." He took a deep breath.

"I met with Rosalee's parents; they're a good Spanish family, very moral. Catholic. I explained to them that Patrick had an awesome future ahead of him. His coach even talked Olympics, but Patrick shut his mind off to his future. Unless Rosalee and his child were a part of it, he wouldn't listen to her family, and certainly I was the bad guy, so he wouldn't listen to me, either. We were all at a crossroad, we wanted what was best for the kids, even if they thought they knew better. They were barely sixteen. Her parents refused to allow her to have an abortion, which is what I suggested, thinking it was best. Her family wouldn't hear of it, so they sent Rosalee to live with a cousin. In Spain, of all places. The baby was adopted, and we've never discussed it since. Patrick's way of showing his disappointment was to quit the swim team. Today's the first day he's been in a pool since."

"Ryan, that's so sad, but I understand Patrick's frustration, how horrible this must've been." Anna took a moment before she spoke, needing to absorb all he'd told her. "He has no idea where Rosalee is? Do they talk? Text?"

"No. Her parents forbade her to have any contact with him."

"They're legal adults now — can't they make that decision themselves?" Anna's heart broke for Patrick and Rosalee.

"I suppose they could, but as far as I know, Rosalee has moved on. I asked Patrick about it once, and he left me with the impression he was over her, but I don't think he is. And maybe he never will be. That's why he spent all of his free time holed up in his room these past two years."

She remembered his story from the ship, and she could have sworn he had said Patrick spent his *entire* four years of high school hiding away, but it was easy enough to allude to two years as four, especially in a situation like Patrick's, worried about his son's future and knowing that his entire life might've been different had he not fallen in love at such an early age.

"That explains why you sent him to so many therapists," she said. "I'm guessing he's depressed?"

"Yeah, he's been on a few medications, though none really helped him. Now, I'm duty-bound to see that he gets to college. After that, he can do whatever the hell he wants. I'm sure it will be something to spite me," Ryan said, disgust in his tone.

"I can't imagine he's too enthused about much, when he was left in limbo, not having any say in a very crucial decision that obviously has deeply affected him. Though look at him. He's like a shark." They turned their attention to Patrick, doing lap after lap in the pool.

"They called him 'Sean the Shark' in school. Sean is his middle name. Funny you picked up on that."

"Well, it's true. Watch him." Anna had never seen such precision, speed, and grace. He was meant to do this, she thought. Later, if things progressed, she planned to give serious thought to Patrick's future as a swimmer, and if she could help him, she would. Such wasted talent.

"I'm glad you invited us. This is a major milestone," Ryan said. "I knew he missed this," he added.

"He's welcome to come over anytime and swim," Anna said. "He's like one with the water. I could watch him all day, but I've been rude." She stood up, holding her hand out to indicate he should stay. "Ginger ale?" she asked.

"You read my mind." He smiled as he watched her.

"Be right back," Anna said, going to the small refrigerator and taking two bottles of ginger ale and two glasses. She filled both glasses from the ice maker. Her mini outdoor kitchen was great at times like this, and even more so, you couldn't see it as it was hidden behind a fancy wall away from the pool. She'd set up the grills early this morning, and the smoky mesquite scent was putting her in perfect party mode. She would film this one day, when her life was calm and settled. She adored playing hostess.

She'd sent Jeb and Mona for booze, for even though she wasn't much of a drinker, she did like to have it on hand. Lubbock County was partially dry, but there was a strip of liquor stores located on a stretch of Tahoka Highway, just outside the city limits. They should be here any minute, unless Mona had to make a pit stop at Walmart, which was highly probable given her love for the supermarket giant. She would spend hours roaming the aisles if you'd let her. Lucky for all of them, she usually went alone, but this was a holiday weekend, and more than likely, she'd find something on sale that she just had to have or something Christina needed. A crazy T-shirt or a pair of shorts that barely covered the cheeks of her butt, as she would say. *Dear Mona,* Anna thought, as she returned to the table. *What would I do without her?*

"Here you go." Anna handed him the glass, along with a napkin.

"All fancy, I see," Ryan said, taking the glass from her.

"It's habit, what I do," she commented, sitting down beside him. She pushed her chair closer to the table in order to get beneath the giant umbrella. The hot Texas sun was shining as brightly as a ball of fire. She used her napkin to wipe the perspiration from her forehead. She'd twisted her long hair into a topknot and wore a yellow tank top with white shorts. The coolest outfit she had that was barbecue-appropriate and comfortable. Maybe she and Ryan would go for a swim later, when the sun wasn't so hot. She'd always enjoyed an evening swim, then a relaxing bath right before bed. It was better than an Ambien, which she used on occasion when she was overworked, overtired, and sleep was nothing but a dream. She would take a pill, sleep like the dead for hours, then roar back to life, to start the cycle all over again. But it's who she was, how she worked. Another secret she kept from Mandy. The Xanax and the Ambien. This was too personal to share with anyone except Mona, who knew everything there was to know about her and Christina, as she was like a second mother to her, and she knew that Mona felt that Anna was the daughter she could never have. Their relationship was as close to perfect as one could get, and she'd been so blessed when Mona and Jeb accepted her offer all those years ago. She paid them a very hefty salary, which they said they didn't need, but that was the way it had to be. Anna would not allow them to work without a salary. End of story.

"It's apparent you do very well," he said, motioning to the house and pool. "I'd like to see your studio sometime, if you wouldn't mind. That way, when I watch *The Simple Life,* I'll have the inside scoop."

"Come on, I can show you now, if you want. Mandy won't be here for at least another hour. Looks like Patrick is making up for lost time, so maybe he'd like a little privacy," she suggested, standing and nodding toward the pool. He was doing the backstroke with such perfection, it was easy to understand why his coach had thought

Patrick had a chance at making the Olympics.

"Great." Ryan downed the last of his drink and left his glass on the table.

Ryan followed Anna inside. She didn't usually allow outsiders in the studio, but at this point, he was much more than that, and besides, she wanted to show him exactly what the process was. Mandy and the crew made it look easy, but it wasn't. It was a good thing that she adored doing this, adored her job. "Over here," she indicated. The door leading downstairs was unremarkable. Off to the far side of the kitchen, with a small rolling cart to one side, and a shelf full of cookbooks lining the other side, the door was easily missed if one weren't paying attention as it had been built to match the walls in the kitchen. Her reason for doing this was part structural and part personal choice. While she loved her work, when she was upstairs in her personal kitchen, she didn't want anything to remind her of her filming kitchen. Strange, she knew, as the decor was quite similar, but it worked for the crew. They would come and go through an outside entrance, while she and Mandy used the stairs that led to the studio kitchen. She flipped on lights as they made their way down the stairs.

It was dark inside since she wasn't filming right at the moment, so she hit the studio lights, filling the kitchen area with the bright light needed for filming.

She watched Ryan. "What do you think?" She smiled.

"It's nothing like I imagined," he said. "*Wow* is the first word that comes to mind."

"Obviously, this half is what you see when I'm doing food videos." She had a long rolling worktable, which on camera looked like an ordinary kitchen countertop. Behind that were two ovens, a microwave, and a giant refrigerator and freezer. All could be moved, as they were also on rollers. The appliances could be tricky, what with all the cords, but they didn't have to move them often. The sink area was the only part of her studio that couldn't be moved, so they always worked around that if they needed to. Another rolling counter, complete with a ceramic backsplash and drawers below, where she kept her utensils, faced the large lights that hung above the set. "This is the biggest area and most used. We can re-arrange the space if we need to, but I like to keep it like this. I'm comfortable, know where I can step. I do change the decor according to seasons and holidays, but it works for me and the crew."

"It's hard to imagine this from your videos. They make it look like you're in the kitchen upstairs."

"I designed it that way. Though upstairs it's permanent." She laughed. "Come on, I'll show you the living area."

She stepped into a much smaller space that housed a small sofa, tables with matching lamps, and a movable wall, which she used to hang pictures on, which were changed according to what she was filming. "I film some of my decorating videos here. Mostly floral designs, sewing." She pointed to another rolling worktable. "This" — she reached down and maneuvered a lever that allowed her sewing machine to appear from an ordinary cabinet — "is for when I sew. It's all designed for convenience when we film. I hired a super crew, and they're the reason why we've been so successful. I'm just the face and the laborer." She laughed again.

"I think you're much more than that. Without your vision, I don't think your crew could've created this."

"Maybe, but it's a team effort when we work. A lot of things I can do without them, like prep and that sort of thing. Unless it's something the viewers need to see. We have a good routine, long hours, but none of us complain. We're doing what we love."

She showed him her small office, which was simply a desk with two laptop computers and a shelf filled with books she used, then the bathroom, where she sometimes filmed beauty videos, but that wasn't her specialty, so filming in there wasn't easy. "This is the bathroom." Basic design, with a shower, sink, and toilet; there was nothing fancy about this part of her studio.

He peered in, shaking his head. "You're a genius, Anna Campbell. I'm impressed beyond words."

"Thanks," she said, and wondered if now was the right time to tell him of her suspicions. They were alone, and it was quiet. "Ryan." She said his name softly. "There is something I've been meaning to tell you. I just, well, the timing is always off. Not sure it's right even now." She stopped, suddenly unsure. She was not one hundred percent sure if she was pregnant. She hadn't tested herself, hadn't gone to the doctor; all that had happened is that she'd missed her cycle last month. No, she would wait until the pregnancy was confirmed by a medical professional. So now, what to tell him?

"What is it?" he asked, concern in his voice. "You can tell me anything, Anna. I'm that kind of guy."

Anna laughed. "Good to know." She chewed on her lower lip, something she did when she was worried. She needed to tell him anything but the truth. "I thought maybe Renée might like to go to school with Christina. At Bishop Coerver. I haven't discussed it with her yet because I wanted to speak with you first. She seemed unhappy about going to Lubbock High." The words tumbled from her mouth as though it were exactly what she had intended to say. She was becoming such an accomplished liar.

He didn't say a word, just stood there.

"Look, maybe it's not my place."

Ryan continued to stare at her. "You're goddamn right it's not your place!"

Stunned, she stood rooted to the floor. Words escaped her. She watched him watch her. His gaze darkened, and she could see the veins pulsing in his neck. Frightened, she stepped away from him. "I'm going upstairs," she said, and went through each room, making sure the lights were off. When she reached the stairs that led to her kitchen, she stopped, turning to see if he was following her. She didn't see him. "Ryan," she called out. "Let's talk about this later."

What else could she say? Glad she hadn't told him the truth, she still should have said anything but what she did say. Probably hurt his ego, but again, he'd become angry so quickly, it scared her. She took another step, waiting for him to respond.

"I'm here," he said.

"Oh." He'd startled her. "Ryan, look, I overstepped. I'm sorry. Don't let it ruin our day."

As she was standing eye to eye with him, she saw someone else. A man who was quick to anger, quick to judge. Not the man she thought she knew. Ryan had a temper, she realized. He'd shown it on multiple occasions, so why she was just now realizing it was beyond her comprehension, but now that she had, she didn't want to stay down here any longer.

She was afraid of what he might do.

He reached for her hand, and instinctually, she pulled it away. "No, let's go upstairs," she told him.

"Hey, I'm sorry. I didn't mean for it to come out the way it sounded."

"It's fine. Really. Let's just forget I said anything." Anna stood on the next step, his nearness intimidating. "I'm sure that if Mona and Jeb are back, they're wondering where we are," she said, and walked to the top of the staircase. Opening the door that led to her kitchen, she breathed a sigh of relief when he followed her.

"Anna, wait," he said, taking her arm. She stood face-to-face with him, unwilling to do anything that might cause him to react.

"I'm here," she said, offering up a half-warm smile.

"You are right to be concerned about Renée and her schooling. She's not happy about Lubbock High. I should listen to you. Again, it's been a while since a woman's had any influence over me."

Did he think he could explain away his temper by agreeing with her, *after* the fact? "You're right, Ryan. It wasn't my place. Let's just forget it and enjoy the rest of the day. I've got enough ribs and a brisket to feed fifty people," she said, her way of changing the subject.

"Sounds great."

Anna went out to the pool area through the mudroom. Ryan followed her, but she didn't speak to him.

Patrick sat on the end of the diving board, swinging his feet back and forth. He was a cute kid who'd had a giant dose of reality much too young.

"I bet you're starving after that swim," she called out to him. She'd heard somewhere that swimmers needed to eat thousands of high-calorie foods a day in order to perform. No doubt her red devil's food cake

229

would fill that need, but not in the healthiest way.

He dropped off the diving board into the water and swam across to the side of the pool. "I am kinda hungry now," he said.

"Tell me what you want." She'd feed this poor guy, give him the calories he needed in order to regain the energy he'd just burned in the pool.

"Whatever you're cooking smells good." He gave a half smile.

"Ribs and brisket," Anna said. "Let me get you a towel." She kept a large supply of pool towels in a cabinet in her outdoor kitchen. She grabbed a handful and gave him one as he stepped out of the pool.

"Thanks."

"No problem. Why don't you dry off while I get you something to drink? Coke, right?" She remembered he'd ordered this, or rather, Ryan had ordered that drink for him the other night at dinner. "Or not," she added.

"Do you have Dr. Pepper?" he asked.

"Now what kind of Texan would I be if I didn't have the soda we're most famous for? I'll be right back." She had a case of Dr. Pepper in the kitchen pantry.

Inside, she located the soda, grabbed six cans, using a small basket she kept in the pantry for the times she needed an extra set of hands. She found the largest cup she had, a metal one that supposedly kept drinks cold for twenty-four hours. She filled it with ice and returned to the pool. "Here you go." She placed the six sodas next to the giant cup of ice.

"Awesome," he said. Anna thought this was the first time he'd actually sounded like a normal eighteen-year-old young man. "Thanks."

"I'm sure some of those ribs are ready. I'll get you a plate. Be right back." She knew that Jeb would be irritated with her for messing with his setup, but there was a hungry young man waiting to be fed, and she knew he'd understand, since he'd spent the better part of his life feeding hungry people of all ages.

Anna had prepared tons of side dishes and kept them inside, as the small refrigerator wouldn't hold all of them.

"I thought we weren't eating until this evening," Mandy said as she entered the kitchen.

Anna jumped. "You scared the crap out of me," she said.

"And a happy Labor Day to you, too," Mandy tossed back. "I take it the gang's all here?"

"They are. Patrick is hungry, so I'm fixing him a plate," she said, explaining why she was taking all the food out of the refrigerator.

"I smelled the barbecue as soon as I opened my car door. I'm starving myself. Mind if have a bit?" she asked, noting the large plastic bowl of potato salad.

"Help yourself. I'm going to get a couple slabs of those ribs for Ryan. Stay here until I come back. I want to personally introduce you to Ryan and his kids."

Mandy nodded. "Sure."

Anna filled two plates with potato salad and a green bean salad she'd featured on the show last week, which had received almost 3 million likes. She guessed that her family and friends would like it as well, given the response from her audience. She microwaved the baked beans she'd prepped and threw in three unheated dinner rolls. He'd have to wait for the corn, as she'd grill it a few minutes before serving.

Balancing the two plates, Anna used her foot to nudge the door open. Mona hadn't closed it all the way, which for once, was a good thing.

Patrick sat next to his dad, though both appeared as though the other didn't exist. Anna could feel the tension between them.

"Start with this. I'll get the ribs," she said, placing both plates in front of him. "Be right back."

Anna removed two slabs of pork ribs from the grill and placed them on the stack of plates she'd put out earlier. She was using the heavy-duty paper plates that, according to the manufacturer, were the best on the market. According to the commercials, they'd hold just about anything. Though she hadn't mentioned this to anyone, she was testing these out today, and if they were all that they claimed to be, she'd accept a sponsorship and, possibly, a feature in an upcoming commercial.

When she returned to the table, Patrick had consumed half of the food. "These are hot; you'll have to tell me if they're any good," she said, placing the two large racks of ribs beside the other two plates. He ate as though he were starving. Hard to believe this was the kid Ryan worried about eating.

"Thanks, Anna."

"My pleasure. There's plenty, so eat as much as you want," she added.

Not speaking to Ryan wasn't going to work, given there were others to consider, so she asked, "You want to try them? I haven't put the corn on the grill, but if you're hungry, I'll fix you a plate."

"I'll mind my manners and wait," he said, getting in a dig at Patrick.

"All that swimming burns calories. I couldn't let a guest in my home starve," Anna said, meeting his icy gaze. More and more, she had doubts about continuing her relationship with this man. However, there was that one little issue she had to settle before making any decisions. She'd bite her tongue for now. She'd already witnessed his temper in the studio — once was enough.

"He's not starving," Ryan said. "But thanks for this." He nodded at the plates of food.

"No worries."

As Anna headed back inside, she heard a terrifying scream. She ran into the house, through the kitchen. "Mandy?" she called out. "What's . . ."

"Oh my God, call nine-one-one. Go, my phone's on the counter!" Mandy shouted, as she held Christina's seemingly lifeless body. "Go, damn it!"

Paralyzed with fear, no one moved. Mandy yelled again, "Call nine-one-one now!"

Anna glanced up to see Renée looking down. She just stood there. A rush of adrenaline forced Anna into action. Running to the kitchen, she found Mandy's cell phone. With shaking hands, she dialed 911.

"What's your emergency," a calm and pleasant female voice asked.

"My daughter. I . . . she's hurt. I need an ambulance. Now!" She recited her address by rote, dropped the phone on the floor, and raced back to the foot of the stairs. Dropping to her knees, she saw that Christina was still breathing, "Christina, it's Mommy," she said, tears streaming down her face. "It's okay, you're going to be okay."

"I think her leg is broken," Mandy said. "She's gonna be fine. I want you to calm down. Anna, listen to me."

"How . . . what happened?" She stared at her daughter, her bright orange bathing suit still damp from the pool. She smelled of chlorine and mesquite smoke.

Christina moaned, turning her head to the side. A single tear fell from her eyes. "Mommy," she whispered.

"It's okay, baby. The ambulance is on its way. I'm right here. I'm not going to let anything happen to you, I promise." She held her daughter's slender body, gently wiping her hair from her tear-stained cheeks. Her thick lashes were clumped together, as though she'd been crying before.

"I'm going to open the gates," Mandy said.

Anna squeezed back tears. "Go, quickly."

"What's going on in here?" came Ryan's voice from the doorway in the kitchen. "Where's Renée?"

"I'm here," Renée said from the top of the staircase.

"Anna, what the hell happened to her?" he said, bending beside Christina. She wanted to push him away, tell him to get out, but she couldn't.

"I don't know. I've called for an ambulance. Please move back," she said, her motherly instinct kicking in. He moved a few inches away.

Anna heard the sirens in the distance. "We're going to get you to the hospital, sweetie. Can you hear me?"

"Mommy?" Christina said again, then blacked out.

Mandy ran through the front door, the paramedics trailing behind.

"Out of the way, please," a man about Anna's age said as he stooped to attend to Christina.

"What happened?" he asked, as he assessed her injuries. "Anyone?" he said, running expert fingers up and down her spine. "Ma'am, you need to move. Let me take over."

Anna scooted a few inches back, allowing

the paramedic to slide a plastic board beneath Christina. "I heard a scream when I came inside," Anna said. "Mandy, did you see what happened?"

By this time, Christina was moaning again. Anna guessed she'd blacked out because she was in so much pain. "Please, just help my daughter," Anna said, her voice several octaves higher than normal.

"All I saw was Christina at the bottom of the stairs. Maybe ask her?" She pointed to the top of the stairs, where Renée was sitting on the top step, looking down at all the activity below.

"Get down here now!" Ryan shouted.

"Okay, okay, geez," Renée said, taking her time walking down the stairs. "What?" she asked when she finally reached the bottom.

Mandy took charge. "What happened?" Her voice was stern, no-nonsense.

Renée shrugged. "I don't know. One minute, she was showing me her Harry Potter books, then she said she had to go to the bathroom. And then" — she pointed to Christina's crumpled body as the paramedics lifted the board onto the gurney — "that."

"Bullshit," Mandy said. "Her bathroom is in her bedroom. You can't leave that room through the bathroom door!" Mandy looked at Ryan. "Ask your daughter what happened — this is important, damn it!"

"Mandy," Anna said, following the paramedics to the front door. "Later. Take care of the food. The grills are on, so turn them off. Mona and Jeb should be back any minute to help. I'll call you from the hospital."

Anna followed the paramedics to the waiting ambulance. Fear ripped through her, her heart rate increased, and her vision blurred. She was about to have a full-blown panic attack. Just when her daughter needed her the most.

CHAPTER 14

"She has a fractured tibia, though it's a clean break," Dr. Laird explained. "There's a slight break in the fibula, here" — he pointed to the X-ray image on the computer with a pen — "this small bone. She'll be in a bit of pain for a few days, which we can manage with low-dose pain meds. Then we can ease off with acetaminophen. I want to keep her here for the next twenty-four hours. She has a slight concussion that I'd like to monitor. It's just routine. She'll be good as new in a few weeks," he explained to Anna.

"This is all my fault," she said to him.

"Anna, kids fall all the time. If they didn't, I'd be out of business." Ed Laird was a pediatric orthopedic surgeon. She'd met him and his wife, Susan, when she was building her house, and they'd become fast friends when Susan learned she was *the* Anna Campbell from *The Simple Life.*

On the ride to the hospital, she'd borrowed a cell phone from one of the paramedics, called Ed Laird, and asked him to meet her at the emergency room. Thankfully, he was home. He'd arrived within minutes of the ambulance.

"How is this your fault?" He tucked his pen into his shirt pocket.

"I don't know. I just feel responsible. She's my daughter; you know how parents can be." She cast a wan smile. "Probably more so than most."

Susan and Ed had four boys under the age of ten.

He smiled. "I do. Kyle broke his arm twice, roughhousing with Keith. It's a constant battle trying to keep them alive. This isn't your fault; get that idea out of your head. I'll arrange for you to stay in a special suite, so you can stay here with Christina, maybe get a bit of rest yourself?"

"Thanks, Ed. I'll take you up on that. You should have all of my insurance information on file."

"I'll let Admissions know."

He explained what she could expect throughout the night, told her the nurses would keep a close eye on Christina, and they could both leave first thing in the morning, barring no unexpected complications.

An hour later, Christina was in a private room, was groggy from the pain medication but able to talk. "Sweetie, I'm so sorry you're hurt. I wish I could take away your pain."

"I'll be okay," she said, though Anna thought she sounded horrible. Alarm bells started to ring. Christina was so out of it, but Anna knew it was the meds talking. She had to stay calm for Christina's sake.

"Of course you will," Anna said. She adjusted her pillow and smoothed the sheets. She was totally out from the pain medication.

A small pull-out sofa gave her a bird's-eye view of Christina in her hospital bed. With a sigh of relief, she sat down and stretched her legs. She still wore the tank top and shorts with her sandals. Not that she cared. Right now, Christina was her only concern. They would get through this, just as Ed had told her.

Though now that she was alone with her thoughts, she couldn't help but wonder if Renée had had anything to do with Christina's fall. They'd been in her room for almost an hour. She needed to talk with

Mandy. Luckily, there was a phone in the room.

The hospital operator connected her to an outside line. She called Mandy's cell phone. "I'm on my way to the hospital now. Mona and Jeb are taking care of your place. I'll see you in half an hour. We need to talk."

She hung up the phone. So much for asking questions on her terms, but she knew Mandy was concerned about Christina, and they'd talk as soon as she arrived. Meanwhile, Anna went to the small bathroom, leaving the door open, so she could hear her daughter. She washed her face, took her hair out of the topknot, raked her fingers through the tangles, then put her hair up in a messy bun. She rinsed her mouth and looked at herself in the mirror. "What have I done?" she whispered. Just a few months ago, her life was as predictable as the days of the week. She thought back to the cruise. That was when her life started falling apart. She should have gone to Orlando and enjoyed the time with Mandy and Christina.

"Mom," Christina called. "Can I have some water?"

Anna moved at the speed of light. A pitcher of fresh ice water had been placed on the bedside table minutes after they'd brought her in. Several plastic-wrapped cups were provided. She took the waxy paper off and poured a small amount in the cup so she wouldn't spill it. "Here, sweetie." Anna held the cup for Christina, then raised the bed just enough so that she could drink without spilling the water.

"Thanks."

She lowered the bed and watched her daughter fall back into a drug-induced sleep. Anna dimmed the lights in the room, then positioned herself on the sofa so she could watch Christina.

She must've dozed for a few minutes, when she was awakened by a creaking sound. "Mandy," she said, beyond thrilled to see her best friend.

"How's she doing?" Mandy whispered.

Anna quickly ran through the list of her injuries. "Ed thinks she'll be fine in a few weeks. I hate this, Mandy. I feel responsible."

"Can we sit?"

"Over here." Anna sat back down, making room for Mandy.

"First things first. I brought your cell phone, purse, a change of clothes, and a toothbrush. You can thank me later. If there's anything else you need, I'll call Mona."

"No, no, this is fine. I wasn't thinking clearly in the ambulance. That was horrible, seeing her in pain and not being able to do anything about it." Tears filled her eyes. Mandy gave her a tissue from a box on the small table beside the sofa.

"Thanks." She blew her nose and balled the tissue up in her hand.

"Anna, I know this isn't what you want to hear, especially in your condition, but it has to be said. I was on my way upstairs to grab some things I'd left in the room a few nights ago, and it was a good thing I did. Who knows what else would've happened had I not been there? I don't feel good about this. While I didn't see her actually fall, I saw that little snot standing at the top of the stairs *watching* Christina just lie at the bottom of the steps. When I screamed out, 'Call nine-one-one,' she had a damned cell phone in her hand, yet she just watched, Anna. Do you see where I'm heading with this? I'm not riding any kid's ass. I'm just giving you my take on what I did see."

"You're sure she had a phone? Maybe it wasn't charged," Anna added, because if she let Mandy's assumptions guide her in the direction she was leading her, Christina's fall couldn't have been an accident.

"I can't say for sure, but tell me what

244

thirteen-year-old kid walks around with a cell phone that's *not* charged?"

Anna nodded. She agreed with Mandy's assumptions. "What happened after I left?"

"Ryan was pissed. Big-time. He ripped the son good, blaming him, said if he'd had any manners, he would have waited to eat with everyone else, and Christina would have been where she belonged. It didn't make sense. He was in such a rage, I truly don't know if he knew what he was saying. He dragged those kids out, cussing ninety miles a minute. Lucky for him, Mona and Jeb only arrived after he left. It's just weird. I know you think he's all that, and maybe to you, he is, but Anna, there's something that's not right about him."

She'd had similar thoughts herself. "Look, about the . . . *you know.*" She nodded toward the bed, placing a finger to her mouth indicating Mandy should not say *that word.* "I don't even know if I am, *you know.* I haven't tested. I'm just late, and a couple times I've felt nauseated like I was with Christina."

Mandy leaned as close as she could. "If you suspect you're . . . whatever you're calling it . . . then you need to find out and make a decision. One way or the other, this could . . . No, it already has affected your

245

daughter, and you need to take charge of this now. I know you don't like it when I speak badly of Ryan and those kids, but I don't care. You're feeling sorry for them, why I have no clue, but while you're viewing them through rose-colored glasses, ask yourself this: How well do you *really* know him? His kids? Today was the second time you've seen them. And something else, and I know it's not really my business, but I'm making it my business anyway. What the hell happened to Ryan's wife? Have you two discussed your histories with each other?"

Mandy held up her hand. "Don't say it. I'm trying to look out for you and your daughter. Think about it. How did she die? When did she die? Has he given you details? I don't think so, because knowing you as well as I do, you would've told me. Don't say you wouldn't either." Mandy was breathing hard, her emotions on full display.

Guilt tore through Anna's gut like a sharp blade. All she knew about Ryan's wife was . . . nothing.

"I haven't told him about Wade."

"Why not?"

"We met on a singles cruise, Mandy. I don't know. I guess we were focusing on getting to know each other, not reminiscing over our dead spouses!" Tears rivered down

246

her cheeks. She let them flow, cleansing the hateful words she'd just spewed.

"Okay, I get that, but that was three months ago. If you're serious about this guy, if you're carrying his child, I'd want to know details about his life before you."

Anna nodded. They should've discussed their past lives, shared what made them the people they'd become.

"Look, there's a twenty-four-hour drug-store across the street. I'm going to get a *you know* test. Sit here and think about your life." And with that, Mandy got up and walked out of the room without saying another word.

Her life was a total mess. Wishing she could erase the past few weeks as easily as she erased the whiteboard in her studio, as much as she disliked Mandy's sermon, and it was a sermon, she was right. Anna was responsible for bringing Ryan and his children into their lives. It was up to her to make this right, to do whatever she had to in order to return her life to normal. Mandy was brutal, and her words hurt, but though the truth was sometimes a hard slap in the face, she'd needed to hear this. Taking a deep breath, she slowly released it, and sat there watching Christina's steady breathing, in and out. She reached for her Louis

Vuitton bag on the table. Inside, she located the amber-colored bottle of pills. If ever there was a time for an anxiety crusher, it was now. She removed the childproof cap; a dozen or so small oval, yellow pills were just waiting to work their magic.

No, Anna thought, *this is not the answer.* She replaced the cap and dropped the bottle into the bottom of her purse.

What the hell was I thinking? No way should I even consider popping any kind of pill in my mouth, given my suspected condition. It was another problem she didn't need and, honestly, didn't want. She enjoyed her life at this stage — being Christina's mom and doing what she loved was enough. At least for now. Thoughts of another child, *Ryan's* child, frightened her. While she'd never terminate a pregnancy, just the fact that she was even *contemplating* doing so unnerved her. Why she'd thrown caution to the wind eluded her, though why it did, she had no answer. Ryan was persuasive, attractive, and intelligent — all attributes any woman could desire. His temper was a huge obstacle, the way he shouted at Renée and Patrick, in her opinion, unforgivable. It was more than obvious that she hadn't been thinking with her mind as opposed to other parts. As she stood next to Christina, whose leg was encased in plaster and who had a concussion, Anna had no one to blame but herself. Mandy was right. Though it had barely been three months since she and Ryan had started dating, it was time to make a major decision.

She'd put off the test that would confirm what she apparently didn't want to acknowledge way too long.

As soon as Mandy returned with the test, she'd find out, one way or the other, and deal with the results regardless. At this point, she didn't have much of a choice.

CHAPTER 15

"Her vitals are excellent," the nurse told Anna. "Try and get some rest, Ms. Campbell. We're watching Christina at the desk, via closed circuit, plus Dr. Laird instructed the folks at Tele-Screen to monitor her room."

Anna was confused. "What are you talking about?"

"Tele-Screen. It's basically a second set of eyes. Similar to air traffic control; only, the blips on their radar are patients. He thought it best given your celebrity. It's a new monitoring system that some hospitals are using now."

Anna nodded. "That's good to know though I doubt anyone knows we're here," she told the nurse.

The nurse was probably her age, maybe a bit older. She had her blond hair in a French braid and wore light blue scrubs. Most importantly, she had a caring smile.

"You haven't heard?"

"Heard what?" Anna asked, warning bells blasting in her head, causing her heart rate to increase, a knot in her stomach. "What are you referring to?"

"Your daughter's accident; it's been on the news."

Mandy pushed through the heavy door, carrying a small paper sack. Seeing the nurse, she stuffed the sack inside her tote bag. "How's she doing?"

"Christina's accident made the evening news. Do you know anything about this?"

"What? Of course not. Who told you this?" Mandy asked.

Anna nodded toward the nurse.

Mandy directed her words to the nurse. "How did this information get out to the public? Aren't patients supposed to have a right to privacy? I need to speak to your public-information officer. Right now."

"Mandy, slow down. I'll call Ed, let him know what's happened," Anna said, then spoke to the nurse. "Could we have a moment?"

"Of course," the nurse said, stepping out of the room.

Anna motioned for Mandy to go into the small bathroom. "Here, give me that test. I want to know what I'm dealing with; then we'll focus on the idiot who's made my daughter's accident public knowledge."

"There's three to a box. Just in case," she said, taking the paper sack from her purse. "Do your thing; I'll keep an eye on Christina."

Mandy closed the door, leaving Anna to do what she should have done weeks ago. Hands shaking, she opened the Quick Results pregnancy test box. She read through the instructions, reminding her of the years she and Wade had tried to get pregnant. Not much had changed other than the waiting period. This test said sixty seconds.

She washed her trembling hands, removed the foil wrapping, and took out the pink-and-white stick that held the power to change her life forever. Before she could change her mind, she followed the instructions. When she finished, she placed the stick on the side of the sink, and counted to sixty. Twice, then once again just to make sure.

Before she viewed her results, she sent up a silent prayer that whatever they were, she would have the courage to deal with them.

With the stick in her hand, she opened her eyes and saw two words, not one pink line or two pink lines like the tests she'd used years ago. No, this test actually gave you the words.

Not pregnant.

Tears filled her eyes. "Thank God," she said out loud. What if it was wrong? Quickly, she used the second test stick.

Not pregnant.

Anna smiled, overwhelmed at the relief she felt. Then, just because she could, she used the third stick.

Again, *not pregnant.*

In her mind, three was a charm. She accepted the results and prayed her period would come when she wasn't so stressed. Though that could be forever, given the mess she'd made of her life. She'd make an appointment with her gynecologist soon in order to make sure there wasn't anything medically wrong.

When there was a slight knock on the door, Anna opened it and showed Mandy all three sticks.

"Thank heavens," Mandy said, embracing her. "I bet you wished you had done this sooner," she said.

"I was afraid of the results, but yeah, I should've. Mandy, what is wrong with me? I'm so screwed up right now." She thought of the Xanax in her purse. She might pop one later, just to take the edge off.

"Nothing is wrong with *you*. Now that we're sure there's just one of you, call Ed, tell him I need to speak to the hospital's public-information officer, tonight. I'll contact the local media, explain their airing the story is a violation of Christina's rights, her being a minor. I think we can wrap this up pretty quickly. Now, go call the doctor." Mandy smiled at her. "I know, I know, I am bossy, but you love it. Now go." She gave her a slight push toward the door.

Anna used her cell phone to call Ed Laird. She explained the situation, and he gave her a name and number. "Before I forget," she brought up the NOTES app on her phone and typed in the information Ed had given her. "Here," she said, and handed her phone to Mandy. "Do your thing."

Anna returned to her daughter's bedside, saw she was sleeping and that her breathing seemed deeper, probably from the medications. She would never forgive herself if something happened to Christina. Her worst fear, one she'd gone through years of therapy trying to overcome. After today's accident, if it really was an accident, she knew she couldn't let it slide. As soon as Christina could speak without the effects of the drugs, she would ask her what happened, and if she was pushed.

Mandy returned to the room. "All done. Apparently one of the admitting nurses recognized you. Her husband is the six o'clock news anchor at KCBD. She thought your trip newsworthy and called him. Not sure what's going to happen to either, but I promise you, we'll keep this as quiet as we can." Mandy motioned for her to sit. "However, if this wasn't an accident, we won't be able to keep it out of the news," Mandy said. "It won't matter who you are."

Nodding in agreement, Anna knew that Mandy spoke the truth. "What now?" she asked, needing direction about where to go from here.

"Let's wait and see what Christina says. Then, depending on that, we'll decide. I still think that little snot had something to do with this. If not, she is one coldhearted bitch. Sorry, I know you don't like name-calling when a kid's involved, but riddle me this. Would your daughter have watched one of her friends if they fell down a flight of steps and not called nine-one-one when she was told to? Would any of her friends?" Mandy walked across the small room to the sofa and sat down.

Anna sat beside her. "Of course not."

"I don't have kids, but I know a bad egg when I smell one. Renée Robertson is as rotten as they come."

Anna sighed. "I think she's mixed up, and that's about all I can say at this point. She was hot and cold at dinner at the restaurant, but I attributed that to her being a typical thirteen-year-old girl. She was mad at Ryan because he told her she couldn't get a sleeve tattoo. I get that kids get pissed at their parents. I'm hoping that's all that's going on."

"Screw that, Anna. Open your eyes and stop being so damned defensive. The girl is weird; she's probably the reason we're sitting here now. How many times has anyone fallen down those stairs? Christina runs up and down them all the time. I've never even seen her trip, let alone take a flying leap and land in a heap at the bottom of the steps. It makes sense; at least it does to me."

"I know."

Anna needed to think. Dozens of "what-ifs" plagued her.

"I should call Ryan, at least let him know how Christina's doing," Anna said.

Mandy bounced off the sofa like she had springs on her feet. In a harsh whisper, she asked, "Are you nuts? Who cares what he thinks? If he were all that concerned, he would've called by now. Anna, what the hell has this guy done to you? It's like you've let him drain you of all the spunk I know you have. He doesn't deserve to know, if you want my opinion, which I know you don't."

"But you're giving it anyway, free of charge," Anna completed.

"Always."

"Did anyone check on Mr. Waffles?" Anna asked. "I totally forgot about him. Shit, I'm going to call Mona." She dialed Mona's cell, and Mona answered on the first ring.

"Mona, it's me. Listen, could you check on Mr. Waffles? I don't remember seeing him around today. Christina is going to be all right. She's got a bad fracture and a slight concussion, but if all goes well, we'll be home tomorrow." Anna listened to Mona, holding the phone away as a string of cuss words filled her ear.

"Call me as soon as you find him," she said, and ended the call. She set her cell phone so that it would buzz instead of ring. She didn't want to disturb her daughter.

"Mona said she hasn't seen him since this morning."

Other than the sound of Christina's breathing, and the bleeping of the heart monitor, the room was silent.

Anna chewed her bottom lip. "I hope he's okay. Probably hiding somewhere. With all the confusion today, he must've been scared."

"Or something's happened to him," Mandy interjected, voicing the thoughts Anna didn't want to admit to having, too.

"He's probably holed up in a closet somewhere. You know how sneaky cats are."

"I do, but Mr. Waffles isn't just your everyday ordinary house cat. He's more like a dog. He doesn't usually hide, does he?" Mandy asked.

"I showed Ryan the studio earlier. He may have followed me downstairs, so he could be trapped there. I'm pretty sure I didn't see him, but I'll call Mona, ask her to look."

Anna called again, told Mona, who was not a happy camper at the moment, to look in the studio, and again, call her as soon as she found him.

"Christina will be crushed if something's happened to him," Mandy said. "I will, too."

Again, all Anna did was nod.

"Mom," Christina called, her voice a hoarse whisper.

Anna hurried to her bedside. She pushed a stray hair away from her daughter's face. "Hey, sweetie, I'm right here. Mandy's here, too."

Mandy stood on the opposite side of the bed. "Hey there."

Anna saw tears in Mandy's eyes, saw how

she was struggling to contain them.

"Mandy" — Christina turned to her — "thanks for being here."

She sniffed. "I wouldn't be anyplace else in the world. I want you to rest, okay? I'll stay with you if you want me to."

Christina nodded. "I'm thirsty," she said, turning back to Anna.

Anna poured a couple inches of water in her cup. "Let's raise you up a little bit, okay? Tell me if I'm causing you any pain." Anna adjusted the bed, though this time Christina was able to hold the glass and drink on her own. "All better?" She reached for the cup.

"A little more," Christina said. "So thirsty."

"It's all the drugs in your system," Mandy explained to her. "Which for now is a good thing. I don't know if your mom explained your injuries." Mandy caught Anna's eye. She shook her head from left to right.

"You broke your leg in two places, and you've got a bump on the head. Ed took good care of you, said we can go home in the morning. He wanted you to stay tonight, just as a precaution," Anna explained, rushing through her injuries as fast as she could.

Christina's breathing became a bit labored, her eyes widening. "No! I don't want

to go home! No!" She was full on scream-
ing now.

"I'll get the nurse," Mandy said, whipping
out the door.

"Calm down, sweetie. It's okay, you're going to be just fine." Anna tried to soothe
her daughter, but she refused to relax.

"Hey there, girl with the broken leg," said
the nurse with the braid. "What's going on?
What's your pain level? One being a wee
bit, ten being you can't stand it." The nurse
watched the numbers on the monitor and
placed the tips of her fingers on Christina's
neck.

"I don't know, maybe a six. I don't have
to go home if the pain gets really bad?"
More of a question than a statement, and
alarm bells were ringing so loudly, Anna felt
as if she needed to cover her ears.

"I'll be right back," the nurse said. "It's
about time for her medication."

"Mom, I don't think I'll feel like going
home tomorrow." Christina squeezed her
eyes, closing them so tightly, they crinkled.

"I'm sure if Ed feels you need to stay an
extra day, he'll tell us."

The nurse returned with a small white
paper cup and a fresh pitcher of ice water.
She filled the cup she'd been using, then
handed Christina a small white pill. "This

will help the pain; it'll make you sleepy, too, which is just what the doctor ordered."

Christina swallowed the pill, then relaxed a bit.

The nurse typed a password in the built-in computer on the wall opposite the bed, her fingers clicking across the keyboard, then closed down the program, leaving a screen saver with the name of the hospital jumping across the screen in small blue letters. "I'll leave you girls; if you need me, just push this," and she showed them the button built into the bed. "I'm just a buzz away if you need anything. If the pain is too much, we can give her another dose. Dr. Laird doesn't like to see his patients suffer."

"Thanks," Anna said.

As soon as the nurse left the room, Mandy spoke to Christina. "Before that pill sends you to never-never land, can you tell me what happened? How you managed to tumble down stairs like a Slinky?"

"What's a Slinky?" Christina asked, her words already sluggish.

"Never mind; it was before your time. Mine, too. Just rest," Mandy said, and sighed.

They both hovered over Christina like two mother hens. Anna was so grateful to have a friend who cared about her daughter almost as much as she did. "I know what you're trying to do, and I appreciate it. I just don't think now is the time. She's so heavily medicated, who knows what she'll say? Let's be patient, Mandy. Please, because if you're thinking what I know you're thinking, this could turn into a three-ring circus."

"I know. Listen, I'm dying for some caffeine, and I know that you must be as well. There's a cafeteria somewhere. I'll go find it." Mandy took her tote bag and left the room, careful not to disturb Christina.

With her daughter zonked out, Anna returned to the sofa, the events of the day finally catching up with her. Her eyes felt like they had lead weights on them. She closed them, just for a minute.

"Hey, sleepyhead," came a male voice. "Time to rise and shine."

Anna jerked awake, stunned when she saw the room pooled in early-morning shadows, the sun rising, casting rays of soft golden light through the slats in the blinds.

"Christina." She pushed herself off the sofa and leapt across the small room, where she saw that her daughter was still sleeping soundly. Pushing herself as close to the bed as possible, trying to put as much distance as she could between her and him, she quickly assessed the room. The only way out was through the door, and she couldn't lift Christina from the bed with her entire leg encased in plaster. No, she needed to face this son of a bitch. Once and for all.

"What are you doing here?" Surprise, shock, and anger siphoned the blood from her face.

"I was concerned. I tried calling you, but you didn't answer. So here I am."

Protective instinct kicked in, and Anna positioned herself as close to her daughter as she could without actually crawling in the bed with her.

"Where is Mandy?" she asked.

"That I couldn't tell you, but there are many other things I can tell you *if* you want to know."

"She went for coffee," Anna said. She felt her heart pumping, prayed that the drugs in Christina's system would keep her knocked out. She eyed the call button on the bed, slowly inching her hand over the bed's heavy, plasticlike railing, ready to push it when suddenly, the door opened.

"Excuse me," said a woman, glancing at the hospital bed. "Wrong room."

He ignored the interruption. "She must have gone to Seattle for it, huh?" he suggested, tossing his head back and laughing maniacally. "Get it? Seattle? Starbucks?"

263

Anna scanned the room for her cell phone. It was on the sofa, wedged in between the cushions. She couldn't get to it without leaving Christina's bedside.

"What the hell do you want?" She spat out the words contemptuously. "How did you find me?"

He moved closer, inches away from the foot of the bed. Anna took a step back, her left hand searching for the call button. She had to distract him. Keep him as far away from her daughter as she could.

"You made the news," he explained, enunciating each word as if he were speaking to a toddler. "You like being on the news. Don't you? All of your fans, or *viewers,* isn't that how you refer to them? They'll feel sorry for poor little, rich Anna and her daughter. Boo fucking hoo." His tone was mocking, yet there was also something else.

Her heart thumped, and anger burned in the pit of her stomach. "Where is Mandy? If you hurt her" — she swallowed, her throat tight and dry — "I'll kill you!"

Tossing his head back, insane laughter spewing from him, he shook his head. "You'll kill *me?* I. Don't. Think. So." Blue eyes she'd once found attractive were now reduced to evil slits.

Anna darted a glance at the door. Wasn't

it time for a nurse, the doctor, *someone* to come in and check on Christina? Full morning sun filtered in through the slats on the blinds above the sofa. How long had she slept? Didn't matter. She needed to take control. Suddenly, Christina moaned in pain, then settled back into her drug-induced sleep.

"What do you want from me?" Seething with rage, Anna had to keep him away from her daughter. "Tell me!" Her voice broke. "What?" she hissed between gritted teeth, wanting to scream, but fearing that doing so would only add to his insanity, and who knew what he'd try? And he was truly insane. How she'd missed that was beyond her, and now it was too late. No, she was not giving up. This bastard was not going to ruin her life any more than he had already.

She eased her left hand to the call button, her eyes never leaving his.

"Anna, Anna, Anna! I see what you're doing. Go ahead," he encouraged. "Call the nurse. Go on," he said, pointing to her hand. "Push that call button. I dare you," he taunted. "No, I double-dare you."

She pulled her hand away from the button. Christina winced in pain, her eyes fluttering open, the effect of the drugs slowly easing off. "Mom?" she said, her voice dry and cracked. "Drink."

She placed a protective hand on Christina's chest. "In a minute, baby. Rest."

"Drink," she repeated. "I'm thirsty."

Wanting to take care of her daughter's immediate needs, needing to keep this sick piece of flesh as calm as she could, she swallowed, her throat as dry as her daughter's, only hers was from fear. "She needs water. I'm just going to get this" — she removed her hand from Christina, located the plastic cup from the table beside her bed, holding it out for him to see — "and this" — she lifted the small blue pitcher with her other hand — "and pour some in here." She poured a splash of water into the cup, spilling it over the blankets, but she didn't care. She would not take her eyes off him. "Here, baby." She held the cup to her cracked lips. "Drink."

Christina took several swallows of water, then collapsed into the pillows behind her. Without making any sudden movement so as not to distract him, Anna slowly returned the cup and pitcher to the side table.

Her full attention on him now, Anna was bitter, her voice guttural when she spoke. "If you don't get out of here, I'm going to scream. I mean it." To her own ears, her words sounded weak and uncertain. Clearing her throat as much as she could, she added, "Just tell me what you want and go. I'll forget you were ever here." All those months of looking over her shoulder, knowing, *feeling* unknown eyes watching her, and now it all came down to this. A culmination of emotions fleetingly passed through her. If only she'd seen what she now saw. *Too late,* she thought, as she stared at him.

More deranged laughter, as he stood at the foot of the bed. With one hand in his pocket, and the other hovering above Christina's broken leg, he slowly wiggled his fingers, taunting her. "I bet a good smack on the cast would really hurt. What do you think? No, never mind, let her tell us if it hurts." He balled his fingers into a fist, raised his arm back, then, as he was about to smash his fist onto Christina's cast, three black-clad men burst through the door, guns aimed and ready to fire.

"Hands in the air!" one shouted while the two others tackled James Banks to the floor.

"Mom!" Christina shrieked. "What's . . . what's —" Anna didn't give her a chance to finish. She leaned forward, wrapping her arms around her and blocking her view of what was taking place on the floor.

"Shhh, it's okay. We're going to be okay," she repeated, shocked at the turn of events.

Steel cuffs clinked, and the sounds of heavy booted feet pounded, evidence of the struggle to contain James. Never in a million years had she suspected he was her stalker. Yes, he'd been upset when she broke it off with him, but enough to devote months to stalking her? It didn't matter. It was over.

Mandy came in, along with the woman who'd entered her room earlier. Apparently, the woman was a police officer. She trilled off a version of the Miranda rights warning as the officers were pulling James off the floor.

"Let us through," one of the officers said. "This scum is going down for a very long time."

The trio stood aside as the arresting officers led James Banks out of the room, but not before she heard him say, "I'll be back for you, bitch."

The adrenaline that had pumped through her veins evaporated as quickly as it came, and Anna collapsed on Christina's bed. Trembling, she struggled to regain her composure. "It's going to be all right, sweetie, I promise." Tears rivered down her daughter's face.

Anna still hadn't fully grasped what had actually taken place. She pushed herself off the bed, straightening the sheets. She said the first thing that came to mind. "I thought you were going for coffee."

Mandy still wore the same clothes as she'd had on earlier. "I was. I'll fill you in on the details" — she glanced at Christina, who had come wide-awake — "later."

Anna knew she didn't want to go into the nitty-gritty details in front of her. "Thanks."

As soon as the room emptied, Ed Laird and a nurse she hadn't met came into the room. "Little bit of excitement here today," he said to Anna. "How's our girl doing?" he asked. "Still hurts pretty bad, I'm guessing?"

"Mom, who was that man?" Christina had no clue, and as far as Anna was concerned, she would leave it at that.

"That was a wacko, who got out of control," Mandy said. "Now, tell Ed how you're feeling." She took charge and for that Anna was thankful. She needed time to absorb what she'd just experienced, time to compose her thoughts. She went to the bathroom, splashed cold water on her face, redid her bun, then stopped. The last twenty-four hours had been bizarre to say the least, and now the shit was going to hit the fan. She'd have to make a trip to the police station. Again. Though this time, she would know who her stalker was, and luck willing, he'd disappear into the far corners of some dark prison cell for a very, very long time.

Christina turned to Dr. Laird. "It still hurts."

"I'm sure it does. You've had a nasty break. Amy is going to give you a bit of pain medication. I'm going to write you a prescription, your mom can get it filled, then as soon as all the paperwork is taken care of, I think you're safe to go home later this afternoon."

"No! I don't want to go to that house. I'm in a lot of pain, really," Christina insisted. "I should probably stay a few more days."

Anna returned to her daughter's bedside. "We'll take good care of you at home. I'm sure Mr. Waffles is wondering where his best bud is." She looked at her dearest friend, silently asking if they'd found the cat. Mandy mouthed, "No."

And the hits just keep on coming, Anna thought to herself. Mr. Waffles would keep. And as much as she hated pushing him aside, right now Christina was her main concern. All the details, police reports, the bullshit with Ryan would keep until later.

Now, more than anything, she had to find out why her daughter didn't want to go home.

CHAPTER 16

"I saw him in the cafeteria," Mandy explained. "Creeped me out, then, when I realized who it was, I decided I'd follow him. I was always a bit suspicious of him. Too slick, too nice. Fake. When you gave him the boot, he was angry, Anna. Like unnatural anger. Seeing him here, well, I thought it best to call the cops and at least alert them. I followed him down the hall, toward her room. I knew something was awry; then I texted you to warn you. You need to keep a spare charger in your purse," Mandy said, as they both knew her phone battery was dead again. "Then I spoke to Rhonda; she's the lady who came into the room, pretending she'd made a mistake entering the wrong room. In reality, she was checking on you and Christina. We all watched on the closed-circuit monitors. Those dudes were ready to take him out when he walked over to her bed and raised his fist. Let's just say I've never seen men in uniform move so quickly."

Anna took a sip of her coffee. "This is all so surreal. I can't wait to testify against him, if it comes to that. Frankly, I'm more concerned about Christina's reluctance to leave. She hates doctors, hospitals. Plus, I know she's bound to ask how Mr. Waffles is doing. Are you sure Mona and Jeb searched the studio?"

"Yes, they both did. Top to bottom. I hate to say this again, but I will. I wouldn't put it past Renée, the little snot, to have hurt him."

"I'll call Ryan later, ask him if Renée saw him."

The hospital cafeteria started getting crowded, as the afternoon shift was beginning in another half hour. Ed signed release papers, and arrangements were made for Christina to return to the house via ambulance. With her left leg in a full cast, there was no way Anna could take her home in her Nissan, which was still parked in the garage at home.

"Not sure she'd tell you if she knew. I'm still ticked at the way she stood at the top of the stairs, watching." Mandy finished her coffee and placed the paper cup on the tray.

"The kid is confused, and yes, I agree, she

should've acted, done something besides watch." Anna wondered if Renée was the troubled child and Patrick just a miserable kid who'd suffered an adult blow much too soon.

"I didn't get the chance to introduce myself during all the commotion, but he's a handsome kid. He was distraught, I could tell. Unlike his sister."

"He is, and I'd like to see him get back into swimming. He's amazing, but I've got to get my own life in order before I can offer him a hand." Anna felt she should encourage Patrick, reach out in some way. Later, she would.

"Don't overstep your boundaries, Anna," Mandy cautioned her.

As she had when she'd taken Ryan on a tour of her studio. He'd said as much, though his words were harsh, hateful. "I won't. Trust me on that."

"Let's see if your daughter is ready to rock and roll." Mandy stood, took the tray with their cups, dumped the cups into the recycling bin, and placed the tray on top of a stack of others.

Anna had arranged for a hospital bed to be delivered in the afternoon. Christina's cast was heavy, and the leg needed to remain elevated and stable. The bed came equipped with some gadget that did both.

They returned to the third floor. Anna would ride in the ambulance, and Mandy would follow. She'd agreed to stay at her house as long as she was needed. A true best friend. Grateful she had no upcoming events, or appearances, all Anna wanted to do was get back the life she'd had at the beginning of the summer. Wipe the slate clean. And she would in time.

As soon as they entered the room, Anna's heart broke. Christina was sobbing, tears dripping down her cheeks, her eyes red and swollen. "Oh, baby, are you in that much pain?" The nurse had given her a second dose right before they went down to the cafeteria for a much-needed coffee. Anna thought she'd be sleeping by now, making the trip home a little easier.

She sniffed, and Mandy gave her a wad of tissues. "Wipe your nose," she said, grinning. "Pain that bad?"

Christina blew her nose, tossing the tissue aside. "The pills help a lot," she answered.

"Okay, then tell us why Niagara Falls is running down your face?" Mandy always came up with a silly comment, anything to get a laugh or, in this case, a very slight smile.

"Mom, could you just ask Dr. Ed to let

me stay a few more nights? Please," she begged.

"No, baby, we can't. You'll do just fine at home. We've got the special bed for you. We're going to keep you downstairs, in the den. I'll make up the sofa bed, and we'll camp there until you're able to move about."

Christina nodded. "I guess that's okay."

"It'll be like a slumber party every night," Anna said, trying to cheer her up.

"What about school? I'm supposed to start *high school* next week!"

Finally, Anna thought. This is what was upsetting her so much. If she were in the hospital, maybe somehow that made a difference to her, and if her friends knew that she'd missed the first day of high school through no fault of her own, it wouldn't be so bad when she was able to go to school. Unsure if this was so, she truly hadn't given much thought about Christina's schooling the past twenty-four hours. Starting high school in the middle of the term, which is most likely when she'd be able to walk again, would be horrifying for anyone. It didn't matter that she'd gone to school with most of the same kids since second grade. High school was different.

Anna remembered when her mother died her senior year. All once-in-a-lifetime activities that were normal for a high-school senior had come and gone without any of the excitement she'd dreamed of when she'd been a freshman. Elizabeth's family had tried to make her senior year as normal as possible, she remembered, but without her mother, it hadn't been the same.

"I'll make arrangements for a tutor, sweetie. I know this must be the worst possible time for you, but we'll work it out. I'll see if Tiffany can hang out, make sure you're current on all the freshman gossip. I'll take care of everything else, I promise." She would; however, she couldn't do anything about her daughter's midterm entry.

"Whatever," Christina said, relaxing into the pillow, the medication taking effect.

There was a knock on the door, and two men entered the room with a gurney with all kinds of hooks and fasteners, ready to transport them home. *Thank God,* Anna thought.

"I take it this young lady is ready to break outta this place," said the younger of the two men.

Christina offered a silly smile, drifting in and out of a drug-induced haze as they maneuvered her onto the gurney.

"I'll meet you at the house," Mandy said, "You, too. kiddo." She tapped the metal pole on the gurney.

"Thank you, Mandy. For everything, and especially that trip to the drugstore." She half smiled. "At least I don't have *you know* to worry about now."

"Enough. Let's get out of here."

Forty-five minutes later, the ambulance drove through the gates, and, much to Anna's amazement, Mr. Waffles stood waiting outside the gate. She stopped the car and scooped him inside, tears filling her eyes. "You had us worried," she said. He appeared fine, though she'd check him out as soon as they were inside. "I know someone who's going to be thrilled to see you." Grateful that Mr. Waffles decided to grace them with his presence, she knew he would cheer Christina through her recovery. She didn't need to know he'd disappeared.

It seemed a lifetime ago since she'd taken that plate of ribs to Patrick.

CHAPTER 17

Three weeks later

Hands shaking, Anna hung up the phone. "Mona," she called, and raced to the kitchen, where Mona was chopping onions on a cutting board. "Listen, something terrible has happened, to a friend," she lied. "I need to leave for a couple hours. I need a humongous favor. Can you sit with Christina, help her with the bathroom if she needs to go?" It'd been three weeks since the accident, and Christina was just now able to get into the wheelchair and move about downstairs. Though getting her into the chair was difficult, they'd been managing.

Mandy was downstairs in the studio, working with the film crew. They were preparing for the first episode of the Thanksgiving holiday season. It was an easy one, for which she'd do voice-overs for the most part. She'd spent the morning putting together her annual Thanksgiving planner, how to organize recipes, a step-by-step plan to make the week prior to Thanksgiving easy and uncomplicated. She read through her viewer e-mail, spent a few minutes giving what she hoped was sound advice to one viewer concerned about the proper way to send out invitations by mail or e-mail. A no-brainer, but this is what made *The Simple Life* so successful. Anna enjoyed everything about her work, right down to the last-minute detail.

"You ain't gotta ask like it's a favor; 'course, I will," Mona said. "I'll make sure she's able to pee and whatever else she needs."

"Tell Mandy I had to leave. It's important. I shouldn't be long." She gave Mona a hug, then headed for the garage. She'd explained to Christina that Mona would be here, and Mandy was downstairs. She'd been using her cell phone to text them when she needed anything, and for once, their cell phones were being put to good use.

She hadn't seen Ryan since Labor Day weekend though they'd spoken on the phone several times. Each agreed Christina needed her undivided attention. They hadn't discussed the accident or what might've happened, but she would soon. Christina clammed up each time she broached the subject, and she'd let it slide, not wanting to upset her daughter. For now.

She was beginning to share Mandy's suspicions about what had happened to cause Christina to fall down the stairs. Renée's behavior was beyond suspicious. The couple of times Mandy had asked Christina about that day, she refused to talk about it. All told, it seemed very likely that the fall was much more than an accident.

Thirty minutes later, Anna parked in front of The Daily Grind. With no idea what Ryan's emergency was, if it was truly an emergency at all, or simply an excuse to see her, she headed inside. Either way, she'd agreed because she wanted to see him face-to-face. It was time to call it quits. She was not pregnant; she'd gotten her period a week after she'd taken the pregnancy test, so there was no reason for her to continue seeing him. She questioned her feelings. And if she was totally honest with herself, she did care for Ryan. But there were many of his traits that she did not like. For starters, the way he spoke to Patrick and Renée. But she'd put those thoughts aside now and see what was so urgent.

Anna spied Ryan sitting at a table in the corner. His hair was in need of a trim, and he also needed a shave. He was handsome, she couldn't deny that, though being handsome wasn't necessarily associated with having a personality to match his outward appearance. You can't tell a book by its cover, her mother used to say.

Her stomach knotted as she made her way to the table. She'd get this over with and move on. Lesson learned.

He stood and pulled her chair out before saying anything to her. "You look good, Anna. I've missed you. How's Christina?"

She sat in the chair he offered. "We're taking it day by day." He didn't need to know anything more as far as she was concerned.

"Renée said to tell her hi."

Anna refused to respond.

"Ryan, you said this was an emergency." If he'd lied to lure her back into his arms, she'd tell him to go to hell.

"It is."

"Okay. Shoot." She sounded like Mandy.

"I lost my house," he said, his sapphire eyes filled with tears.

"What? I don't understand. What happened? How?"

"Last night. It burned to the ground. There is nothing left. Nothing."

"Oh God, Ryan, I'm so sorry. The kids, they're safe?" she asked, hating herself for

281

her previous mean thoughts.

"Yeah, fortunately, they were both gone when it happened. We're staying in a hotel tonight, and they're both distraught, losing all their possessions, keepsakes, things that belonged to their mother. I don't know what to do."

Perplexed as to why he hadn't called her immediately, she was unsure why he needed to tell her this in person now. "What happened? Was there an electrical problem? A gas explosion?" She didn't know much about house fires, but she was sure he was about to give her the lowdown.

"They're not sure yet. What's left of the place is full of arson investigators. It's a damned nightmare, and as I said, I'm at a loss, not sure what to do."

For an educated man, a professor, Anna thought, he sounded awfully naïve, almost childlike. "Have you contacted your insurance company? I'm sure they'll instruct you on what steps to take."

"That's just it. I let my homeowner's insurance lapse, so there's nothing."

Who lets their frigging insurance lapse?

"You're uninsured?" She was stunned to hear that any reasonable adult in this day and age would allow something as important as homeowner's insurance to expire. It was practically unheard of. At least in her world.

"Are you sure? Maybe there's been a clerical error, a mistake?"

Ryan took a sip of coffee. "I wish that were the case, but no, I didn't make the payments the past three months. I'm screwed any way you look at it. As I said, I don't know what to do. That's why I called. You're so . . . savvy, I thought maybe you'd help" — he coughed — "have an idea, something I can do, I don't know. Maybe you've got a connection. A GoFundMe page maybe."

For three months he'd wined and dined her. The expensive restaurants, the hotels. What in the name of Pete was he thinking? Not paying his insurance premiums was beyond irresponsible. She took a sip of the coffee he'd bought her. It was lukewarm, but she needed to do something in order to stall him for a few minutes. She needed to think, wished she could run this by Mandy, but her best friend would croak if she knew she was here with Ryan, and worse, if her suspicions were correct, that he was about to hit her up for a loan.

While Anna had plenty of money to lend him, she was hesitant to even say the words to him, as she knew this was where the conversation was heading. If he'd wanted to set up a GoFundMe page, surely his colleagues at Texas Tech would assist him, take charge. They'd treated him with the cruise on his birthday, which was quite a grand gift as far as she was concerned. If he'd lost everything he owned in a fire, surely they would step up to the plate for a tragedy of this magnitude? She didn't know. He'd never introduced her to his colleagues, or friends, neighbors, nothing. For that matter, she'd never been invited to his home. The one time she'd said she was in his neighborhood, he'd asked her to wait, telling her Patrick and Renée would feel awkward seeing another woman in their mother's home. It didn't make sense then, and it didn't now.

"Look, I should go. I don't know what I . . . I'm going to do," Ryan said, sounding defeated. "I never should've called you. I'll figure this out on my own," he said, pushing his chair away from the table.

"No! Wait," she said. Maybe there was something she could do to help him. "Stay." They were almost the exact words she'd said to him at dinner the night they met on the cruise ship, she recalled quite clearly now. "I need to think. I'm sure we can figure something out." There, she'd once again put herself in a position she'd regret, but too late. It just wasn't in her nature to *not* help her friends. Ryan had been much more than a friend, and though she'd wanted to tell him their relationship was over, now wasn't the time. Obvious now, Renée had been telling the truth the first night she'd met them at The Shallows. Her dad didn't have the finances for a private school, and apparently it was even a struggle to pay Patrick's reduced tuition.

"Thanks, Anna. You're too good to me." He pushed his chair back. "You're not drinking your coffee."

She took a few sips of the lukewarm, bitter brew. "Sorry," she said, and finished what was left in her cup. "I'll take care of the hotel until you find something permanent." The words flew out of her mouth fast, too fast to take them back. She could do this. At least until he figured out his future. Anna was fair to a fault. "Where are you staying?" she asked. "I'll make sure they send the bill to me."

Lowering his eyes, he said, "The Crown Hotel."

Anna knew of it. Everyone in Lubbock knew The Crown Hotel, home to some of the biggest cocaine busts in Lubbock County. "You can't stay there, Ryan. The kids."

"It's all that was available at the last

minute," he said, defending his choice.

"I'll see what I can find," she added. No one with kids should even consider staying at that dive. Drug runners and prostitutes called the place home. The place was in the news at least once a month. "You're sure about the insurance?" she asked again.

"Anna, if I wasn't, I wouldn't be here begging for your help," he said, his expression clouding with anger. "Never mind," he said, standing, pushing his chair aside, almost toppling it over. He threw a five-dollar bill on the table. "Have another cup of coffee on me." Before she could react, he bolted out of the coffee shop, as several customers glanced at her.

She hurried out, hoping to catch up with him. His tires squealing, she watched as he peeled out of the parking lot. "Jerk," she said. She shouldn't have agreed to meet him. She stood in front of the coffee shop, amazed and shaken. Ryan Robertson was trouble with a capital *T*.

She returned to her car and headed back to the house. Feeling bad, knowing Patrick and Renée would be spending who knew how long in that dumpy hotel, she accepted Ryan's choice. Apparently, offering to pay for their hotel wasn't enough. She shouldn't have asked him about the insurance that second time, but she had. Too bad he couldn't control his temper for the sake of his kids. He — *they* — were not her problem. If he tried calling her again, she wouldn't take the call. Better yet, she'd block his number; then she wouldn't be bothered at all. Enough was enough. It was time to move forward. The holidays were coming up, and she would have her hands full; this was her busiest filming season. They stuck with the weekly one-hour segment, but Anna liked to film fifteen-minute surprise specials during the holidays, and her viewers liked it as well. No, she was way too busy to deal with Ryan's screwed-up life. While she was slightly sad for Patrick and Renée, she was not their mother.

As soon as she pulled into the garage, Mandy came bursting out the door. "Where have you been? Have you heard the news?"

Anna rolled her eyes. She loved that Mandy cared so much, though sometimes it was suffocating. Now was one of those times. "News? No, and I was meeting . . . a friend." She didn't need to know about her meeting with Ryan. As far as Anna was concerned, that was the last time she'd ever see him. Fire or not. His irresponsibility wasn't her problem. She locked the car and went inside.

Mandy trailed her. "Your old boyfriend's house went up in flames last night. It was just on the evening news. They suspect arson."

Anna went to the kitchen and took a Coke out of the refrigerator. "Arson? Are you sure?" She'd just left Ryan thirty minutes ago. He said the investigators were still at the house.

"You don't seem that surprised," Mandy said. "You know something you're not telling me?"

She might as well spill the beans. "I just left Ryan, we met at The Daily Grind. He told me about the fire, said the investigators were there when he left, something to that effect. Apparently, they've finished."

"You actually met the guy, alone? After what his daughter . . . Never mind. I can't believe you'd do something so stupid. He's a con man, Anna. Surely, you've figured that out by now?" Mandy said. "For all we know, he could've burned his house down, hoping to collect the insurance money. He strikes me as the type that would do that, and again, I know, I don't know him, but I don't have to."

As usual, Mandy's assumptions were pretty accurate. "Except he doesn't have any homeowner's insurance."

"What?" Mandy asked, raising her voice. "How do you know?"

"That's why he wanted to meet. He said he hadn't kept up with the premiums, and there was nothing left." When she thought about it, he hadn't seemed all that upset. He'd been more concerned about money, which, sadly for him and his kids, was a bit too late.

"He asked you for money?"

Anna took a drink of Coke. "Not in so many words. Said he needed my help, a Go-FundMe page. Did I know how he could get some kind of public assistance?"

"And?"

"He's staying at The Crown, that drug haven that's on the news all the time. I offered to arrange for another place to stay, foot the bill. When I asked him if he was sure about the insurance, it pissed him off, and he walked out. End of story. I'm done with him, and you're right, he's probably a con man, and I was just too dumb and desperate to see it. So we're done. I'm not going to take his calls." Anna took her cell phone from her pocket, scrolled through, and blocked his number. "There, he's blocked."

"I'm not so sure this is the end, Anna. I just left Christina after hearing about the fire on the news. We had a nice talk, and she finally opened up to me. She told me exactly what happened on Labor Day weekend."

"She did?"

Mandy nodded. "It's just as I suspected. Renée shoved her down the stairs."

CHAPTER 18

"You're sure?" Anna asked, stunned by what she had just heard. "I need to talk to her now." Hurrying to the den, where Christina lay in the hospital bed watching TV, Anna took the remote from the side table and turned off the set.

"Mom! I'm watching that!" Christina whined.

"You can finish it later. We need to talk, *now.*" Anna sat on the edge of the bed, scooting Mr. Waffles to the side. The contraptions to stabilize her leg had been removed since Ed had freed her to start using her wheelchair. "Tell me exactly what you told Mandy and how it happened. I'm serious. This isn't the time to worry about what anyone thinks, other than me. Now, start talking." She hated that she had to be so forceful, but this was serious. More serious than her thirteen-year-old daughter knew.

"Mom, come on, I'm gonna be walking soon. All I want to do is forget that this ever happened. Aren't we supposed to forgive people? Isn't that what you've taught me all my life?"

"Christina Michelle Campbell! Listen to me, and I am not joking. A crime was committed against you. Mandy said you told her that Renée pushed you. I suspected as much, but I don't expect you to lie for her, or try to cover this up, pretend it never happened. Forgiving and allowing someone to harm you are two completely different issues. Now, tell me. I'm not leaving your side until you tell me the truth. No fairy tales, Christina."

Her daughter sighed like a woman ten times her age. "I'm not stupid, Mom."

"No one said you were. Stop stalling, and tell me what happened," Anna said, her tone stern.

"We were in my room, and I was showing her some of my stuff, my Harry Potter collection, the necklace that belonged to Grandma." Anna felt her blood pressure soar. She'd given the necklace to Christina for Christmas last year, along with the responsibility of its care. It was the only expensive piece of jewelry her mother had ever had.

"I'm listening," Anna persisted.

"She liked the necklace. Duh, who wouldn't? Anyway, she asked if she could borrow it, for the first day of school. Said she'd give it back, but I told her no."

She saw how upset Christina was getting just remembering that day. This was just the beginning; who knew what kind of damage she'd suffer down the road?

"Renée called me a couple of names, said I was nothing but a spoiled, rich bitch — sorry, but that's what she said. I took the necklace to put it away. I was taking it to your room, thinking if I did, she'd just forget about it. I stepped out of my room, and she followed me. I didn't say anything. I just thought she was kinda weird and all. Then it happened so fast, but I remember, I felt her hand on my back as I walked past the top of the stairs, and she shoved me."

Anna was sure her skull was going to explode. Anger, unlike anything she'd ever felt, possessed her. She sat on the edge of the bed, a million thoughts running through her mind.

"Are you okay?" Christina asked.

"No," Anna said. She wasn't sure if she'd ever be okay again. She'd brought this man and his children into their lives. Could she do what the law required? To stop Renée from harming, possibly killing, some other innocent person? Possibly get her the help she needed?

"The necklace," Christina said. "Did you find it?"

Until that moment, Anna hadn't known it was missing. Maybe this explained why Renée had lingered upstairs. "Mandy, did anyone locate a necklace after we left in the ambulance? You know, the ruby-and-diamond necklace my mom had." Anna had told Mandy the story behind the necklace; it had belonged to her mother's great-great-grandmother, and was the only piece of jewelry she'd ever cared about. Keeping it in the family was a tradition. Her mother always told her that if something were to happen to her, to take the necklace and pass it on to her daughter. It was like she'd known about Christina before Anna had even graduated from high school. To this day, she believed her mother had had a premonition about her death.

"No one mentioned a necklace to me," Mandy said. "I can ask Mona."

"Let's forget the necklace for now; it's not important," Anna lied, knowing that if it were found in Renée's possession, Christina's story would hold more weight. Given the time that had passed, coming forward now could be seen as some kind of revenge against her. Law enforcement would question why they'd waited so long to report an attempted murder.

"I don't want either of you to discuss this until I speak with my attorney."

"Mom! What do you mean? I don't want to get Renée in any more trouble. She's a weirdo and all, but let's forget this. Please? This will be all over the school, and I'll never live it down. It's bad enough that everyone talks about that stupid YouTube channel of yours!"

"Both of you, calm down," Mandy hissed. "Mona will hear you for sure."

Anna took a deep breath, her heart thundering against her chest, panic clouding her ability to reason. In and out, just like she'd learned in therapy. In and out. Dizzy, she grasped on to the bed.

"Mom! What's wrong," Christina cried out.

"Calm down, she's okay. Anna, you're having a panic attack. Relax, take deep breaths, in and out. Just like you're doing," Mandy coaxed in a calming voice.

Anna nodded. "I'm fine, just give me a minute." It took a few minutes for her to regain her composure. She'd never experienced a panic attack around her daughter, and as far as she knew, Christina didn't even know she had them. She'd done her best to keep that part of her life a secret. Luckily, this hadn't been a full-blown panic attack.

"I'm fine," she said again. "Mandy, could you get my purse? It's in the kitchen."

She was going to take a Xanax, and she wasn't going to sneak. She had issues that she knew she had to deal with, and now, this. It was all her fault; she'd been so . . . *loose* on the cruise that night. Now this was the end result. She hadn't been herself since. Anna planned to make an appointment with her therapist. But only after she phoned her attorney.

Mandy returned with her Louis Vuitton bag. She took out the amber bottle of pills, and in front of Mandy and Christina, she broke one of the tiny yellow pills in half, placed it under her tongue, waited for it to dissolve, a technique her therapist suggested when she was in full-blown panic mode as this allowed the anti-anxiety medication to enter her bloodstream faster.

"Mom, I'm sorry what I said about your YouTube channel. All my friends think you're the coolest mom ever; I guess I get a little jealous sometimes."

"Oh, baby, it's okay. I know it's hard for you sometimes, but it's what pays our bills and keeps the house running. I started this after your dad died. It was my way of dealing with grief, opening up to others. When my grieving was tolerable, I branched out, cooking, decorating, and the channel took off. I can't apologize for keeping a roof over our heads, but I do understand where you're coming from." Tears were running down her face. She wiped them away with the edge of the sheet. "I started having these attacks after I lost your father. I felt like I was a bad-luck charm — everyone I'd loved died. I've spent years trying to come to terms with this, and I know that I'm not to blame, but that's the reason for these crazy panic attacks I have."

"You don't have to carry the guilt around, Anna. It is what it is. We're not always in control of what we do, nor can we always control what happens to the people we love. I've known about your panic attacks, you know that. And the medication. I have snooped in your purse a few times. Looking for a lipstick, keys, whatever. I saw the pills. Actually, while I'm in this confessing mode, I've plucked a couple of them myself."

Anna burst out laughing. "You sneaky bitch! Sorry, Christina," she said, placing her hand on her daughter's hand and the other on Mr. Waffles. "I'm just kidding, just so you know."

"I know — me and Tiffany say bad words to each other. But not all the time," she added.

"As long as it doesn't become a habit. I'm no saint in that department myself, but it's a trait I've never really cared for. Let's not worry about using bad language. It's the least of my concerns right now. Christina, we have to report what happened to you. This is serious. Renée needs help. And we have to protect others from what she could do if she is allowed to keep doing what she has done."

"Does she ever," Mandy interjected. "She's a little . . . rat."

"She is," Anna agreed. She could have said much worse, but she'd already lost her cool in front of her daughter. She wouldn't say what she really thought, not in front of her. Later, she and Mandy would talk. For now, she needed to get Christina to understand the importance of reporting her accident to the proper authorities.

"Seriously, I'm going to call Simon Goldstein. He'll advise me. Christina, I want to make sure you understand what you need to do. No matter how embarrassing, or scary, you have to do what is right."

"This sucks, big-time, but yeah, I know

what I have to do." She fell against the pillows, resigned. Anna wished this had never happened, along with a dozen other things she'd experienced in the past few months. *Will I ever get my life on an even keel again?*

"I'll leave you with Mandy if that's okay. Just for a few minutes while I make a phone call."

Mandy spoke up. "Go do what you have to do. We can finish watching the movie you interrupted."

"Thanks, I won't be long."

Upstairs in her office, Anna called Simon. Explaining what happened was easy enough. He advised her and Christina, and Mandy as well, to keep quiet until he arrived. He would be there within the hour.

CHAPTER 19

Simon Goldstein had been her personal attorney for five years. He was short, bald, and wore Benjamin Franklin glasses, the epitome of what one imagined for a lawyer. When he spoke, his voice was soft and kind. She valued his advice, and it was agreed that Christina should cooperate with authorities, but she would need a criminal attorney. Daniel Alan Lowande was the best in West Texas, according to Simon.

"I've called him. I told him your daughter, Christina, wasn't able to travel, so he's agreed to come to your house first thing tomorrow morning. Understand, he's just here to advise. You're the victim, not the criminal," Simon said, directing his words to Christina.

She nodded. "What will happen to her?"

"That's up to the system. First, we have to establish that a crime was committed."

"Isn't the fact that she's telling what happened enough?" Anna asked. "She's lying in this bed because she was pushed down the damned stairs!"

"Calm down, Anna. I'm on your side. I'm only telling you what you can expect to happen. Given that she's a minor, we can keep this quiet, or at least try to. Given your popularity, I can't promise some kook won't leak this to the press, but it's against the law to release Christina's identity."

Anna took a sip of coffee. "It won't be too hard to guess who she is if this gets out. Most people she knows, the school, her friends, their parents, all know who I am. It won't be hard to put two and two together."

"Let's not worry about what may or may not happen. Daniel will advise you tomorrow. Now, if we're finished, I have a late appointment at the office." He looked at Christina, still in the hospital bed in the den. "Hang tough, kiddo. You're a brave girl, just like your mother."

"Thanks," she said.

"I'll walk you out," Anna said, closing the door behind her.

As soon as they were out of earshot, she spoke. "Do we really need a criminal attorney?"

"Yes. Christina isn't going to be charged with a crime, though it will be up to her to convince the authorities an actual crime took place. Don't worry, Anna. I would do the same if I were in your place. Now, I've got that appointment. Stay in touch, and I'll do the same."

"Thanks, Simon," she said, and closed the door behind him.

She and Mandy had spent a couple of hours searching for the necklace that Renée felt she had the right to. There was no other explanation for its loss. They hoped the little rat had held on to the necklace, that it hadn't been burned up in the fire, since finding it in her possession would do a great deal to assure law enforcement that Christina was telling the truth.

Before she returned to the den, Anna went to the kitchen, where she found Mona and Jeb. It was time to tell them what had happened, assuming they didn't suspect already.

"Can we chat for a minute?"

"Only if'n I can stir this pot of chili while I'm talkin' to you. I promised Christina this mornin' I'd make her a pot of chili. I ain't gonna break a promise. So, what's up?"

"I suspected somethin' was going on when I saw Simon's car," Jeb added. "Ya'll ain't in trouble with the law, are ya?"

She wasn't going to say they weren't, but she needed both to be aware of what might happen if what had happened to Christina was made public. Anna explained about Christina's fall, her hesitancy to tell them what had actually happened, and now that she had, that things might not be pleasant. "If you two want to go to Idalou, I'll understand. We're good here for the next few weeks. I'm cooking and filming, so it's not like we'll be without food."

"You tryin' to scare us off, forget about it," Jeb said. "We're family, and family sticks together."

"You two are the best. Of course, Mona knows this, right?" Anna teased, the first time she'd done so in days.

"Mona does; now git on outta here. I'm goin' to bring trays in for you three brats. We're gonna watch that show where the dead people walk," Mona informed them in her twangy way.

"Sounds good," Anna said, then left the pair to finish dinner. Before returning to the den, Anna made a pit stop in her bedroom, checking through her jewelry box once more, in case they'd missed locating her necklace earlier. She pulled the tiny drawers out, searched through each one. The necklace was not there. Sad that a family heirloom was lost, it saddened her more to think how Christina felt when she'd learned it was nowhere to be found. Anna told her people were more valuable than things, and to always remember that. As she was about to return to the den, her landline rang, and she answered, thinking it could be Simon, or the new attorney calling to confirm tomorrow's visit.

"Hello," she said in her best vlogging voice.

"Anna, it's me," Ryan said. "Don't hang up."

"What do you want?" she asked, reverting to her normal voice.

"I wanted to apologize for the way I stormed out of the coffee shop. I'm upset, the kids are freaking out. I took it out on you and just wanted to tell you I'm sorry."

"Fine, then." She wanted to hang up, but then she had a thought. Maybe she needed to keep Ryan dangling a little while longer. "The news said it was arson," she said. "The fire."

"Yes, we're all terrified," he told her. "This is going to sound crazy, but poor Renée said that *you* could be responsible. Maybe you were pissed at her, blamed her for Christina's accident. I told her no way, but you know how kids are when they become fixated on something."

"What?" Surely she hadn't heard him correctly. "Tell me again." She took her cell phone out of her pocket and texted Mandy: Come to my bedroom ASAP. Mandy answered, On my way!

Anna hit the speaker button on the landline. Mandy entered the room, and Anna placed a finger over her lips, indicating she should be quiet.

"So, Ryan, what you're telling me is Renée thinks I was in some way responsible for *burning down your house*? Because of Christina's fall? That's what she believes?"

Mandy clicked the CALL RECORDING app on her cell phone. Anna gave her a thumbs-up. She placed her cell phone next to the receiver.

"Crazy, huh?" he said.

"It's only crazy if you actually believe her," Anna said, trying to see if he agreed with his daughter.

"I didn't say that, just that she's got this idea in her head. You know how young girls can be."

"I do, yes."

"So, that offer you made, the hotel. You still good for that? This place is not fit for rats, let alone my children. You were spot-on, again."

Anna looked at Mandy, mouthed, "What should I do?"

Mandy shrugged.

"Let me make a couple of phone calls, I know the managers at the Garden Inn and the Hyatt. Let's see what they have, and I'll call you back." Despite not being certain that Anna was making the right decision, Mandy nodded.

"I knew I could count on you, love. I'll wait to hear from you," Ryan said, then clicked off.

Anna stared at Mandy. "He's one ballsy SOB. I'll give him credit for that," Anna said. "I think I should call Simon."

"Yes, see what he advises."

Anna dialed Simon's cell phone. He picked up on the second ring. "Simon Goldstein."

"Simon, it's Anna. Listen, I just had the most bizarre phone call. From Ryan. He told me his daughter, Renée, believes I'm responsible for burning down their house, then he had the gall to ask me if I could put them up in a better hotel. He's waiting for me to return his call. What should I do?"

"An arrogant man. Get him a room. This might work to our advantage, though I'm advising you not to discuss your daughter's fall or that necklace that went missing. Play it by ear, but don't say anything that might be incriminating. You're simply his friend helping him out."

"If you're sure," Anna said, "I'll arrange things now."

"Go ahead, but remember, you're helping a friend, nothing about the fire or the fall."

"Thanks, Simon. I'll keep you posted if anything changes."

"You'll tell this to Daniel tomorrow morning," he advised.

Anna ended the call.

"What a dirtbag," Mandy said. "Not Simon, Ryan."

"Frigging nerve of that rat Renée, accusing me of burning down their house. The girl must have a mental problem. Let me call Barb at the Hyatt. She owes me a favor."

Anna called Barb and made arrangements for *two* rooms. One for Ryan and Patrick. One for Renée.

"Maybe he'll think I rented two rooms so we can be alone. Turn your recorder on — I want this documented."

When she dialed Ryan's cell, he picked up instantly. "Hey, that was fast."

"I've got two rooms waiting for you at the Hyatt. Ask for Barb, and she'll take care of you." Anna forced herself to be civil.

"Well, I am impressed once again, Anna. I can't thank you enough. You said two rooms, right?"

"Yes, I'm sure" — she started to say "Renée needs her privacy" but remembered Simon told her not to talk about her — "you all could use the extra room."

"You're sure that's why you rented two rooms? I can keep the kids out for ages, trust me. If that's what you're hinting at, I'm all for it."

Anna's eyes doubled in size. "Uh, no, I really think you could use the extra room."

"Have it your way, Anna. I'll head that way then, and I'll call you first thing in the morning."

"Ryan, don't you have school tomorrow? Or have you taken time off?" She had to ask.

"Uh, I'm on leave, or rather, I took some leave. It's going to take a while for me to figure out what's next. I'll call you first thing in the morning. 'Night, Anna."

"That's one creepy son of a bitch, and I don't care what you say," Mandy said. "He doesn't sound too broken up about losing his house, everything he owns, and all that."

"No, he doesn't. Though he did manage to muster a few tears at the coffee shop this afternoon. I'm sure they were for my bene-fit. Something isn't right; I can feel it in my gut."

"Wait and see if he calls back. You might

have to make a booty call later tonight," Mandy joked.

"In his dreams," Anna said.

"Probably, and wet ones, too," Mandy teased.

"You're nuts, but in a good way. Let's get out of here. I'll take the extension to the den. If he calls back, just follow me with your cell phone, and we'll record whatever crap spews out of his mouth."

"Now, that's more like it," Mandy said. "You're going to be just like me when you grow up."

"Heaven help me," Anna said.

"You will need that, too, if you follow in my footsteps."

"Come on, let's go have some of Mona's chili. It's better than mine, but don't tell her I said that."

"Deal," Mandy said.

Mona had placed TV trays in front of the sofa, and two armchairs. Christina had a tray specifically for her bed. She'd arranged bright red bowls of chili on each tray, along with plates with a slice of corn bread stuffed with jalapeños, and shredded cheese. "Mona, this smells hot," Anna said, thinking was there any other way to eat chili in Texas? "Spicy hot."

"Yep, ya'll gonna be . . . well, let's just say

you'll be visitin' the ladies' room a couple o' times tonight," Jeb said, and they all burst out laughing.

Comforted by her hodgepodge family, for a few minutes, Anna felt like she'd returned to her old life.

Then the phone rang.

Anna grabbed the extension, racing to her room before Mona or Jeb picked up on her conversation.

"I need a bathroom break," Mandy said, her excuse for following Anna upstairs.

She closed the door as soon as Mandy followed her inside. "So, I take it the rooms are to your liking."

"They're great, much better than The Crown. Listen, I asked Barb to run a tab; hope you don't mind. The restaurant here is decent enough, and the kids are starving as usual."

"Of course, I meant to tell you that you could. They have a gift shop, too. Any toiletries, shaving gear, get whatever you need. The kids, too."

"You're too kind, Anna, and I mean that," Ryan said, lowering his voice. "I don't know how I can ever repay you. Actually, I do, but we'll work on that another time."

"Just helping out, Ryan, that's all. Nothing more," she assured him. The last thing she wanted to do was lead him on. She almost felt sorry for the guy. What an idiot she'd been.

"We're going to have dinner, so I'll catch up with you later. 'Night, Anna," he said, and hung up.

She tossed the phone on the bed. "He's got nerve, I'll give him that," Anna said. "I'm going to call Barb, ask her to send me his tab each night in an e-mail. Not because I care about the money; I just want to know if he's actually feeding his kids."

"I would, too; if nothing else, just to be nosy," Mandy said, grinning from ear to ear.

"That, too."

Anna used her cell to call the Hyatt. She told Barb what she needed, asked that she be as discreet as possible, and now she owed Barb a favor.

"Done," she said. "I'm going to finish that chili. It's so hot, who knows, I might be arrested for arson?"

"That's not funny, Anna. If that weirdo kid of his actually tells that to the arson investigators, they'll have to question you, at the very least."

"I think she's just being a strange kid, running her mouth. I'm not worried."

"I hope you're right," Mandy said. "Come on, I want to watch that dumb program they're glued to. See what the hype's all about."

CHAPTER 20

Daniel Alan Lowande arrived promptly at nine o'clock. When Anna saw him, she wished she'd taken more time with her appearance. Ruggedly handsome, dusty-blond hair, light blue eyes, and at least six-four, he looked like a Texan. He dressed like a Texan, in his snakeskin boots and Armani suit. Maybe the suit wasn't typical Texan, but Anna could tell that he was a man's man. A Texas man. He reminded her of Chris Hemsworth, the actor who portrayed Thor in the Marvel Studios movies. His hair wasn't as long as the actor's, but it was long enough. He was, simply put, a hunk.

"Please, Mr. Lowande, come in. I'm Anna Campbell. My daughter is waiting to speak with you. We appreciate your coming to the house. Christina hasn't been able to do much more than roll around this place in her wheelchair. Otherwise, we would've come to your office." Okay, she was blabbering. She hadn't expected this. She hadn't expected to be reminded of Wade.

"It's my pleasure, Ms. Campbell. Now, if you wouldn't mind offering me a cup of coffee first, we can get down to business. I'm an addict. Coffee, that is. Can't seem to function without at least a pot in the morning. I overslept and had to settle for the drive-through at Starbucks. I need something stronger."

Anna laughed. "I get where you're coming from. I've just made a pot of Kaya Kopi. Cream, sugar, or both?" she asked.

"Good brew — black, thank you," he told her.

"Follow me into the kitchen," Anna called over her shoulder. "If you don't mind," she added.

"Best place in the world to figure out a person," he observed. "See what they like." He grinned at her. "You know, Cheerios or Frosted Flakes."

"Very true. We're more of a Fruity Pebbles crew here when we have cereal," she said as she filled a large yellow mug with coffee. "Though I do like to toss in a banana; makes me feel like I'm eating healthy."

He took a sip of coffee. "Excellent."

"It's my favorite," she said.

"You've got good taste," he said.

Anna would swear he was flirting with her. Or maybe this was just his way with everyone. Regardless, he was here to advise Christina and nothing more. She was through with men. For a while.

"Simon briefed me last night, but I'd like to speak to Christina first. Straight from the horse's mouth, if you will. Sometimes kids are frightened of authority figures, so since most likely we'll have to chitchat with the police, I'll want to advise her what to say. I'll see if I can help you all get this matter settled, then let her get back to being a kid again."

That was exactly what Anna needed to hear.

"Here," Anna said, "let me refill your cup and you can bring it with you. We've been camping out in the den since the accident. Dr. Laird is hoping to put her in a walking cast in the next week or two. Follow me," she said, bringing her mug of coffee with her.

Mandy was downstairs with the crew, shooting layouts for the thumbnail. This could take hours, as Mandy was a perfectionist in all that she did. One more reason she was so successful.

She'd asked Mona and Jeb to give her and Christina time alone with the attorney.

When they saw him, *if* they saw him, she could only imagine how they'd tease her.

"Right this way," Anna said to Mr. Lowande.

They walked past the double staircase, toward the den. He stopped, looked up. "Can you show me," Mr. Lowande asked, "which staircase she fell down?"

"Of course," Anna said. "This one." She went up the stairs, stopping at the landing on the second story.

He followed her. Walking along the landing, he stooped, ran his hands over the smooth oak floors. "Smooth."

"But not slick," she added. "They don't have a lot of varnish just for that purpose." They were more natural, rough-hewn.

"I see that." He stepped down the first few steps, which were the same rough-hewn oak, but Anna had had slip-proof rugs made for both set of stairs, the rubber backing specifically designed to prevent falls.

"Anyone ever fall or trip on these?" He ran his fingers along the edge of the rugs.

"No. They're sealed with a special glue. They're guaranteed not to budge. Go on, try tugging at that corner," Anna said. "Though I suppose anyone could fall; they're not a hundred percent foolproof. As with anything else, nothing is perfect, but this is close, as far as stairs go."

"I see," he said, standing. "Mind if we go to Christina's room?"

"Not at all." She directed him to follow her. He appeared as though he was actually investigating a crime scene, which in essence, he was.

Anna opened the door, stood aside as he stepped into her daughter's room. *No big mystery here,* Anna thought. A typical teenage girl's room. Purple bedcovers, pink-and-lavender pillows on the bed, with a half-dozen stuffed bears, another of Christina's collections. These were from her many trips to Build-A-Bear Workshops when she was much younger. One bookshelf held all of her books, the Harry Potter series that she was so proud of, as all were signed first editions. Her dresser was scattered with hair ties, barrettes, and a few compacts. Blushes and powders because that's all Anna allowed at her age. Maybe lipstick and mascara if it were a special occasion, but she wanted to keep her daughter thirteen *while* she was thirteen. A MacBook Air was in a charging station on her desk, along with her Kindle and a set of rechargeable earbuds.

Mr. Lowande walked around the room, looking but not touching anything. "Lots of interests, I see," he said, as he perused the titles on her bookshelf.

"She's a reader, like me," Anna explained.

"Readers make for good kids," Mr. Low-ande said. "My mother's words."

"She's right. Nothing like an escape with a good novel. I need to read more myself."

"Good habit to have, I'd say. Okay, I'm ready to meet Christina," he announced. "Lead the way."

Both walked down the staircase, but he walked much faster, purposely careless, as though he were trying to make himself stumble or topple down the rest of the stairs.

"I take it Christina flew up and down these steps a dozen times a day," he added, looking up.

"Probably, more so when she's not in school. This is a big house," she added, stating the obvious. "She spends a lot of time in her room, doing the usual girl things."

"I want to meet her," he said.

Anna led him around the staircases to the den, which covered at least a third of the downstairs. "In here," Anna said.

Christina reclined on the hospital bed, her grayish-white cast splayed on the bed, while her other leg was tucked beneath her. She wore a pair of black shorts, and a gold-and-black T-shirt that read BISHOP COERVER in gold letters. A gift from Tiffany. She was

318

playing a game on her cell phone, saw them, and placed it on the table beside the bed.

"I'm Daniel, and I know you're Christina," he said, smiling. "Looks like you've got a rad setup here," he said in teen speak.

"Sort of," she agreed, then looked toward her mother, raising her eyebrows, smiling. Anna felt her cheeks turn pink.

"Your mom gave me permission to discuss what happened on Labor Day with you. As you're a minor, I'd like to make sure you're comfortable talking with me; I don't want you to feel nervous in any way." He looked at her, waited for a response.

"I know, I have to do the right thing, and Mom says it's wrong to cover this up, but really, I just wish it'd never happened. Anyway, you can ask me whatever you need to." Christina raised herself up a bit higher.

"I want you to tell me your take on what happened, and if you need to stop, tell me. If you can't remember something, tell me. You good with that?"

She nodded.

"Tell me what happened," Mr. Lowande asked in a gentle voice. He sat in the chair next to the bed, Anna took a seat in the chair beside him and placed the mugs of coffee on the small table between the two chairs.

"I wanted to make her feel comfortable because she was a guest. Mom's rules. I didn't mind because at first I thought she was kinda cool. She has pink hair, lots of piercings. She didn't say much, so I asked her if she wanted to see my room. We were at the pool, and Mom and Ryan were there with Patrick. He's the swimmer. Really good, too."

Anna disliked her name being linked to Ryan's, but it couldn't be helped.

"We went upstairs to my room. I showed her some of my stuff, the Harry Potter books. I don't think she's a fan. Then I showed her the necklace mom gave me for Christmas last year. It's like a family heirloom thing. Renée asked me if she could borrow it to wear the first day of school. I told her no. She called me a couple of names, said I was spoiled. I figured I'd better put the necklace away, so I headed out of my room to go to Mom's room, which is at the opposite end of the landing. If we leave the doors open, we can see into each other's rooms. Anyway, as I was going to Mom's room to put the necklace away, right when I was about to pass the steps at the top of the landing, she put her hand on my back. Then she pushed me."

"Anything else you can think of, any hint

that she intended to do this to you *before* she actually pushed you?" Mr. Lowande asked.

"I don't know what she was thinking before she pushed me. She followed me and waited until I was lined up with the staircase, so maybe she thought about it before, at least a second or two. Why does that matter?" she asked.

"Premeditation," he replied.

"You mean like she planned ahead?" Christina asked, her face a couple of shades lighter.

"It only takes a second to make the decision, so yes," he answered, his voice completely sober, the light teasing tone gone.

"So where do we go from here?" Anna asked. "This is . . . another nightmare." She felt her chest beginning to tighten and quickly took a deep breath. In and out, slowly releasing it because she needed to stay calm. No panic attacks.

"We'll have to file a formal complaint with the police department, they'll investigate, then take their findings to the prosecuting attorney. Given that we're dealing with a minor, we'll see what the state recommends, then go from there."

"It sounds so easy," Anna said. "What will they do to her? If they decide there's enough evidence to do anything at all, what do they do with a child in these kinds of circumstances?"

"Lots of options. I don't want to guess, so we'll take this one day at a time. If you're sure I'm your man," he added.

"Yes, I'm sure. Christina, are you happy with Mr. Lowande?"

"Yeah, okay," she said.

"I'll need you to sign a few papers, I'll need a retainer, then we're good to go."

"Of course," Anna said. This wasn't a favor; this man was doing his job, and he didn't work for free. "In my office, we can take care of all the paperwork."

"Thank you. Christina, you'll do just fine. Listen to your mom here, and we'll get this taken care of so you can put it behind you and move forward." He glanced at her cast. "When your cast comes off, of course," he added, chuckling.

CHAPTER 21

Mr. Lowande — *Daniel,* as he insisted she call him by his first name — stayed with them when two of Lubbock's finest came to the house to file the report. It wasn't as difficult as she'd expected, but she didn't care for the fear she saw in her daughter's eyes when the two officers questioned her.

"Like I said, I just wanted to take the necklace, put it in Mom's room so it would be safe," Christina reiterated.

"When she called you those names" — the officer looked at his notes — " 'a spoiled brat, and a bitch,' you didn't react?"

"I said no. Why would I? She was kinda weird, I got that. I just wanted to put away the necklace Mom had given me," Christina said, her voice edging up an octave.

"John, she's said this three times." Daniel knew one of the two officers, and he wasn't about to let them browbeat Christina into making any false statements or suppositions.

"You've got enough in your report."

They'd been over the incident several times. "Yes, we do. Now, we'll file this. It may take a day or two, then it'll go to the prosecutor's office. Not sure what happens, once it's in their hands, but they'll contact you and your mother." He spoke directly to Christina.

"Okay," she said. "Then I can forget all about this?"

"That's up to the prosecutors, not us. We just write the report," the officer named John explained. "Daniel, good seeing you. Not ideal circumstances, but you understand."

Daniel shook hands with both John and the other officer, whose name Anna hadn't gotten, but it didn't matter. This was the beginning of getting their lives back to normal.

To before Ryan.

Anna walked the officers to the door, Daniel trailing behind. "Thanks, guys," he said, then she closed the door.

"That was not the most encouraging pair," she said. "They seem to think this is some kind of childish prank, payback for not letting Renée have the necklace."

"They'll question her, and it's possible they'll search for the necklace. May not be much of an area to search since the place is literally ashes now." She'd told him about the fire.

"Mom, Renée had luggage in the trunk of Ryan's car. Remember, he said she'd packed up a bunch of stuff the day of the barbecue. He did say that, I remember!"

"You're right, or something like that. He said she'd packed like she was going on a trip. Maybe some of her things are still in the trunk of Ryan's car," Anna suggested, feeling a glimmer of hope that they might find her mother's necklace, but more than that, that Renée would be found out, and, she hoped, get the treatment she so desperately needed.

"Something else, I just remembered," Anna said. "Excuse me," she said, and whirled out of the den and into the kitchen. She'd forgotten all about the gifts Patrick and Renée had brought on the day of the barbecue. In all of the excitement, if you could even call it that, she'd never bothered opening their gifts, hadn't given them much thought, until that moment. Someone had tucked them away in a drawer; she remembered seeing them the other day. Probably Mona. She pulled several deep drawers open, then saw the two little boxes sitting in the drawer where she stored extra napkins.

Taking the boxes with her, she handed them to Daniel. "Ryan's kids gave these to me. I never opened them during all the commotion," she said, thinking she was being extremely fair, calling attempted murder a commotion.

"Do you mind if I open them?" Daniel asked.

"Of course not," she replied. "Do whatever you need with them." Personally, she wanted to toss them into the garbage, but that was being childish.

Both boxes were identical and looked to have been prewrapped. "You haven't tried to open this one?" He held one of the packages toward the light. "This looks like it's been opened and maybe resealed."

"No, I'd forgotten they'd given them to me, though I did run across them when I was searching through the kitchen drawers a few days ago. I closed the drawers and didn't think of them again until just now. I can ask Mona if she opened them or tried to."

"No need. Why don't you open them now? I'll snap a few pictures with my cell phone. Just in case."

"In case of what?" Anna asked. *Does he think there's a bomb or something inside?*

"Just to be on the safe side. I don't think

there's anything to get alarmed over, just being overly cautious."

The boxes were approximately three-by-four inches. The wrapping paper was a white glossy with gold trim. Whatever was inside, the boxes were prewrapped. Carefully, she used a fingernail to break the seal without tearing the paper. Daniel snapped a photo, then she peeled the paper back, revealing a dark brown box. He snapped another picture. She opened it up. Four pieces of assorted chocolates, the kind you could purchase at any drugstore. One more flash from his cell phone.

"Open the other box now," Daniel directed, then added, "please."

This was the box he thought might have been tampered with, though seeing what was inside now, it could've been like this when they'd given it to her. Truly, she hadn't paid that much attention then. Anna went through the same routine, allowing Daniel to snap a picture as she took the paper apart, removed the dark brown top to the box, and revealed a second box of chocolates. She sighed with relief. "Nothing unusual here," she said. But as she was about to pluck one of the chocolates out of its paper, she saw a light green powdery substance that looked like it was oozing from a crack in the chocolate. "Wait, look at this," she said, pointing to what she was seeing.

Daniel took another picture. "Whatever you do, don't eat that."

"Of course not," Anna said. "Any idea what this could be?" she asked Daniel.

"Maybe. Do you have a plastic bag?"

"Sure." She ran to the kitchen and returned with a small box of plastic sandwich bags.

"Mind opening one?" he asked, then picked up another bag in his hand, using it as a glove to pick up the box and drop it into the bag Anna was holding open. They repeated the process with the other box of candy even though it appeared to be fine.

"Want to tell me what you think this is?" she asked.

"Let's wait until we get the lab results," he answered. Clicking through his phone, he hit a number, then spoke. "Listen, I need you two to come back. I've got something that could be connected to the crime scene. I need to get it to the lab ASAP. Thanks," he said, then ended the call.

"Why does this need to go to a lab? I need to know," Anna insisted. "In the kitchen," she said, leaving Christina to wonder what was going on. She'd tell her soon enough.

Daniel sighed. "Ms. Campbell —"

"Call me Anna, please," she interrupted.

"Anna, I don't know for sure, but that green powder, it looks like a pill that's been crushed."

Her heart rate quadrupled. "What do you mean? What kind of pill?"

"There's been a string of young women at Tech who have been roofied. That is exactly what it looks like when it's crushed up. Do you happen to know where those chocolates were purchased?"

Stunned, Anna took a minute to reply. "No. As I said, they were a gift from Ryan's kids. I suppose I could call him, ask if he remembers where he bought them."

"If you wouldn't mind, Anna, it'll be a big help to me and the investigators."

Ryan was the last person on earth she wanted to speak to, even more so now, but she'd do what she needed to help with the investigation. "Excuse me, I'll be right back." Anna used the door in the kitchen to go downstairs to the studio.

They were still snapping pictures on set in the kitchen. "Mandy, I need to speak with you for a minute. It's important."

"Sure. Guys, let's call it a day. I think we've got enough stills to work with," Mandy said to the three members of the crew who were still there.

Normally, Anna would've chitchatted with them, but now wasn't the time. She did give them a wave to let them know they weren't the cause of her emergency. The crew was more like extended family, as far as she was concerned, and she made sure they knew this and all were extremely well compensated for their hard work.

"In the office," Anna said.

Mandy followed her to her small office, where she usually tended to work-related e-mails and such. "Daniel, he's the attorney Simon sent over, never mind. Follow me. You need to see this." Anna hurried upstairs, Mandy at her heels. In the kitchen, Daniel sat at the bar, the two plastic bags on the counter.

Mandy looked at Anna.

"Mandy, this is Daniel Lowande. He's helping Christina. Daniel, she knows what's going on. You can speak freely in front of her."

"As I was telling Anna, the candy, at least one piece of it, appears to have been tampered with. I can't say for sure, but the green powder looks like a crushed-up roofie."

"A roofie? As in a date-rape drug?" Mandy managed to spit out.

"I'm not one hundred percent sure, but I suspect it could be," he told her.

"Where did this" — she pointed to the boxes of candy in the plastic bags — "come from?"

"I'd forgotten all about them. The barbecue. Patrick and Renée brought me gifts. I was busy, so I put them on the counter in the kitchen. I forgot I had them. There was so much going on that day. I think Mona or someone put them in a drawer, and I totally forgot about them. Daniel wants me to call Ryan, see if he remembers where they were purchased."

"Then do it," Mandy said.

"I was about to, I just wanted you to do what you did last night. With your phone." Anna knew it was legal in Texas for her to record a phone conversation without the person's consent. But even so, she didn't want to go into it with Daniel just yet.

"Excuse us," Anna said. "I'll see if I can find where they were purchased."

Anna hustled out of the kitchen to her bedroom upstairs. "Get the app ready to record." Anna dialed Ryan's cell number.

"Hi, love," he said.

Anna rolled her eyes. "Hi, Ryan. I, uh, wanted to see how you all were. Any news on the fire?" She'd been instructed by

Simon *not* to discuss this, but she needed to give him a reason for her to call.

"Nothing yet. I'm waiting to hear myself."

"Oh, well, I guess I assumed since they'd ruled the fire as arson, you would know the details by now."

"You would think so, but no, nothing yet," Ryan said.

"Ryan, listen, there's something I've been meaning to ask you. With everything that's happened, it escaped my mind. Do you remember the chocolates Patrick and Renée brought that day? They were a gift. They were placed in a drawer, and I just saw them again. I wanted to thank them, but also I wanted to know if you recall where they were purchased? I'd like to . . . do a segment on the show on how to reproduce the candies, boxes and all. I thought with the holidays around the corner, it might be a great gift idea. For kids to . . . give their teachers."

Mandy shook her head.

"Hmm, seems like we were at a CVS earlier that morning. I'm pretty sure we bought them there."

"Oh, thanks. I know it sounds crazy, but do you remember which CVS?"

"Sure, the one on East Braun; it's closest to the house."

"Okay, well, thanks. I'm . . . tell Patrick and Renée I said thank you."

"Hey, don't hang up. Why don't you stop by the hotel later tonight? I'd love to see you. Catch up."

While she thought it tacky to dump a guy over the phone, it's exactly what she needed to do. "Look, Ryan, with all that's happened, Christina's accident, your house fire, I think it's probably a good idea if we stop seeing each other." As far as she was concerned, they were over the day of the barbecue, but she hadn't told *him* yet.

"What!" He shouted so loudly, she had to hold the phone away from her ear.

Deep breath in and out; she knew he'd react this way, which made calling it quits over the phone a good idea. Anna suspected that, if pushed too far, Ryan could become violent. She was finished with him. "You heard me, Ryan. I have a lot going on, you're going to have a lot on your hands, dealing with your house, the fire. I just think it's best we end this now."

"Anna, just stop! I know you're upset about your daughter. I would be, too. But we're just getting started. Remember what I told you that night in the parking lot at The Shallows?"

"Yes, Ryan. I do, but I don't feel the same."

Mandy was getting more than an earful.

"Anna, you might not have said as much, but trust me, a woman like you in the sack, you weren't just a tumble in the hay. You might not even realize it yourself. Your actions showed me exactly how you feel; don't deny it." His voice was calm, but in a scary sort of way.

A mistake of massive proportions, Anna feared what Ryan might do if she were to continue this line of conversation.

"We'll talk another time, maybe. Goodbye, Ryan." Anna ended the call before she said things she'd regret.

"He's a frigging loony, Anna! What is he talking about? The parking lot?"

"The night I met him at The Shallows for dinner with the kids, he walked me to my car. His kids were already in his car, and he whispered in my ear, told me he loved me. I thought it an odd place to make such a serious statement, but you hear what I'm dealing with. He's not right."

"You're not kidding. I think he could be dangerous. You need to tell this to the police. He could be one of those kinds of boyfriends who stalk and kill you. I'm not joking, Anna, so don't take this lightly. I know he played you; it's not your fault, so don't blame yourself. The guy's a wacko."

"Mandy, I agree. Listen to this, then tell me what you think. Okay, we both know I'm not loose, or whatever they're calling it now. Hopping into the sack with a guy I just met isn't me, not that I'm judging. You know this, right?"

"It's not my business what you do, Anna. But yes, you're not a tramp, if that's what you want to hear.

"Why would he lace candy from his kids? Doesn't make a lot of sense, but nothing about him or those kids has ever left me with a good feeling. They're all weird, if you ask me, and again, we both know, I don't know them, but from what I've heard, I don't want to know him or those kids. Maybe the son, but who knows about him? He could be a psycho in the making."

"I shouldn't tell you this, but what the hell. Ryan told me Patrick got his girlfriend pregnant, the summer before his junior year. The girl's parents sent her to live with family in Spain. Apparently, Patrick never got over her or the baby she put up for adoption. Ryan said this is why he quit the swim team. I told Ryan I wouldn't mention this to anyone, but I think I'm past keeping my word where he's concerned."

"Wow, that's terrible. Did he say where the girl is now?" Mandy asked.

"From what I gathered, she's moved on with her life in Spain. That's all I know. Now, let's get downstairs before those cops come looking for us up here."

"Gotcha," Mandy said.

Daniel was still seated at the bar; the two police officers who had left were back. "I understand you received these boxes of candy as a gift from Mr. Robertson's children? Any reason why they'd want to drug you? The son, he got a thing for you maybe?"

"No! Not hardly. I've only met him twice. That's ridiculous," Anna said, her voice laced with shock. "I can't believe you would even suggest something like that."

Daniel spoke. "He's just doing his job, Anna. We have to cover all possibilities. Please don't be offended."

"I don't know of any woman in their right mind who wouldn't be offended at such a suggestion."

"I agree. Guys, get the tests done on this as soon as you can. If I need to make a few bribes to get to the head of the line, tell Birch I'll buy him a bottle of scotch, the good stuff."

"Now, you know if we said that, we'd be

in a heap of cow dung, Daniel. Go on and make that call, and we'll take this to old Birch now. Ma'am, I'm sorry this is so distasteful. My wife watches your show all the time. She's gonna be impressed when I tell her I met you." The cop's way of trying to make nice, Anna knew.

"Wait, just a sec," she said. The bookshelf on the side of the door that led to the studio held several copies of a cookbook she'd authored two years ago. While it wasn't much, she might make someone happy, if only a teeny bit.

"You have a pen?" she asked the officer.

"Sure," he said, handing her a nice Cross pen.

"It was my dad's. He was a cop, too. Lost him last year," he said to Anna as though he had to explain the pen's history.

Anna looked at him. "I'm sorry. I lost my father when I was seven. What's your wife's name? And yours? I don't believe I caught it."

"Julie Myers. I'm Jim."

Anna signed the inside cover of the cookbook to Julie and Jim. "Here. Give this to your wife. Tell her I appreciate her watching my show."

"Her birthday's next week. This will be the perfect gift, so thanks, Ms. Campbell."

"It's Anna, and you're welcome."

Both officers left.

She turned her focus to Daniel. "I need to get back to my daughter. She's probably wondering what happened to me. Is there anything more we need to do today?"

"No, we're good. I'll call Birch, get him going, and as soon as I know anything, I'll be in touch. Don't worry, Anna. Jim and John are good police officers, and they take their jobs seriously. They'll get the report to the prosecutor ASAP. Then we wait, see what happens, take it from there. Just keep Christina entertained until she's on her feet."

"Of course — thanks, Daniel. I'm glad you're on our side," she added. "Mandy, could you see Daniel out?"

"Absolutely," she said, giving Anna a sly wink.

"I'll see you soon, Anna," Daniel said.

When she returned to the den, Christina was sound asleep.

CHAPTER 22

The phone jolted Anna awake. She looked at the time. "Is this Anna Campbell?"

She tossed the covers aside. It was just after six in the morning. "Yes, this is she."

"This is a courtesy call from the Lubbock Police Department. We need to speak with you. We're on our way." The line went dead.

Anna wasn't sure the police even made courtesy calls. Not caring about the time, she dialed Daniel's cell number.

"Morning, Anna. I take it they called," he said.

"The cops? Yes. Said it was a courtesy call. What does that mean?" She was in the bathroom, running a brush through her long hair, which was still damp from the shower last night.

"They're bringing you in for questioning in the Robertson arson case. I told them I'd bring you in myself. No need to go to your house, make a big scene."

Time stopped. Anna felt like she'd been punched in the gut. Rage took over. "What? Surely you don't think I had anything to do with that?"

"Of course not. Apparently, the daughter told the investigators you had it in for her because you think she pushed Christina down the stairs. It's Christina's word against hers, though I don't think it's going to be a problem proving she had something to do with it. Certainly anyone who knows you wouldn't expect you to retaliate by burning their house down. It's not pretty, but I'm headed your way. We can go to the police station together. Clear this up, and you'll be home in time for lunch."

"You're sure?" she asked.

"As sure as I can be. I'll be there in fifteen minutes, Anna. Don't worry. I'll have this cleared up soon."

Anna quickly slid into a pair of jeans, a cream-colored blouse, and a pair of ballet flats. She twisted her still-damp hair into her usual topknot, then called Mandy, who was in her room here at the house.

"Listen, the cops are bringing me in for questioning. Renée told the arson investigators I might have something to do with the fire. I need you to look after Christina. Mona and Jeb left for Idalou late last night.

340

They won't be back until tonight. You good with this?" Anna asked, racing around her room, gathering her cell charger and stuffing it inside her bag. "Daniel is taking me down to the station. Keep this as quiet as you can. I don't want Christina to get wind of this."

"Wow, no worries. I'll take care of everything on this end."

"Thanks, Mandy. When this is all over, remind me to send you on the vacation of your dreams."

"I will. Now, go do what you have to do to settle this mess."

Anna went downstairs quietly, careful not to make any noise. With Christina in the den, it was tough to sneak out of the house so early, but she was waiting outside the gates when Daniel pulled up in a silver Ford truck. *Pure Texan,* she thought.

He stopped outside the gate and jumped out of the big truck. "I thought you might need a boost; you're such a tiny little thing."

"Thanks," Anna said, as he helped her step up into the truck.

"I would've brought my car, but it's in the shop."

He did a three-point turn, then directed the Ford toward the police station in South Overton.

"I didn't have time to make coffee, so we'll go through the drive-through at McDonald's, if that's okay. I like their coffee a helluva lot better than Starbucks'."

"Thanks," she said. Though coffee was the last thing on her mind, she could use a dose of caffeine, no matter where it came from.

Anna didn't pay much attention to the staticky voice at the drive-through, her attention fully on what lay ahead. How in the world did Renée think she could accuse her of something so vile and get away with it? Especially knowing she was responsible for pushing Christina down the stairs. The girl had issues, and Anna was through playing nice. That girl didn't need treatment for issues; she needed to be locked away to protect society from her.

"Here, you'll need this," Daniel said, handing her a large cup.

"I'm sure I do." She thought of the bottle of Xanax in her purse. She needed one now more than ever, but there was no way she'd take one while heading into the police station to be questioned for arson. Even the thought was so absurd, she could hardly contemplate being in such a crazy situation. Did these so-called arson investigators really believe a confused and vicious thirteen-year-old? She would soon find out.

Daniel parked in the back, leading her inside through a private entrance.

The inside of the Lubbock police station appeared to be just like police stations she had seen in TV dramas. Gray walls and horrible fluorescent lighting. The smell of burnt coffee and the stale odor of cigarettes permeated the long hallway they walked down. "Anna, you let me answer for you, if you're unsure what to say. You're innocent, you've got an alibi, so this is just a formality, remember. You'll be just fine." He took her hand. "You can trust me. I promise."

She felt a rush of heat when he took her hand but couldn't focus on her physical attraction to her daughter's — now *her* — attorney. Wasn't that forbidden or something? No matter. "Thanks, Daniel. It means a lot. I've had some serious trust issues lately," she added.

They were led to a small interrogation room by a female officer. A table, a few chairs, and a glass window where she knew they watched suspects when they were being questioned about a crime. *She* was a suspect now.

"Relax," Daniel said, tossing back the last of his coffee.

They had been there for about five minutes when two plainclothes officers entered the room.

"This is special investigator Gary Furdale, and his partner, Lindsey Patterson." Daniel made the introductions. "Anna Campbell."

Was she supposed to shake hands, say "Nice to meet you"? With all of her etiquette savvy, she had no clue. She just nodded, acknowledging their presence.

They sat down in the two chairs across from her. Neither seemed like they were ready to read her her Miranda rights, toss her in jail, and throw away the key. Gary was a short guy with a perfectly groomed goatee with the gray just starting to show. Anna would guess him to be around her age. Friendly brown eyes, he made her feel at ease as soon as he spoke to her. "This is just a formality, Ms. Campbell. We have to follow all leads, regardless of how inadequate we may believe them to be."

She nodded, unsure if she was expected to say anything. Her mother's words came back to her. *If you don't have anything nice to say, don't.* Not quite what the words implied, but she couldn't help but think of them.

Lindsey Patterson was a cute redhead. She wore her hair cut in a pixie cut, which went perfectly with the freckles that dotted her face. When she smiled, her clear blue eyes sparkled. "Ms. Campbell, I'm sorry we have to meet under these circumstances, but as Gary said, it's simply part of our job to follow all leads."

"She understands," Daniel said.

"Can you tell us where you were the evening of September 26th?"

"I was at home taking care of Christina, my daughter."

"And you have someone who will verify this?"

"Yes, three people." She gave Mandy's, Mona's, and Jeb's full names.

"Do you ever shop at Candle City in the mall?" Lindsey asked. "They've put all their holiday candles out already, hard to believe. You know the store?"

"Yes, I've been there a few times. It's been a while," Anna said, trying to remember when she was there last. It had to be last year, but she couldn't pinpoint an exact day if she were asked.

"You weren't there on the night of October second?" Gary asked her again.

"No, I was not. I haven't been there in at least a year," she added.

"You're fine, Anna," Daniel encouraged.

"I could check my bank records if you need an exact date. I purchased red tapered candles for a show we filmed a couple of weeks after. You can look at my playlist; it should be there, under 'holiday decor' if you want to check now."

Daniel took his phone out, clicked a few times, then handed his phone for Gary and Lindsey to see.

"I watched that episode," Lindsey said. "I'm a big fan, but don't tell anyone I told you that, especially now."

Anna smiled. "Your secret is safe with me."

"You can go now, Ms. Campbell, I think we've established you have an alibi, and we'll need your bank record showing you were there on the day of, or about two weeks prior to, filming your show."

She breathed a sigh of relief. "Can I ask why you are all so interested in Candle City?"

"It's part of the arson investigation, so I can't give you the details, but sooner or later, this will all be made public," Gary explained.

"Daniel, can I tell them about Christina's accident?"

"I told Gary on the drive over to your house. He's already checking with John and Jim, the officers who came to your house to write up the report."

"I see," she said even though she didn't.

346

As long as she was free to leave this building without handcuffs being slapped on her wrists, she didn't see the need to go into the story again. Maybe she'd have to when or if this investigation was finalized, but for now, all she wanted to do was get the hell out of there and go home to her family.

Gary and Lindsey both stood up at the same time. "We're sorry we had to bring you in this way. John and Jim were jumping at the bit to go back to your place. Thanks, and we'll be in touch." They shook hands, and Daniel led her back down the overly bright hallway, out the door they'd entered, and into his truck.

Once they were buckled in and headed back to her house, she asked Daniel, "Why didn't they just call me if that's all they had to say?"

"It's what's required. Plus nothing like checking the suspect out in person. Kind of like learning about someone when you see her kitchen."

She laughed. "I would've been more than happy to invite them over for coffee."

"I'm sure Lindsey would like that. She was starstruck," he teased.

"Please, I am anything but. I cook and decorate, that's it. I'm not a movie star."

"No, but you're a humongous sensation

on YouTube. You have a huge following. I have to admit, I watched a few of your videos last night. I'm intrigued, to say the least."

Anna's heart fluttered but in a good way. "I'm very flattered. So what did you watch?"

"Dinners for one," he said.

"That's an easy one to film."

"What do you do with all the food? I know that's crazy, but I have to know," Daniel said, a smile on his face.

"We eat it, or the crew does. It doesn't go to waste, I can tell you that."

"Good. I wondered about that."

"Well, I'm happy to clear that up for you."

As they turned down the drive to enter the gates, Anna was dumbfounded when she saw that two local news crews had gathered outside the gates.

"This is what I was hoping to avoid," Daniel said. "You have another entrance?"

"In the back. The crew parks there, though this is too early for them to be here. We can go in through the entrance they use." Daniel maneuvered the large pickup truck, pulling as close to the door as he could without ramming into the house. "Go on inside. I'm going to get rid of the media before this gets out of hand."

"Thank you so much, Daniel. I'm grateful

Simon contacted you."

"Don't say that until I send you my bill. We're not finished, remember? There's still the possibility your daughter may have to go to court if the state decides to prosecute Miss Robertson."

"I wish I could forget. I wish a lot of things. I'll make us a cup of coffee if you'd like. You might need some replenishment after dealing with that group."

"Deal," he said, getting out of the truck. "I'll be back."

CHAPTER 23

"The popular YouTube sensation Anna Campbell was questioned this morning in the arson case of Texas Tech University professor Ryan Robertson's house fire. Sources tell this station that the former lovers had a dispute during a Labor Day event, hosted by Ms. Campbell. Her minor daughter, whose name we're not permitted to release, suffered a fall and was hospitalized with a severe broken leg and a minor concussion. It's believed that Mr. Robertson's minor daughter had a conflict with the Campbell daughter, and the fire was set as retaliation. More on this breaking news . . ."

"This is bullshit," Mandy said, tossing the remote across the den.

"Mom, this is a nightmare! Everyone at school will know it's me! Can't you do something?"

"Daniel is taking care of it. He's a lawyer, honey, and he knows what he's doing. Let's allow him to do his job. I know this is the worst thing that will ever happen to you. If there were any way I could change what those nasty reporters said, I would. Just know that it's not true. Any of it."

Christina wheeled around the room in her wheelchair so she could sit beside her mother. She leaned over as far as the chair would allow. "What about the lovers part, Mom?"

Anna knew this was coming and wasn't sure how she should handle the situation, but when in doubt, telling the truth seemed to be the way to go. "Mandy, could you give me a minute alone?" She nodded toward her daughter.

"Yep, I'm going to make lunch for all of us today."

"God help us, but thanks," Anna said, realizing it was almost noon. Daniel hadn't returned for the coffee, but he'd texted her telling he would stop by later.

As soon as Mandy left the room, Anna positioned Christina's wheelchair so that she faced her. "Ryan was never my lover in the way they're reporting it. Lovers are just that. They love each other. Like I did your father. Like Mona and Jeb. That's gross to hear when you're thirteen, I know, but it's the truth. The news is most likely going to

351

get nastier, since Renée seems to think I burned their house down to get even with her for pushing you. I told you that."

"Mom, duh. I can't see you burning anything. Even food."

"Thanks, sweetie. Your trust means more to me than you know. I can't lie, and I know this isn't what you need to hear; it's hard for me to say this to you, but you know I try to be up-front with you as much as I can."

She nodded.

"I did have a physical relationship with Ryan. I was never in love with him, though at one point I thought I cared about him. He is pretty rough with Patrick, and Renée. Cusses at them, and I think it's rubbed off on Renée. The night I went to dinner to meet them, he was rude to both of them. I'm not sure why; I don't think there is any support system in place, and I think he has financial issues. Maybe he takes that out on his kids. I can't say for sure, and it's just a guess. I feel terrible for bringing this drama and embarrassment into your life. I don't know what I can do to change this, or how to keep you from hearing things on the news, but I will try to keep this out of the public as much as I'm able. Daniel is working on that as we speak."

"I know it's not what you wanted. I kinda liked Ryan, but he seemed cold to me, like his eyes were empty. Does that sound crazy or what?"

"Not at all." Anna thought her observations were on point.

"Mona and Jeb said you can stay at their house in Idalou if you want. When this is over, you'll probably have your walking cast on, or I hope it's going to be off, and you can start school after the Christmas break. It's not like you're lagging behind. They're willing to stay there with you, but I said this was your decision."

Anna had hired a tutor who came to the house in the afternoon during the week. Christina was up to date on all of her lessons, and Tiffany stopped over at least a couple times a week to catch her up on the latest freshman gossip. Plus, she stayed in touch with her other classmates through social media. She would not be the pariah she'd thought she'd be when she was finally able to walk through the door at Bishop Coerver. Anna cringed when she remembered she'd considered footing the bill in order for Renée to attend the school with her daughter. Thank God her relationship with Ryan hadn't gotten to that point.

Barb sent her a daily e-mail with copies of

all the receipts Ryan and his kids accrued. She continued to foot the bill for their hotel, food, and items from the gift shop. She had the money, and it wasn't as if it hurt her finances any. She didn't want to see them back at The Crown, no matter how rotten Ryan and his daughter were. However, this would have to stop soon. She couldn't take care of the world, and especially a family that was doing its best to rip hers apart.

"What about Miss Holmes, my tutor?"

"I'm sure she'd be more than willing to drive the few extra miles to Idalou."

"Do I have to give you an answer right now?"

Anna acted like she was in deep thought. "I don't think you do. You don't even have to consider it. It's simply an option I'd like you to have. You didn't ask to be dragged through my mess."

"I'll think about it. More than anything, I just want this stupid cast off. I bet the hair on my leg is as long as the hair on my head, and it feels gross."

Anna chuckled. "We can take you and get them waxed when your cast is off."

"Really? I thought you said that was too much upkeep when I asked you the last time."

"It is, but you're worth it. It hurts like

crazy the first few times, though the upside is that the more you have them waxed, the less hair you'll have."

"Okay, I'll think about that, too. Mom, do you really believe Renée wanted to . . . like, *kill* me?"

Anna had wondered about that herself. "I don't know, baby. Like I said, she's had a rough life. I'd like to think not, but I can't say that and be sure."

"What about her mom? She died when Renée was a baby, right?"

Once again, Anna realized just how little she knew about Ryan's past. Mandy was right when she told her they should've been up-front about their spouses. Her only defense was that she'd met Ryan on a singles cruise. She hadn't thought it the most pleasant topic, but they should've had this conversation when they'd started seeing each other once they'd returned to Lubbock.

"I believe her mother passed away when she was just a baby; I think she might've been one or two years old. Ryan said she's never had a female figure in her life."

"What about grandparents? Aunts, uncles, or anything?"

"Ryan told me his family died when he was in college." Anna realized in all the conversations they'd had, that was the only time he'd ever mentioned family. It never came up again, and it should have. She'd told him she'd lost her father when she was a little girl though she hadn't elaborated on the details. He knew she'd lost her mother, but that was all. Now that she was really thinking about the dates they'd had, all Ryan had talked about was money, or he had tried to show her that he had money. The fancy dinners, the hotels. How much *he had.* Or hoped to have? He drove a new Honda. His clothes fit well. He always looked like he'd stepped off the pages of a men's fashion magazine. He was put together. *All fake,* she thought. *Every bit of it an act created to . . . what? Attract gullible women?*

She suspected she wasn't far off the mark, but she would obtain answers to these questions in time as the arson investigation proceeded. And if a case was brought against Renée, assuming the prosecutors decided there was a case, it made it almost certain that she would learn more about his past.

"So he's kind of like you. I mean, without a family."

"Baby, you are my family. Mandy is family, and Mona and Jeb. They're as good a set of grandparents as you could wish for."

"I know. I just thought that's what you and Ryan had, you know, in common, why you hooked up."

"Sadly, we don't have much of anything in common other than the fact we're both single."

"Daniel is cute, don't you think? He looks like Thor. Tiffany about croaked when she saw him leaving. Said he was a hottie."

"Don't get any ideas, kiddo. Daniel is a nice-looking man, and he's kind and smart. He's our attorney, and nothing more, so don't you get any ideas in that pretty little head of yours."

"I was just telling you my opinion, that's all," Christina whirled around in her wheelchair. "Think Mandy has lunch ready? I am starving."

"Sit tight, and I'll check."

Anna felt better for airing her dirty linen, if you wanted to call it that. She wanted to clear the air, especially after that news report. Sure, there would be more news in the upcoming days ahead, but she'd deal with it. She had a loving family and knew they were all standing with her and would always be there for her. Blood didn't always make family.

"Christina is starving, and I said I'd check

on lunch. Something smells good."

"Look at this," Mandy said, opening the top oven to reveal a pizza with cheese bubbling. The smell of garlic and onions made her hungry.

"Looks delish," Anna said. "Want me to see if I can get my daughter in here, or do you want to bring this to the den?"

"I'll bring it to her. I used that garlic crust you had in the freezer. Someday, I'm going to actually watch your videos and learn to cook. Directing the crew doesn't leave a lot of time to stand by and take notes." They both laughed.

"I'll get the drinks," Anna said.

"Thanks. Be there in a minute."

Anna took three cans of Coke to the den, not bothering with ice. She put them on the coffee table. She took her cell from her pocket and checked to see if she'd had any messages.

There was one from Daniel.

Major news. Be there when I can. Might be late.

Major news. Anna hoped like heck this wasn't going to send the local news vans back to her gates, just waiting for another piece of half truths to fill their allotted three minutes of live-on-air news.

Just as she'd explained to her daughter,

whatever happened, they would deal with it, and she would do whatever it took to make this up to her. First things first.

Mandy came into the den carrying a serving tray over her shoulder like they did at Mario's Pizza Parlor in downtown Lubbock. "Be careful." She moved the cans of Coke to the side so she could place the tray on the coffee table.

"I don't know about you, but I'll be glad when we can eat in the kitchen again. Girl, you need to do whatever it is you're supposed to do to get that monstrosity off your leg," Mandy said, as she served slices of hot, crusty pizza.

"I'm getting a walking cast soon. I'm sick of this room, too. I can't wait to have some privacy in my bedroom."

"As soon as you can hoof it up those stairs, your room is waiting," Anna said. For the next fifteen minutes, they munched on pizza and talked about the upcoming holidays. Mandy said she really needed to be on top of her game this year, given the news. Anna agreed. Hopefully, this wouldn't damage her reputation too badly.

CHAPTER 24

"I know it's late, but I could not get away before now, and I need to tell you this in person," Daniel said. Anna had spent half an hour soaking in the tub, the first time she'd truly relaxed since this ordeal began. She'd just put on her sleep shirt and planned to read in bed, but this was much more important.

"Come in through the back. I'll unlock the studio entrance."

She quickly found a pair of comfortable jeans and a sweatshirt. The evenings were starting to cool. Though West Texas rarely had much of an autumn, she felt a crispness in the air when she'd left Mona and Jeb earlier. She'd gone to the cottage, or the little house as Jeb liked to call it, and taken a few minutes to fill them in on the latest events, at least the ones that she knew about.

She hurried through the studio, hitting a set of lights so Daniel could see. She'd just unlocked the entrance when she heard his pickup. She opened the door and stepped aside to let him in.

"I don't want to hear what you have to say, do I?" she said as she went back upstairs.

"I think you might be surprised. Any coffee? I know it's late, but the stuff does not keep me awake."

"I'll make us a cup in the Keurig." She fixed their coffees, bringing them to the bar. He took a sip, then ran a hand through his hair.

"Christina's memory paid off."

"How so?"

"She remembered what Ryan told her the day of the barbecue. Something about Renée's packing like she was going on a trip, brought along her entire bedroom. That's not too far from the truth. It seems Gary and Lindsey were able to get a warrant to search the trunk of Ryan's car. Just as had been said, there was a small piece of luggage inside. She had all kinds of personal items, just stuff a kid her age would have, but she also had a ton of photographs of her mother."

"Oh" was all she could say.

"I was able to take a few snapshots with my phone. Not routine, but nothing about this case is routine." He showed Anna several photos of a woman of whom Renée was the spitting image.

"She looks like her mother, don't you think?" Anna said, handing the cell back to him. "Poor kid."

"Wait, there's more. While I wasn't able to get my hands on it, I thought this might bring a smile to your face." He opened the pictures again and handed her the phone.

Tears sprang to her eyes. "Oh, it's Mom's necklace! I'm so relieved. Christina's been so bummed about this. Where did they find it?" She was pretty sure she knew the answer but needed to hear it anyway.

"In the luggage, along with the rest of her stuff."

"So this is good, right? Proof that Christina is telling the truth about what happened."

"Yes, it will hold a lot of water if this goes to court. Speaking of which, I know this isn't my case, but I heard that James Banks pleaded guilty to first-degree stalking. Not sure what kind of deal he's getting, but he'll be off the streets for a while."

"As crazy as it sounds, I haven't thought too much about him since they arrested him. What I never understood was why me? He's a good-looking guy. He could've had any woman he chose, even the wife he lied about."

"He was obsessed with you and apparently had some sort of mental breakdown when you broke it off with him. He was in therapy for a while. I don't know who the therapist is, but he or she will most likely be asked about his mental evaluation, which might have some bearing on his sentence, but that's not all."

"I see why you never made it back this morning. Did we get the gag order?" He'd told her he was going to ask the judge for a temporary gag order in an emergency chamber hearing due to the age of the girls.

"We did. Temporary, but it's a good thing. Now, this isn't what I wanted to tell you, and it really goes to Patrick's or Renée's state of mind, but Birch called me an hour ago. That chocolate was loaded with Rohypnol, or roofies as they call them on the street. Birch says it's the same crap that's been seen in a few cases at Tech. A couple of girls almost died a few months ago. It didn't make the news; someone at the college kept it quiet. So, that's where we're at. I'm guessing with the necklace, and this roofie mess, the prosecutor will decide sooner rather than later if he's going to bring charges against that messed-up girl.

It's sad in a way; she's so young. Anyway, I appreciate the late-night coffee. I'm out of here, and if you don't mind, I'll leave through the mudroom."

"Now that there's no chance of the media hanging out, plus, the news hour is over, go on, get out of here. And thanks, Daniel. I appreciate all you've done."

"As I said, you'll get my bill."

She smiled, closed and locked the door behind him, and went upstairs, ready to relax and read for a while. It had been a helluva day, to quote her attorney.

CHAPTER 25

Anna did her best to try to wiggle out of that night's charity event, but at the last minute decided it wouldn't hurt to show her face in public and let folks know she wasn't hiding.

Every year, the local garden club hosted an event, Sun 'N Fun, a home and garden show where most of the proceeds went to one of her favorite charities, Habitat for Humanity. She would make an appearance, shake a few hands, and hope to help to meet their goal of one hundred thousand dollars. Anna always matched whatever amount they raised — it was for a good cause — and it was something she felt good about.

She chatted, made the rounds, talked to a few dozen people, posed for the camera, and even though she wasn't all that comfortable, given the state of her private affairs, she had to return to the vlogging world eventually.

"Anna, I adored those Halloween treats on your show," said one guest.

This was followed by others, complimenting her on the show, her recipes. No one even hinted at the scandal that had been reported on. This gave her hope that, in time, it would be forgotten, nothing more than a bad memory. She stayed an hour longer than she had planned to. On the drive home, she chatted briefly with Mandy, revisiting the events of the past few months. There was one task she needed to tend to, and she would do so as soon as she was alone.

She pulled her Nissan through the gates and parked in the garage. Mandy was still staying over a few nights a week. Christina had a walking cast on, and tonight she'd had Tiffany over to spend the night, a celebration of sorts.

As soon as she changed into her sleep shirt, Anna went to her personal computer and sent Barb an e-mail telling her that she would no longer continue to cover Ryan's hotel. Then she went to the website of the credit card she had used and sent a message asking that the card be cancelled, then paid the balance. A whopping seventy-three hundred dollars. That done, she logged on to her Facebook page and read a few posts, seeing that she had a friend request from someone named Laura Jones. Anna thought she was probably the friend of a friend, and though she was not sure, she was in a good mood, so she accepted the request.

She clicked on the page, a bit surprised to find photos of the event she had just attended. She recognized a few of the people in the photos, but she wasn't sure who this Laura Jones was. She clicked the mouse and enlarged the picture, and though she had never met this woman, she knew she'd seen her recently.

Then she remembered. This was the face in the photographs Daniel had taken of the pictures in Renée's luggage. Only, she was much older and hadn't aged well. She looked rough, unlike the usual glammed-up women who attended the event. These weren't photoshopped, some kook trying to play mind games with her. This was real.

The implication behind the photos blew her away. How could this be? Was she seeing more than was actually there? She examined the pictures again. This was definitely an older version of the woman in the pictures he'd shared with her.

If she put two and two together, and she was quite capable of doing so, she had to conclude that Laura Jones was none other than Ryan Robertson's *dead* wife.

She glanced at the clock, saw it was after one in the morning but didn't care. She called Daniel. He needed to know what she'd just discovered.

Ryan's wife was alive and well.

"Hey, it's late. This better be important."

"It is." She relayed the evening's events, then explained about the friend request. "I'm going to send these pictures to you while you're on the phone, and I need someone to tell me I haven't completely lost my mind. Give me a minute." Anna clicked and pasted the photos in an e-mail, then sent them to him. "You should have them any second."

"Let me boot up my laptop. Two seconds," he said.

Anna heard his fingers clicking across the keyboard.

"Okay, I have them. Give me a minute to look at them."

"Sure," Anna said. This had to be the ultimate lie. And his kids? Did they believe their mother was dead? And if so, what could possibly keep a father from telling his children the truth?

"You're right, it's her. Aged, and not too kindly, but it's her. She's using a different name, obviously. I don't know what this means or how it relates to your case, whether or not she's involved in some way. It's hard to get something past me, and this, well, let's just say I'm shocked. I'm going to make a few calls, see what I can find out. Are you going to be up for a while?"

"I'll never be able to sleep unless I pop an Ambien, and I'm trying to ease off those things. So, yes, I'll be awake."

"Talk soon," Daniel said, ending the call.

Anna was also in a semi state of shock. Nothing made sense. Poor Renée. She didn't like the girl. She had tried to kill her daughter; whether that was her intent or not was yet to be determined, but still, to not know your mother was alive. It couldn't be good, whatever the reason for her disappearance, if that's what it was. Or maybe she'd left and decided after all these years to return.

The publicity surrounding her daughter — had it brought her out of hiding? Anna was at a total loss for any reasonable explanation.

Her phone rang, and it was Daniel. "Did you find out anything?"

"I did, and I hope you're sitting down because you're not going to believe what I learned about this woman. This story just keeps getting stranger by the minute."

Daniel told her what he'd found out. As he had predicted, Anna was shocked. Though she'd just told Daniel she was trying to lay off the Ambien, she took a whole one and didn't even bother to crawl beneath the sheets.

EPILOGUE

The media went crazy when news of Ryan's very-much-alive wife was made public. So many questions Anna had had were now answered, though the why behind the answers was something she would probably never have.

Laura Jones, also known as Leticia Elise Robertson, had spent the last eleven years locked away in Texas's Huntsville State Prison. Patrick had suffered extreme abuse at the hands of his mother. Not beating, whipping, or slapping. No, the abuse Patrick suffered was much worse than that.

It started when he was three. So-called viruses. Seizures. High potassium levels. The list was lengthy and horrifying. Anna's heart broke with each word she read, the suffering Patrick had gone through as a child. When Renée came along, he was six, old enough to know that he was only sick with Mommy, according to the records Daniel had. Wanting to protect his baby sister from all the trips to the doctor, getting poked and pricked, and needles, the endless emergency room trips, he'd finally told a doctor that Mommy made him sick.

An undercover investigation was launched after the child told the doctor, and Leticia Elise Robertson had been arrested, the papers said, a clear-cut case of Munchausen Syndrome by Proxy. She was tried, convicted, and sentenced to fifteen years in prison, but was released after only serving eleven years, her sentence reduced by four years for good behavior.

"No wonder that kid is so freaking evil," Mandy said. "Looks like she's taken after her wack job of a mother."

Anna and Daniel, along with Mandy, Jeb, and Mona, were enjoying a break after a long workday. The holidays were right around the corner, and it had been nonstop for all of them.

Christina was out of her cast, and had been able to return to school right after Thanksgiving. She walked with a limp, but her physical therapist said Christina was a bit fearful she'd break it again. But she was getting stronger by the day.

Given the history of the Robertson family, the prosecutor declined to press an attempted-murder charge against Renée. However, she didn't go scot-free. She was placed in a psychiatric hospital until her twenty-first birthday. Anna doubted she would be released before then. If she were, Anna would do whatever she had to in order to keep her in a safe place, where she couldn't harm anyone else.

Ryan. A liar, a player, and a con man, just as Mandy had said.

And then there was Patrick.

A mixed-up young man who was going to need lots of therapy before he was ready to face the world. Anna had set up an account for him to finish college in California. He wanted to get back into his swimming, and she felt it was her obligation to support his choice. Given what he'd been through, she was glad she could help him out even if it was just financially.

Daniel smiled at her, and yes, she felt all mushy inside. She wasn't sure if her friend-ship with her attorney would go beyond that, but something told her it was going to be so much more than that. He winked at her, and it almost took her breath away.

"Gary is sure Renée set fire to the house. Clever, but nonetheless insane. She used a pushpin to put the string in the ceiling, hung the balloon filled with kerosene, lit a candle, and left the house. It didn't take long for the balloon to meet the candle. That's why they asked you about your trips to Candle City. The metal part of the candle where the wick was attached is their brand. Renée had been seen the night before at the mall, in Candle City, purchasing the exact kind of candle used to start the fire. She denied it, tried to blame it on her dad, said he needed the insurance money. Little did she know that Daddy hadn't kept up with the premiums."

"They's one messed-up bunch o' folks, is all I got to say," Jeb observed.

"Hell, messed-up, that ain't good 'nuff. All of 'em is downright nut jobs," Mona said, as always adding her two cents whether you wanted to hear it or not.

"So what do you think they'll do when they find Ryan and Leticia?"

"Leticia is a free woman. I can't imagine the two of them are together, but it is what it is. Patrick told me that his father always blamed him for the breakup of the family. He told Patrick that his mother died in a car accident, and that that was his fault, too. No wonder he was so aloof. I think that girlfriend he had, the one from Spain, has contacted him. They had a baby, though he or she was put up for adoption. I think that was for the best, but still, if Patrick walks away with a normal life a few years from now, maybe his suffering all those years can be put in the past, where it belongs." Anna took a sip of her coffee. Amazed at the events since she'd taken that cruise, she still hadn't told Daniel all of her suspicions about Ryan. What in his life had caused him to be such a mean, demented man, such an uncaring and cruel father? She would never have those answers, and she could live with that.

"I think Ryan was your first stalker," Mandy said. "If you think about it, what were the odds? The guy had no money. Apparently what he did earn was spent on trying to impress people." Anna had told her this a few nights ago during one of their girl talks.

"He said his colleagues gave him the cruise as a birthday gift. I remember thinking what an extravagant gift. Those friends, colleagues, never made an appearance in the short time I knew him, so who knows? Maybe he was stalking me. I guess a person can have two stalkers. What are the odds of that? He was quite familiar with my shows. He said he never missed them, and I'm sure he was telling the truth. Maybe he had some sick hang-up? I don't know. But what I do know is that we've beaten the subject to death. I say it's time we bury it and move forward. I don't know about the rest of you, but I'm calling it a night." Anna put her cup in the dishwasher, kissed Mona and Jeb, and told Mandy she could go home.

"What about me?" Daniel said. "Can't I at least get a good night kiss?"

Anna turned around so fast, she lost her balance. A strong, muscular hand steadied her. "I haven't had a girl fall at my feet since . . . never."

Anna stood on her tiptoes and placed a kiss on his cheek. " 'Night, Daniel."

" 'Night, 'night, pretty girl."

ANNA'S RIB RUB

Ingredients
1/3 cup chili powder
1/3 cup light brown sugar (dark can be
  substituted)
1/4 cup kosher salt
1/4 cup crushed black peppercorns
1 1/2 tablespoons cumin
1–2 tablespoons garlic powder
1–2 tablespoons smoked paprika
1 tablespoon onion powder
1 teaspoon lime zest
1 teaspoon Mexican oregano
1/2 teaspoon chipotle pepper (seeds
  removed)
1/2 teaspoon coriander
1/4 teaspoon cinnamon

Instructions
Mix all ingredients together, mashing any
lumps of brown sugar, and store in an

airtight container. Give a good stir before using.

How to Use

Use paper towels to pat the ribs dry.

Cover ribs with a light coating of olive oil on both sides.

Rub Anna's Rib Rub into the meat, giving it a good massage and working the spices in.

Seasoned ribs can be refrigerated overnight, covered with plastic wrap.

Allow ribs to reach room temperature before cooking or grilling.

ENJOY!

Anna

ABOUT THE AUTHOR

Fern Michaels is the *USA Today* and *New York Times* bestselling author of the Sisterhood, Men of the Sisterhood, and Godmothers series, as well as dozens of other novels and novellas. There are more than ninety-five million copies of her books in print. Fern Michaels has built and funded several large day-care centers in her hometown and is a passionate animal lover who has outfitted police dogs across the country with special bulletproof vests. She shares her home in South Carolina with her four dogs and a resident ghost named Mary Margaret. Visit her website at fernmichaels .com.